Also by the author
Behind the Night Bazaar

Angela Savage travelled to Laos on a six-month scholarship in 1992 and ended up staying in Asia for six years. She was based in Vientiane, then Hanoi and Bangkok where she set up and headed the Australian Red Cross HIV/AIDS subregional program. Her love affair with Asia continues and she has returned many times since, most recently spending 2008 in Cambodia with her partner and their young daughter. Her first book, *Behind the Night Bazaar*, published by Text in 2006, won the 2004 Victorian Premier's Literary Award for unpublished manuscript. Angela lives in Melbourne.

The Half-Child

ANGELA SAVAGE

TEXT PUBLISHING MELBOURNE AUSTRALIA

The Text Publishing Company
Swann House
22 William Street
Melbourne Victoria 3000
Australia
textpublishing.com.au

First published in Australia by The Text Publishing Company, 2010
Reprinted 2013

Design by Susan Miller
Typeset by J&M Typesetting
Printed and bound in Australia by Griffin Press

National Library of Australia
Cataloguing-in-Publication entry

Savage, Angela, 1966-

The half-child / Angela Savage.

ISBN 9781921656545 (pbk.)

A823.4

For Olgamary Savage, née Whelan
Much has she loved

PROLOGUE

Pornthip heaved herself up on her elbows to look at the baby.

'*Look ying*,' the nurse said.

She held the squirming newborn aloft, tilting her so Pornthip could see. A bloodied cord dangled like rope from the baby's belly, sticky white cream smeared on her skin. The nurse dabbed at the mess with a cloth.

Pornthip had wanted a son, someone to grow up and look after her, but it was not her fate. She'd given birth to a baby girl, another body to protect. She forced herself to sit up.

'Please give her to me.'

The nurse hesitated, looked to the other woman in the room. *Asian but not Thai*, Pornthip realised. The woman also wore a nurse's uniform, but the medical equipment around her neck and her manner denoted seniority. She mouthed something to the Thai nurse and shook her head.

Pornthip lunged towards the baby. 'Give her to me!'

Shocked, the Thai nurse handed over the baby. Pornthip eased herself back down on to the pillow and laid her daughter on the papery gown covering her chest. The baby, eyes squeezed shut, opened and closed her mouth like a little bird.

'*Nok noi*,' Pornthip whispered, adding in a louder voice, 'She looks like a baby bird.'

Nok—that would be her cheu len, *her nickname.*

'Would you like to try and feed her?' the nurse asked.

The foreigner protested, using words Pornthip didn't understand, and moved to pick up the baby.

'Let her be,' Pornthip said. She tried to tighten her hold on her daughter, but the outburst had drained her last reserves of strength. 'Why is she here?' she asked the nurse, nodding at the *farang*. 'I don't understand.'

The nurse said something in a low voice. The foreigner turned on her heel and left the room.

Nok snuffled like a piglet. The nurse gestured for Pornthip to raise her head, untied the strings of the hospital gown and tugged at the neckline to uncover Pornthip's breasts. Nok latched on to Pornthip's nipple and began sucking noisily.

Mae Yai's voice came back from across the years, warning Pornthip's mother not to put the baby on the breast before the milk came in. Pornthip couldn't remember which of her eight siblings, all born at home, her grandmother had been referring to, or why the first milk wasn't good for the baby.

'Don't worry,' the Thai nurse reassured her. 'It's good for the baby.'

Pornthip felt a stab of pain followed by a wave of pleasure, and sank back against the bed. If her mother was still alive, she'd have taken charge. Pornthip would be confined to the house to lie with the baby in a heated room for thirty days while her relatives tended to them. Her body would have had time to recover from the birth.

Instead, she was alone with her daughter in a strange

place. She had no money, no job, no idea who the baby's father was—not that it would make any difference. In the months leading up to the birth, she'd slept rough on the beach or streets. Eventually a security guard took pity and let her doze in his sentry box for a few hours in exchange for a nightly blow-job. No place for a baby girl.

When she'd gone into labour at twilight on the beach, she'd panicked. She'd only ended up at the hospital because a farang woman found her, bundled her into a *songthaew*, and paid to have her admitted. But the foreigner had gone away, and Pornthip had no idea what to do next.

Her mouth was dry and her body ached with exhaustion and hunger. After months on the street, she was nothing but skin, bones and distended belly. What Nok found to suck from her underfed body Pornthip did not know, though the baby seemed content shuffling from one nipple to the other.

When at last she broke away, Nok lay on Pornthip's chest, opened her eyes and met her mother's gaze with a look that might have been wonder.

'*Sawadee Nok*,' Pornthip said.

The baby frowned and opened her mouth.

'Don't ask me,' Pornthip whispered. 'I don't know what we're going to do.'

At that moment the door to the delivery room opened and the boss-nurse reappeared with a white man in tow.

Pornthip blanched, hastened to cover her exposed breasts. The abrupt movement upset Nok, who started to cry. To her surprise, the farang man took a white towel and draped it over mother and baby like a blanket.

'She'll be feeling cold,' he said in Thai, rubbing the baby's back through the cotton.

Nok stopped crying and fell asleep.

3

Pornthip stared at him. He had blotchy skin and a huge nose. Wiry grey-brown hair sprouted from inside his nostrils and ears, like tufts of grass from rock. He looked like the buffoon in a village *talok* troupe.

'Hello little sister, I'm *Khun* Frank,' the man said. 'Connie here—' he tilted his head at the boss nurse '—tells me your name's Pornthip.'

She nodded, kept one hand on the small of Nok's back, raised the other in a half-*wai*.

'And you've just had a beautiful baby girl,' Frank continued. 'Congratulations.'

Pornthip tried to speak but her mouth was too dry.

'You need a drink?'

The Thai nurse approached but Frank dismissed her with a wave. Pornthip thought she choked back a cry as she scuttled out of the room.

Frank gestured at Connie, who came forward with water. He held the glass so Pornthip could drink through the straw.

'*Khop khun na ka*,' she said, lying back down again.

'So tell me, Pornthip, how do you plan to care for the baby?'

Pornthip's eyes filled with hot tears. Could he read her mind? Was another farang about to come to her rescue?

'*Mai roo*! I don't know.'

Connie handed Frank a clipboard.

'That's okay,' he said. 'You've been through so much. And it says here—' he leafed through some papers '—that you're only sixteen. Is that right?'

Pornthip nodded.

'You're exhausted. You should rest. Connie here will give you something to take away the pain and help you sleep.'

4

He might look like a clown but his voice was calm and serious. Pornthip watched the farang nurse prepare a needle.

'Just relax,' Khun Frank said. 'We'll take care of everything. We know you want what's best for the baby and so do we.'

Pornthip nodded.

'Family?' he asked.

'Brothers and sisters in Kalasin,' she said. 'Mother and father dead.'

'Would you like us to help you go home to Kalasin?'

The prospect brought on a fresh wave of tears.

'Can you do that?'

The nurse moved forward and inserted the needle into Pornthip's arm.

'Yes, we can do that,' Frank said. 'And we'll also make sure the baby is well looked after. I mean, it's not realistic for you to take her with you, is it?'

Pornthip frowned, confused, as the words penetrated the euphoria washing over her.

'She'll need food, clothing, shelter. And you know you can't provide for her,' he continued.

'I don't want to leave my baby.'

The words came out slurred, without the force she intended.

'Don't think of it as leaving her,' Frank said. 'Think of it as giving her the best possible start in life. She'll be cared for by a mother *and* father who'll be able to provide her with all she needs. And when she gets older, you'll be able to visit her.'

Pornthip smiled, her anxieties fading.

He snapped a sheet of paper on to the clipboard and placed a pen in Pornthip's hand.

'All you need to do is sign here and leave the rest to us.'

He balanced the clipboard on her chest, blocking her view of the baby. Pornthip didn't read well at the best of times and the words danced on the page.

'I can't see it,' she muttered.

'That's okay,' Frank said. 'Here, let me help you.'

Pornthip felt his hand close over hers. She peered where he pointed, scrawled on the dotted line.

'You'll look after my Nok, my baby bird?' she yawned.

'Don't worry about a thing,' he said.

Pornthip smiled and closed her eyes on the image of her daughter's sleeping face.

The farang bundled the baby in the towel and lifted her off the young girl's chest.

I

At four o'clock on Tuesday morning a concrete girder as big as a bus fell from the sky and crushed a taxi, killing the driver. There were no passengers in the vehicle— fortuitous but not surprising. A driver would have to be desperate, wired on *ya ma* and Red Bull to be trawling Sukhumvit Road for a fare at that hour. Like most of his ilk, the deceased was a failed farmer from the northeast. He left behind a widow, three sons and a daughter, whose future now depended on how many of their chickens survived the cool season.

Tragic though this was, the Thai press couldn't help speculate on how much worse the accident would have been had it occurred at almost any other hour. The front page of *Thai Rath* featured a diagram demonstrating how an incident of this kind during Bangkok's peak times could kill dozens, if not hundreds of people.

The diagram came to life in Jayne Keeney's imagination as she was forced to a standstill on Silom Road alongside an orange crane dangling a metal strut from its jaws above her head. She could picture the crane opening its maw, the beam plummeting towards her. She inched her motorbike forward, narrowly missing a hole in the bitumen, and brushed up against the flimsy blue-striped plastic sheeting, all that separated her from the Skytrain building site. There was no escaping the sense of impending doom.

The girders in this stretch, the site of what would be Silom Station, were wide enough to cast a shadow over six lanes of traffic. Concrete pipes stacked in pyramids threatened to tumble on to the road at any moment, flattening labourers, pushcart vendors and traffic police. Great bundles of metal rods would gouge out the eyes of any who veered too close. On a nearby footpath, all that remained of a pedestrian overpass was a set of stairs leading nowhere.

Jayne had always thought Bangkok would make a great setting for a disaster movie. The Skytrain construction sites strewn across the city made it look as though disaster had already struck.

The bus in front of her belched thick, black smoke that crept under the visor of her helmet and stung her eyes. She cursed herself for taking the motorbike, but after more than four years in the Thai capital, it simply didn't occur to her that she might walk anywhere. Only crazy farang tourists walked. Even pushcart vendors left their carts locked by the side of the road at night and set aside enough *baht* to take a motorcycle taxi or *tuk-tuk* home.

At the end of Silom Road, Jayne turned right into the relative peace of the Dusit Thani Hotel grounds and parked her motorbike beneath a teak tree. It was a mark of the hotel's quality that such rare trees were preserved in its grounds rather than sold off for timber. To the amusement of the doorman, she paused to check her reflection in the spotless exterior windows, fluffed up the black curls flattened by her helmet and wiped the grime from her pale skin before nodding for him to let her in.

The spacious hotel lobby was carpeted in red and gold, with pillars covered in tan leather. Elaborate bouquets of tropical flowers almost brushed the ceiling. Jayne had dressed up for the high-class venue, substituting her usual T-shirt, chinos and runners for a dark-green blouse, black A-line skirt and strappy sandals. But creased and grubby from the journey, she fell way short of the grooming standards set by the women at the reception desk. Their crimson silk jackets and matching skirts looked ironed on, hair pulled into buns tight enough to cause migraines. Jayne was reconciled to the fact she could never compete with local women's commitment to the *riab roi* principle of tidiness and decorum. Still, she thought it was excessive for the receptionist to wince when Jayne asked her to page Mister James Delbeck.

The man who appeared was stocky and ginger-haired with a weather-beaten face, as ill at ease in his expensive suit as Jayne felt in her semi-formal attire. His red-and-white striped tie was knotted loosely, the top button of his pale blue shirt undone. Gingery curls crept above his collar at the back of his neck. The same fuzz coated the wrist that extended from his sleeve as he introduced himself as Jim. The backs of his hands were dotted with the round pink scars of excised cancers. Similar scars marked the bridge of his nose.

He smelled of something loud and pricey, and carried a flash leather briefcase. New money, Jayne guessed. Farmer or tradesman turned entrepreneur. But for all the props, Jim Delbeck lacked the pomposity and nervous energy typical of the Australian businessmen who came to Bangkok to negotiate deals. Puffy-eyed and greying, he looked defeated.

His thick, shiny business card bore a logo in the shape

of a truck and listed his position in corporate jargon that suggested authority and a six-figure salary. She felt sheepish exchanging it for one of her own, a modest scrap of paper with her name, 'Discreet Private Investigator – Speaks English, French and Thai' and her mobile number, printed in English on one side and Thai on the other. Jim responded with a satisfied nod and gestured towards the lobby bar.

Jayne followed him to a corner table. He pulled out a chair and waited until she was seated before taking his place. A single white lotus floated in a glass bowl in front of them. An indoor fountain bubbled in the background.

Jayne ordered a juice from the waitress shadowing them.

'You won't join me in a beer?' Jim said.

'Normally, yes,' she said. 'But I'm driving.'

'In this traffic? Bloody hell. You're a brave girl.'

Jayne didn't know whether to feel flattered or offended. While she liked to think of herself as brave, it was a while since she'd thought of herself as a girl.

'Probably a good thing, given your line of work, eh?' Jim continued. 'Speaking of which...'

He cleared his throat. 'My daughter Maryanne allegedly committed suicide in Pattaya last year. It was in all the papers. You might have read about it?'

He handed her a plastic sleeve containing a newspaper article from *The Bangkok Post*. It featured a photograph of a wide-eyed young woman with a smile not even newsprint could dull. Fair hair in a ponytail and daypack slung over one shoulder, she wore a T-shirt with the logo 'Young Christian Volunteers' on her chest and carried a boarding pass, held out for the benefit of the photographer, for Qantas Flight 01 to London via Bangkok on Saturday 18 May 1996. Less than five months later, according to the article, twenty-one-year-old Maryanne Delbeck jumped from a hotel rooftop in Pattaya, falling fourteen storeys to her death.

Even without the T-shirt, Jayne would've taken the young woman for a Christian. Unlike Jayne whose skin showed the signs of regular, often excessive, alcohol consumption and a fifteen-year smoking habit, Maryanne had the wholesome air of the clean-living. A look in her eyes suggested she had her sights set on something further away from her home in rural Queensland than the seedy Thai coastal town of Pattaya.

Jayne skimmed the article, raised her head. 'I remember seeing something.'

'Maryanne couldn't have committed suicide,' Jim said. 'I don't care what the Thai cops say. She was a good girl. Didn't drink, didn't smoke. Never gave her mother and me a moment's trouble.'

The drinks arrived. Jim waved away the glass and took a swig from his bottle of Tiger beer.

'No way was Maryanne the type to...to do that to herself.'

'The article said something about your daughter being clinically depressed—'

'I don't believe that,' Jim interrupted her. 'She was always so bloody cheerful. Too cheerful. Used to drive me crazy.'

He grunted, the sound of a man choking on emotion, and upended the bottle too quickly; beer spilled from the corners of his mouth.

'Bugger.'

Jayne looked away as he wiped his face with a serviette.

'There are some conditions where people swing between excessive cheerfulness and depression,' she said cautiously. 'Is there any history of mental illness in the family?'

'No there bloody well isn't,' Jim said. 'We're fourth generation Queensland farmers. We don't have time to get depressed. We work for a living.'

Jayne toyed with the swizzle stick in her drink.

'Besides, she'd have told Sarah if anything was wrong. Maryanne and my sister were as thick as thieves. Told her she was going overseas long before her mother and I knew about it. Not that we could've stopped her. Maryanne was too bloody headstrong. Guess she got that from me.'

Jayne stirred her juice, taking a moment to choose her words. 'Some people are very good at hiding their depression, even from people closest to them—'

'I know where you're going with this,' Jim said. 'I'm in denial, right? I'm only her father. What would I know?'

'I didn't mean to imply—'

'I got the same response from those useless bastards at the Australian Embassy. As for the Thai cops, they pretend they can't speak English when they don't want to answer my questions. And the YCV won't cooperate. They're shit-scared of the investigation being re-opened 'cause it means more bad press for them.'

'YCV?'

'Young Christian Volunteers.'

He pointed at Maryanne's T-shirt in the photo, then took a swig of beer as if washing a bad taste from his mouth.

'So if I'm going to find out what really happened to Maryanne, I have to do it myself. That's where you come in. You're a private contractor. I'm a paying customer. I've a job that needs doing and I'm prepared to pay you to do it.'

'You want me to investigate a case both the Thai police and Australian Embassy consider closed?' Jayne met his gaze. 'I won't bullshit you. It's a long shot.'

Jim smiled. 'And I won't bullshit you either. I was planning to hire a professional out of Australia. Then I met with this guy at the embassy—a bit of a poof, but he seemed to know what he was talking about—and he suggested I try someone who speaks the language, knows the place. He gave me your card.'

Her friend Max Parker, Second Secretary at the Australian Embassy. Jayne made a mental note to call and thank him.

'Find out what happened to Maryanne,' Jim said. 'I don't care what it costs.'

Jayne raised her eyebrows. She wanted the job, but she didn't want to dupe a grief-stricken father to get it.

'Say I agree to take the case. Are you prepared for the possibility that I might not come up with anything new?'

'I just want someone I can trust.' He reached into his briefcase. 'I had my lawyer draw up a contract. It's the company standard—unless of course you'd prefer to use your own.'

Jayne shrugged as though she signed contracts all the time. Her usual arrangement rarely involved more than a handshake—a *wai* for her Thai clients—a cash advance and more cash on completion.

She scanned the text. There were sections on the responsibilities of Mr James H. Delbeck ('the client') and the responsibilities of Miss Jayne Keeney ('the contractor'), together with a timeline ('one month, subject to review'). His proposed budget allowed for an advance that, like the price of the drinks at the Dusit Thani, was five times what she was used to.

'This looks fine.'

'I'll get another copy made—' Jim signalled for a waitress

'—and we can sign before you leave.'

'Do you have any background information that might help?' Jayne asked.

He dipped into his briefcase and handed Jayne a large envelope. 'I made copies of Maryanne's letters. I don't know if they're useful, but they give you an idea of what she was like and the work she was doing. There's a photo in there, too. Might help. And there's this.' He handed her a document. 'The embassy report, though I'm not sure how useful that is.'

She glanced at it, recognised the author's name. He was a staffer at the embassy whom Max described as 'ballast', code for one who never rocked the boat. Jayne thought he was an arse-licker.

She scanned the text, a testament to the minutiae of bureaucratic procedures, both Thai and Australian. She added this and the other material to her daypack, wedging them amongst her camera, maps, drink bottle, and the crime novel she was reading, and took out a notebook and pen.

'When are you leaving Bangkok?' she said, testing the pen.

'I'm flying back to Brisbane tonight.'

'Mind if I ask you a couple of questions while we wait for the photocopy?'

'Shoot.'

'Did Maryanne know anyone in Thailand before coming here as a volunteer?'

He shook his head. 'Far as I know, she applied to YCV and they came up with the job in Thailand. I thought she should have finished her degree first, then gone somewhere more civilised, like America.'

For some reason a quote popped into Jayne's head:

Mahatma Gandhi, when asked what he thought of Western civilisation. *It sounds like a good idea.*

'What was Maryanne studying?'

'Social work. Said she wanted to work with children. I told her there was no money in it. But that's what she wanted to do and like I told you, once she put her mind to something, she was bloody well determined to do it.'

'And she hadn't been to Thailand before at all? On holiday?'

He frowned and shook his head.

'What about Maryanne's Christian beliefs, was she...' Jayne searched for the right words. 'Was she very religious?'

'She didn't ram her beliefs down other people's throats if that's what you mean. We're a church-going family. Nothing unusual in that.'

Jayne made a note to find out more about the YCV.

'The article mentioned a brother.'

'Ian, two years older.'

'Were they close?'

'Not particularly. Like I said, Maryanne was close to her aunt Sarah, my younger sister. Sarah's the black sheep of the family, and I think Maryanne favoured her just to piss me off.'

'Oh?'

'Maryanne and I didn't always see eye to eye.'

'Can you give me an example?'

'She wanted to help those less fortunate than her, though she'd say it was patronising of me to put it that way. We argued about it a lot. In my experience, if you're prepared to work hard, you can be anything in this world. Maryanne believed in handouts, or a "hand up"—' he drew inverted commas in the air '—as she put it. Said I was a cynic. I thought she was naïve, trying to change the bloody world.'

He leaned forward across the table.

'She was too confident. She trusted people too easily. It'd make her a sitting duck in a place like this.'

'What do you mean?'

He made a sweeping gesture with his hands. 'Bloody Asian hellhole.'

Jayne thought the Dusit Thani Hotel failed to qualify as any kind of hellhole, but the death of his only daughter was bound to colour Jim Delbeck's view.

She closed her notebook.

'Jim, what do you think happened to Maryanne?'

'I don't know,' he said.

'Accident?'

'Maybe.'

'Foul play?'

'I don't know,' he said again, shaking his head.

'You must suspect something or you wouldn't be hiring me.'

He drained his beer.

'You hear a lot of stories about the shit that goes down in a place like this and—' He stared for a moment at the lotus floating in the bowl in front of him. 'I don't know why anyone would want to hurt Maryanne. I just know that if they did, she wouldn't have seen it coming.'

His shoulders slumped, and Jayne resisted the urge to take his hand.

'I'm sorry for your loss,' she said.

His sad smile was short-lived. 'You know, you're the first person to say that since I arrived in this place. One bastard even had a stupid bloody grin on his face the whole time he was talking about Maryanne's death. If he hadn't been a cop, I would've bloody well decked him.'

Again Jayne held her tongue. Smiling in the face of tragedy was a form of stoicism in Thailand, but this wasn't the time to give Jim Delbeck a lesson in cultural sensitivity.

The waitress reappeared with the contract. They signed both copies and took one each. Jim signed the tab for their drinks, too.

'You can contact me on my mobile number any time,' he said as they walked back towards the entrance.

He extended his hand. 'Good luck.'

'I'll do my best,' she found herself saying.

'One other thing,' Jim said, still holding her hand. 'If you do find out there was foul play involved, I want you to come to me first, not the cops. I don't trust those bastards.'

Again Jayne bit back the impulse to point out that there were good cops and bad cops wherever you went in the world. She didn't want to know whether Jim Delbeck was angry with the Thais because of his daughter's death or if his antipathy ran deeper. She wanted to accept what he offered at face value: an intriguing case that got her out of the demolition site that was downtown Bangkok.

She zigzagged back along the rubble of Silom Road. The meeting made Jayne think of her own father. She wondered how he would describe her to a stranger. Would he highlight their differences, as Jim Delbeck had done with Maryanne? Or would he persist as he always did in finding common ground, no matter how hard he had to scratch around for it?

As far as her parents were concerned, Jayne was an enigma. Once she'd been a normal girl with a nice fiancé and a good job at a Melbourne girls' school. Then she'd tossed it all in and run off to Europe with a visiting French teacher. Somehow she'd ended up alone in Bangkok and for reasons they couldn't understand, insisted on staying there. She hadn't told them about her work as a private investigator. They still thought she taught English for a living and since her father was a teacher, she let them believe it. He loved to think she'd followed in his footsteps; she couldn't break it to him that she'd strayed from the path.

Jim Delbeck seemed to take it personally that his daughter's values differed from his own. To their credit, Jayne's parents never felt that way. They might not understand her, but they respected her right to be different. Once she did get around to telling them she's a PI, she had no doubt they'd take it in their stride.

It rarely happened, but meeting Jim Delbeck left Jayne feeling homesick.

2

Max stood to kiss Jayne European style before resuming his seat. The weather was cool by Bangkok's standards—a balmy thirty degrees by day, mild nights just below twenty. They made the most of it by sitting outside. Max had chosen their rendezvous: the patio at the Sphinx Bar, a little corner of Ancient Egypt in the middle of the Thai capital. Tucked down the end of Soi 4 off Silom Road, the exterior was rendered to look like sandstone, the entrance guarded by a replica of Tutankhamen's sarcophagus. The interior walls were a royal-blue honeycomb of niches containing faux Egyptian artefacts backlit in blue light, and the bar boys wore gold and blue kilts and matching headdresses inspired by the acolytes in the Temple Karnak. A classy joint compared with some of the venues in a lane affectionately known as 'Gay Soi'.

'Long time, no see,' he said as Jayne sat down.

'Too long.'

She pointed to his gin and tonic and signalled for a bare-chested waiter to bring another.

'You look good, Jayne.'

'Thanks Max. I feel good.'

She took a packet of *Krung Thip* out of her pack.

'Still haven't given up that filthy habit I see.' He pushed the ashtray towards her. 'Is that wise, smoking the local brand?'

'Are you kidding? Using a filter is the only way to get a breath of fresh air in this city.'

She drew on her cigarette with exaggerated pleasure and Max smiled. It was a relief to see her looking so relaxed. He was fond of Jayne, but she risked becoming one of those embittered expatriate women who complain about being passed over by expat men in favour of the locals, persist with living in Bangkok, but won't date Thai men. *Khan thong*, literally 'golden bowl', the Thai term for spinster. Too precious to put anything inside. For Max, dating Thai men was the only thing that made Bangkok life bearable.

They chatted for a while, before Jayne brought up the Delbeck case. Max knew what was coming. Three years earlier, she'd used her detective skills to expose the affair Max's then-boyfriend was having with the Australian Defence Attaché. She refused payment at the time, saying she'd done it as a favour. Ever since, she regularly provided Max with opportunities to return the favour. And she had the uncanny ability to make him feel pleased to show off his generosity.

'Jim Delbeck's employed me to look into the circumstances of his daughter's death. Thanks for putting in a good word.'

'Not at all.'

'He gave me a copy of the embassy's report into Maryanne's death.' She put the document on the table between them. 'It has all the hallmarks of Mister Ballast's style: dull bureaucratic language, conservative analysis. But I digress.'

She opened the cover and leafed through a couple of pages. 'It says Maryanne Delbeck came to Thailand as a volunteer in May last year—'

She looked up.

'May last year,' Max repeated, reaching over to touch her arm. 'We were in Chiang Mai.'

Nine months earlier, a friend they'd both loved had died in violent circumstances. Jayne had risked her own life to pursue his killers and clear their friend's name of falsified charges. For this, too, Max owed her.

'I miss him,' Jayne said.

'Me too.'

They raised their glasses and drank a silent toast.

Jayne spoke first. 'What can you tell me about the Young Christian Volunteers?'

'They're a non-government organisation that sends young people on volunteer placements in Asia and the Pacific. Most of their funding comes from churches, but they get a bit of AusAID money.'

'Are they fundamentalists?'

'They wouldn't qualify for AusAID funding if they were. It's in the guidelines. NGOs aren't allowed to use Australian taxpayers' funds for proselytising.'

Jayne raised her eyebrows. 'What, even under the Liberals?'

Max smiled, though she'd hit a raw nerve. Since the election of the conservatives in Australia the previous year, unwelcome policy changes were coming thick and fast. In the latest, Foreign Affairs had issued advice that funds from the Australian Agency for International Development were not to be used to provide information or services related to abortion or emergency contraception. For Max, who oversaw several sexual health projects funded by the Australian government, the directive was causing major headaches. He dreaded what they might come up with next. No more funding for AIDS projects that worked with gay men and drug users?

'So how does the YCV identify placements?' Jayne said, lighting another cigarette.

'Through church networks, I think. But hang on...' He took a diary from the inner pocket of his beige linen jacket. 'If I'm not mistaken, YCV's Asian program coordinator is due here for a monitoring visit. Yes, here it is. Kate Murchison. I've got an appointment with her tomorrow at two.'

'Hot on the heels of Jim Delbeck's visit,' Jayne said.

Max hadn't thought of it like that but she might have a point.

'Any chance you could arrange for us to meet?'

'I'll get her to call you?'

'On the *meu theu*.'

He ignored her use of the lingua franca, knowing she did it to show up his own ineptitude when it came to speaking Thai. French would continue to be the only damn foreign language Max bothered to study, determined his superiors would eventually concede that his next placement could only be the Australian mission in Paris or Geneva.

'Gone high tech have you?' he asked.

'Wouldn't be without it,' Jayne said as she waved her mobile phone in the air before noticing something on the screen. She pushed a few buttons.

'Sorry Max, I've gotta go.'

She stubbed out her barely smoked cigarette, drained her glass and rose to her feet. 'You won't have dinner with me?' Max was disappointed.

'I'd love to, but when you said you wanted to meet here, I assumed you'd made plans for the evening.'

She took two hundred baht from her wallet, ignored his attempts to give it back, and placed it under the ashtray.

'Besides, I have a date,' she said.

'*What?*'

In the time he'd known her, Max had never heard Jayne talk of a date. He knew she had flings, but it wasn't the same thing.

'Oh my god, no wonder you're looking so well. You can't go now. You've got to tell me all about it. Who's the lucky man? Do I know him?'

'You don't know him. It's early days, but he's lovely. And if things work out, I promise I'll introduce you, okay?'

'Jayne, this is outrageous! How about bringing him to my next Friday night *salon*?'

'Relax,' she smiled. 'I told you, it's still early days. Besides, I have to go to Pattaya to follow up on this case.'

Max was poised to protest, when he caught sight of an attractive Thai man on the terrace of a bar called Telephone across the *soi*. The man had an old-fashioned black telephone on the table in front of him, painted with the number twenty-nine in white. Max knew from past forays that if he took a table at the same bar and dialled twenty-nine on the phone in front of him, he could speak anonymously with the guy. Suss him out. Flirt a little. See what transpired.

Max made eye contact with the Thai man over Jayne's shoulder as he stood to kiss her goodbye.

'I'll let you off the hook for now,' he said, smiling at the private pun. 'But I expect all the juicy details next time.'

3

Jayne turned as she walked away and caught sight of Max making a beeline for Telephone. Once she resented her friend's single-mindedness, but the promise of romance made her magnanimous.

She made her way on foot towards the river. Even without the added chaos of the Skytrain construction, the quickest way to her destination this time of the evening was by Chao Phraya river ferry. It was also a journey that showed *Krung Thep*—'City of Angels' as it was known in Thai—in one of its most flattering guises. Jayne caught a local boat from the Central Pier and stood on the outer deck to take in the view. The rays of the setting sun combined with Bangkok's veil of pollution and the dry season dust to turn the muddy waters of the Chao Phraya bronze and bathe the city in a fiery glow. As the ferry traced the serpentine route north, the silhouette of Wat Arun appeared on the west bank, its spires like fingers pointing to the red sky. The temple was named after Aruna the Indian god of dawn, an item of guidebook trivia that came to mind on account of the man she was on her way to meet.

They'd met a month earlier when Jayne ventured across

town to trawl Khao San Road's bookstores for second-hand crime novels. While most resident expats avoided the backpacker precinct, Jayne had a soft spot for Banglamphu, the part of town where travellers from all over the world congregated to swap stories over cheap local whisky that gave them killer hangovers and doubled as a disinfectant for their ulcerated mosquito bites and newly inked tattoos.

The largest bookshop on Khao San Road was Seema's, named for the granddaughter of the proprietor, a genial Indian man known as 'Uncle'. The books at Seema's teetered in gravity-defying stacks taller than Jayne's 1.6 metres and filled all available floor space. The shop smelled of sandalwood, dust and the fragrant tea Uncle drank from a gold-frosted glass. Though the books appeared to be piled up randomly, he knew his stock by heart. From his perch behind the counter, he would dispatch one of his runners with instructions on how to locate a title, which they'd extract with such speed and precision that the stacks barely moved. Uncle would write receipts by hand and place carbon copies with the purchases inside plastic bags, before returning to his perusal of nineteenth-century atlases that he liked to spread across the counter.

People shopped at Seema's for the spectacle. If she didn't have something specific in mind, scanning the stacks for crime fiction could take Jayne hours. So it was a shock to walk in and find books neatly shelved by genre in alphabetical order, the atlases and tea glass cleared to make space for a computer, and Uncle's place behind the counter usurped by a handsome young Indian man.

'What happened?' she wondered aloud.

'Please, not another dissatisfied customer.' He shook his head. 'And here I was, thinking it would be helping my uncle's business to put everything in order.'

His smile showed pronounced eye teeth. A neat moustache and short pointed beard framed his mouth, and his thick lips were tinged purple.

'Where *is* your uncle?' she asked, trying not to stare at those lips.

'He had a heart attack about a month ago.'

'Oh, I'm sorry to hear that.'

The man wiggled his head. 'Happily, he is recovering, although he is still very weak. The doctor says it will not be being safe for him to return to work at this stage. My cousins were wanting to keep the bookstore open, but nobody could find anything. Uncle had a system, but he wouldn't tell anyone what it was. They asked me to step in and as you can see—' he gestured towards the shelves '—I have alienated my uncle's loyal customers by replacing his esoteric arrangement with a modern and efficient alternative.'

She couldn't tell whether he was being ironic or genuinely apologetic.

'For what it's worth, I think it's an improvement.'

'Thank you, Madam.'

'Oh god, don't call me Madam. It's Jayne.' She handed him a business card.

'Rajiv Patel,' the man said, exchanging it for one of his own.

Though only a month since his uncle's heart attack, Rajiv's card bore the logo of Seema's Bookshop and listed his profession as Acting Manager and Information Technology Consultant. A string of qualifications after his name suggested he was older than he looked.

'So, Miss Jayne,' Rajiv said, nodding towards the computer, 'how can I help you?'

'Just Jayne, please.'

He wiggled his head again. She took it as a nod.

'I'm after novels by Carol O'Connell,' she said, 'an American crime writer. I've read *Mallory's Oracle* and I'd like to see if she has any others.'

Rajiv tapped at the keyboard.

'We have one called *The Man Who Lied to Women*,' he said, looking at the computer screen. 'Sounds ominous, isn't it?'

He issued instructions to one of Uncle's runners, and they watched as the man shuffled across to the bookshelves and pulled out the paperback.

Rajiv winked at Jayne.

'Do you read much crime fiction?' she asked as she paid for the book.

'I try to read a bit of everything to build my general knowledge. If what they say about a little knowledge being a dangerous thing is true, then I am becoming a very dangerous man.'

That smile again. Jayne looked once more at the letters on his business card. Rajiv Patel was becoming increasingly attractive. She decided to take a chance.

'Would you like to have coffee with me?'

'Yes.'

They looked at each other, both surprised.

'Though the coffee around here is not so good,' Rajiv added.

'And on a hot night like this, maybe cold beer would be better?' Jayne said.

'You are reading my mind.'

Since then they'd gone on several dates. At least Jayne assumed that's what they were. She'd almost forgotten what it was like to be romanced, so much so that spending quality time in the company of a straight man whilst not getting laid messed with her sense of equilibrium.

The venue on this occasion was a floating restaurant on an old pontoon near the Phra Athit pier. Jayne disembarked from the ferry, taking care not to brush up against the orange robes of the Buddhist monks, and checked her watch. Rajiv managed to be so punctual despite the vagaries of Bangkok traffic, she could time it for a cold beer to arrive at the table just as he did.

Rajiv sighed as his mobile phone screen lit up yet again with his uncle's number. He hit the loudspeaker button.

'Yes, Uncle.'

'Are you already leaving the shop?'

'Yes, Uncle.'

Rajiv slipped the phone into his shirt pocket, dragged the accordion gate across the shopfront and snapped the padlock into place.

'Do you think you should be going back and checking that you have turned off the electricity?' his uncle's voice buzzed against his chest.

'I have turned off the electricity, Uncle-*ji*,' Rajiv said, retrieving the mobile and speaking into it like a Dictaphone. 'I checked.'

'It will be very important,' the old man said. 'My own brother's wife's father's business burned down two years ago due to a malfunction in the electrical circuitry—an accident that could have been avoided if only the master switch had been left in the off position.'

He paused to clear his throat and Rajiv acted quickly to fend off an impending lecture about the myriad misfortunes, acts of God and other catastrophes that had the potential to destroy Uncle's businesses and those run by his extended family members, friends and associates in Thailand.

'Rest assured, Uncle, I have followed your instructions to the letter. Your reminder call is always appreciated. I will see you later. Tell Auntie not to keep dinner for me.'

He hung up before the old man could rabbit on further and headed for the river. Rajiv toyed with the idea of turning off his phone altogether, but for his relatives who prised their mobiles from their ears only to sleep at night, this would suggest he'd been robbed, kidnapped or left for dead in a gutter. Better to know who was calling and how often, so he could manage any concerns before they became catastrophes.

Rajiv supposed his relatives were like any minority, always on edge, never trusting the foreign soil beneath their feet. He supposed, too, they derived comfort from their 'Little India' in Bangkok's Pahurat district, where the air smelled of cumin and sandalwood rather than coriander and jasmine; where you ate your curry with chapatti instead of rice; where conversations took place in Hindi, Urdu, Punjabi instead of Thai; and where, amongst the bolts of fabric, costume jewellery and kitchen implements, you could make your offerings at shrines dedicated to the elephant-headed Ganesh as well as the Lord Buddha.

For Rajiv who'd left India in search of adventure, Pahurat was a disappointment. His mother made him promise to visit his family there, and it became their sole topic of conversation each time he phoned home during his first week in Bangkok. She was glad to know he'd arrived safely but had he spoken with Auntie Priti and Uncle Sunder yet? Sightseeing was all very well, but when exactly did he plan to contact his family? Would he guarantee that by the time they next spoke he would have first-hand news of her beloved sister? Rajiv hadn't planned to let his relatives know he was in the country until the end of his trip when, after a year on the road, he might have welcomed some home cooking and familial banter. But his mother wore him down. Once he met his aunt and uncle, they invited him to stay with them in Pahurat, as they were bound to do, and he accepted their invitation, equally duty bound.

Not only did they choose to live in Little India, Rajiv's relatives felt compelled to maintain standards now considered outmoded in the Mother Country—another liability of immigrant life—making them more conservative than the extended family he'd left behind. His cousin-brothers who were not much younger than him had a curfew of ten o'clock. His cousin-sisters seldom left Pahurat at all. And while Rajiv was told he could take responsibility for himself, on the rare occasion he stayed out late, Auntie made such a fuss about losing sleep, it hardly seemed worth it.

The bookshop was Rajiv's saving grace. Though aware that Khao San Road didn't resemble the 'real' Bangkok any more than Little India did, working at Seema's got him out from under the family's constant surveillance, mobile phone notwithstanding, and gave him the chance to explore what kind of a man he might be in another context.

It turned out he was the kind who dated farang girls. This surprised him. Though a farang girlfriend was considered an essential accessory by most single, male traders on Khao San Road, and a good deal of the married ones, too, Rajiv wouldn't have guessed he could be such a cliché.

To be fair, his relationship with Jayne didn't really fit the norm. For one thing, most Khao San Road romances lasted about as long as it took to shop for souvenirs and arrange a minibus back to the airport. Rajiv had been seeing Jayne for several weeks and he liked her. She was unlike any girl he'd ever met. She lived on her own and did everything for herself. She didn't even have a cleaner. Rajiv had never met anyone who didn't have a cleaner. She ran her own business as a private investigator, which Rajiv was sure must be thrilling, despite what she said. Her modesty only made her more attractive.

She reminded him of 'Fearless Nadia', née Mary Evans, a circus performer turned Bollywood film star from the nineteen-thirties and forties. Fearless Nadia performed all her own stunts—sword fighting, whip cracking, lion taming—her signature act was fighting villains on top of moving trains. And like Jayne, Fearless Nadia was born in Australia.

Rajiv's attraction to Jayne both excited and unnerved him. He'd been in love once before, and he'd had sex once before, but not at the same time. His girlfriends back home came from nice, middle-class Bangalore families like he did. They'd permit a bit of 'Eve-teasing'—a grope, rub, pet—sometimes even under their clothes. However, they drew the line at anything that might technically constitute deflowering. They were 'saving themselves', though not for him.

Rajiv longed for sex *and* romance, and falling in love with a foreigner—with Jayne—seemed at last to provide a means to that end. But as yet he'd been unable to take their relationship to the next level. Admittedly, they'd only been on a few dates, exchanged a chaste kiss at the end of the night. Contrary to popular wisdom, Jayne appeared happy to let things develop between them with no sign that 'all

Western women want is to jump into the sack at the drop of a hat,' to quote his *Mama-ji*.

As much as it unnerved him, Rajiv wanted more. He wanted to spend the night with Jayne, not just have sex and leave as if she were a prostitute. That meant explaining his absence to his relatives. He might contrive to spend a day with her but the thought of making love in daylight made his heart race with anxiety, and he still faced the problem of accounting for his whereabouts. Even in a city of eleven million people, he felt trapped by the scrutiny of his family. Rajiv was stuck in Little India when his heart's desire was to run wild in a foreign country.

He stepped down from the street on to the floating dock that housed the open-sided Ton Pho Restaurant. The interior was bright with the stark light of naked fluorescent tubes. A fly-spotted poster of a fruit bowl, an outdated Tiger Beer calendar, and faded plastic roses in vases on each table passed for decorations. He nodded in greeting to the elderly lady cooking in the veranda-style kitchen off to one side, and spotted Jayne sitting at a table by the river's edge.

She looked up as he approached. She didn't greet him with a kiss for which he was grateful, being brought up to believe it was rude to display affection in public, but there was warmth in her smile. A waitress appeared with a bottle of cold beer and a menu as he took his seat. Rajiv's Thai was basic, but he got the gist when Jayne declined the menu and deferred to the woman in the kitchen. They'd just opened a second bottle of Tiger Beer—that was another thing Rajiv had learned about himself, he liked cold beer—when the food arrived. Prawn *tom yam* soup, glass noodle salad, deep-fried snakefish with a spicy dipping sauce, stir-fried greens and steamed rice. They ate with gusto and when they pushed back their empty plates, Rajiv caught a return nod of approval from the old auntie.

Jayne took out a cigarette and he leaned over to light it for her, before helping himself to one. He didn't smoke before he met Jayne, and he certainly didn't smoke as much as she did, but he'd discovered he liked one or two after his evening meal. She drew back deeply and exhaled the smoke high over their heads.

'I took on a new case today.'

He nodded his head, encouraging her to elaborate.

'Alleged suicide. Twenty-one-year-old girl. The father thinks there was foul play involved.'

'Now *that* sounds exciting,' Rajiv said, rolling the tip of his cigarette in the ashtray to bring the glowing end to a point. 'You cannot be telling me that this is just another dull case.'

'It's a welcome change of pace,' she said, smiling. 'That's the good news.'

'There's bad news?'

She exhaled more smoke.

'It requires me to go away,' she said, 'to Pattaya on the central coast. It could take a few weeks.'

'Perhaps I can visit you there.'

Rajiv spoke without thinking, but as soon as the words were out of his mouth he knew he had to make it happen. It was the chance he'd been waiting for. At the same time, he didn't want to seem obvious.

'I mean, I haven't seen much of Thailand,' he added quickly, 'and I'm keen to visit the seaside. It would be the perfect opportunity.'

'I don't know about perfect, Rajiv. I mean, Pattaya is a bit of a dive.'

'A dive?'

'Not exactly a romantic holiday destination. Foreign navies use it as an R&R port for their personnel and the bay is surround by petroleum plants. The beaches are polluted— you wouldn't want to swim there.'

Rajiv shrugged. 'Perhaps I would be in the way of your work.'

'No, no, no.' She shook her head. 'You'd be more than welcome. Once I get settled I'll give you a call and we can work out the timing. I'll find out if there are any sights worth seeing before you arrive.'

It was on the tip of Rajiv's tongue to say that the only sight he needed to see was her naked body in his arms, but felt he lacked the heroic quality necessary to deliver such a line without sounding corny.

'I am confident we can find some way to occupy our time,' he said.

His mind was already ticking over with thoughts of which cousin-brother would be most susceptible to bribery.

4

Every weekday morning, Police Major General Wichit paused by the *sarn phraphum* in the compound of his apartment building to light a cigarette and place it on the balcony of the small house-shrine for the guardian spirit who lived there. Although Wichit was not a smoker, the *phra phum* was and the Police Major General was keen to express his gratitude to the spirits that looked after him.

He used the time afforded by the slow pace of Bangkok's peak hour traffic to count his blessings. Wichit was the proverbial *nou tok thang khao sarn*, the lucky mouse who falls into the rice bin. As a young man, he had the sort of looks that made women gaze at his face longer than was considered polite. It was the juxtaposition of ruggedly handsome features—dark eyes and eyebrows, high forehead, strong jaw, thick mane of black hair—with the mouth of a pretty child, that accounted for his allure. He looked like a warrior who would salvage flowers from the same field where he'd slain enemies. Never mind that Wichit was neither brave nor romantic, but a lackadaisical man who liked a quiet life and did a remarkable job of avoiding conflict for a police officer. The promise of his looks was enough for him to win the heart of Sangravee and marry into her well-connected family, a move that would have been unthinkable if he'd been an ordinary looking traffic cop. In time his hair thinned and his sedentary lifestyle dulled the sharper edges of his beauty. If Sangravee was disappointed, she never let on. They got along well enough and their union produced two adored children, a boy and a girl, Nathee and Naree.

With a father-in-law in the Interior Ministry and a grasp of English learned at the knee of his grandmother, a former housekeeper to a British diplomat, Wichit secured one of Bangkok's most enviable postings as head of the Tourist Police. He worked in air-conditioned comfort where his toughest challenge was not to laugh in the face of reports made by exasperated farangs. How they'd paid a large sum of money for a handful of Burmese rubies that turned out to be red glass. How they'd given their passports to a tour guide who said he could get them cut-price visas to Vietnam, only to lose the man and their passports in the crowd. How they'd agreed to a friendly game of cards with a fellow who said he worked as a croupier at the casino, only to be robbed of all their travellers' cheques. How they'd exchanged money with an agent *outside* the currency exchange booth only to come away with a wad of 'Hell Bank Notes'—fake money the Chinese burned at funerals—sandwiched in between a few baht. It never ceased to surprise Wichit how people kept falling for the same old tricks. He almost longed for his countrymen to show a little more ingenuity in the scams they pulled.

Youthful good looks, gracious wife, healthy children, cushy job—these were the blessings Wichit counted as he crawled from one intersection to the next amidst four lanes of traffic. When he approached Wat Benchamabophit, the resting place of King Chulalongkorn who saved Thailand from European colonisation, Wichit counted his final blessing, the one that saved him from ruin when he stood to lose all the good fortune that came before. As he took his hands off the steering wheel, pressed his palms together and raised them to his forehead in a *wai* of respect for the King's ashes, the irony of giving thanks for a foreigner was not lost on him.

Wichit first met Jayne Keeney in connection with a timeworn card scam. She'd come to him with information on a group of Filipinos who were targeting farang tourists at the temple sites. Wichit was impressed: she brought him names, addresses and a detailed account of their modus operandi. Most farangs seldom got beyond 'Asian appearance' on their report sheets. Of course, it helped that she spoke Thai.

When she gave him her business card—'Discreet Private Investigator'—he wondered in passing about her visa arrangements, but figured that was the business of his colleagues at Immigration. Jayne's information resulted in a successful prosecution that made his office look good. But it was her work in relation to a personal matter for which he was indebted to her.

Wichit had insisted his children study English. Sangravee was unenthusiastic, but he knew from experience the difference it could make to their future employment prospects and income. As a result, Nathee and Naree attended a private English language college after school three days per week. However, unbeknownst to their parents, Nathee skived off to play video games with his friends at Panthip Plaza, leaving sixteen-year-old Naree—who'd inherited her father's good looks and her mother's romanticism—unchaperoned and at the mercy of a lecherous American teacher. All was revealed when Naree tearfully confessed to her father that she was pregnant.

If word got out, Wichit and his family faced insurmountable shame—'loss of face, eyes, mouth and hands' as the villagers would say. And it would be Wichit's fault, his daughter's indecency blamed on his association with foreigners. He would lose his job, his reputation and probably his marriage. Naree's life would be ruined, regardless of whether or not she kept the bastard child or gave it to one of their relatives in the countryside to raise among their own. She'd be damaged goods. No respectable man would ever marry her.

In desperation but acting on instinct, Wichit dug up Jayne Keeney's business card and enlisted her help to find a discreet, farang doctor to perform a termination—a procedure illegal in Thailand except on medical grounds. Jayne took the girl to and from the clinic and even volunteered her apartment for three days' recuperation following the procedure when, as far as the rest of the family was concerned, Naree was on a meditation retreat.

Wichit didn't know what Jayne said to his daughter during this time, but Naree had returned home calm and clear-eyed and proceeded to apply herself to her studies with renewed diligence. Of course, he'd seen to it that the American teacher was deported on a visa technicality and replaced with a suitably matronly type. Naree hadn't given Wichit cause for a moment's concern since.

Thus did Wichit count Khun Jayne among his blessings. And while he would never be comfortable owing his honour to a farang woman some twenty years his junior, he respected Jayne as he would a Thai person when it came to *sam neuk boon khun*—to honouring his debts. He welcomed any opportunity she provided to demonstrate his gratitude.

Wichit parked his car in the small area reserved for officials and entered the Tourist Police Bureau through a tinted plate-glass door. He acknowledged the *wai* from his secretary and proceeded to his office where he found the document Jayne requested on the top of his in-tray: the police report into the death of an Australian girl in Pattaya. Wichit often looked over his colleagues' reports into cases involving foreigners in the Kingdom. They sought his advice on everything from how best to phrase their findings, to the size of the fines they should impose for traffic infringements and other minor offences. Sometimes he looked over the translations in order to ensure use of appropriate language. He remembered doing so in this very case.

He was leafing through the English version when his secretary buzzed to announce Jayne's arrival.

'*Sawadee ka*, Police Major General,' she said.

'*Sawadee krup*, Khun Jayne.'

He returned her *wai* and nodded for her to take a seat. 'How are you?'

'Fine thank you, sir. And you?'

'Fine.'

'How's your family?'

Wichit assumed this was politeness on her part and not a subtle reminder of the debt he owed her.

'Everyone is well thank you. Now regarding your request,' he handed over the reports. 'The paperwork on the death of Maryanne Delbeck, in Thai and English.'

Jayne accepted it with a nod.

'Anything else I can do to help?'

'I might have questions after I've read through this,' she said.

'Of course.'

She thought for a moment. 'Do you know anyone in Pattaya?'

Wichit turned to a card file on the desk in front of him. 'I have a nephew there, he's a businessman.' He leafed through the cards. 'Here it is, Santiphap Accounting. My nephew's name is Kritsanachai, Chai for short. Take it.'

Jayne looked at the business card. 'Will you let him know I'll be in contact?'

Wichit nodded. 'Anything else?'

'Thanks, that's all for now.'

She slipped the card into her pocket. 'Say hello to Naree for me.'

'Of course,' Wichit lied.

While he would continue to give thanks to the forces, human and spiritual, that saved his family's honour, it would only be inviting bad luck for Wichit to ever remind his daughter of her narrow escape from disgrace.

Jayne spent the day preparing for her trip to Pattaya: collecting surveillance photos from the print shop, finalising another case report, invoicing two clients, arranging a deferral from another.

Kate Murchison, the YCV coordinator, called mid-afternoon from Max's office. She seemed unenthusiastic about a meeting, but Max must have put in a good word for Jayne as, after some muffled conversation, Kate proposed they get together later that evening after she'd had the chance to do some shopping. Jayne would have preferred to spend the night at home but supposed she should be grateful Max didn't rope her into going along on the shopping spree, too.

She arrived at Kate's guesthouse at the designated time

of nine o'clock. Twenty minutes later, she was still waiting. She leafed through *The Bangkok Post*. Yet again the only news from Australia was Pauline Hanson and her One Nation party, that had risen to prominence in the wake of the previous year's election. The local media had a macabre fascination with One Nation's racist agenda and gave Hanson so much coverage most Thais assumed she was the Australian Prime Minister.

She turned to the comics to lighten her mood and had just unscrambled the day's nine-letter anagram when a voice asked, 'Are you Jayne Keeney?'

The woman was heavy-set with a halo of frizzy red hair around a freckled face. Jayne nodded.

'I'm Kate,' the woman said, shaking her hand. 'Sorry to keep you. I just *had* to have a shower. You know what it's like. I can't *believe* how hot it gets here.'

Kate was wearing a sleeveless top, long skirt of flimsy material and sandals, a film of sweat on her forehead despite the shower. Jayne, who was wearing a jacket, felt cold in the air-conditioned lobby and wished she'd worn a long-sleeved T-shirt as well.

'So I guess you'd rather not sit outside?' Jayne said.

'Are you joking?'

Jayne started to think it might be a short meeting.

'What would you like—apart from air-conditioning, I mean? Tea, coffee, something stronger?'

'Oh, God, just because I work for a Christian organisation, doesn't mean...' Kate stopped herself with a laugh. 'I'd love a cold beer, if that's okay with you.'

'That's fine with me.'

'I saw a pub nearby that looked good. What was it called...the Shamrock?'

'The Rose and Shamrock,' Jayne said without enthusiasm.

Irish theme bars had proliferated throughout the world until the pale imitations way outnumbered authentic pubs in Ireland. The Rose and Shamrock was one of several Bangkok versions, a hang-out for soccer hooligans, sunburned tourists and backpackers en route to Australia for working holidays. If that wasn't enough to put her off, Jayne once had a fling with the head barman.

Kate was keen and if pseudo-Celtic was what appealed, then Jayne figured the charms of Bangkok's unique and quirky bars would probably be lost on her. She led the way to the pub and winced as she opened the door on a group of pink-faced men and women drunkenly singing along to U2's 'Sunday bloody Sunday'. She gestured across the room, away from the crowd.

'I'll get us a table if you go to the bar.'

'What do you want to drink?'

'Whatever you're having.'

Jayne slipped into a corner booth and sat with her back to the crowd in an effort to block them out. The green vinyl of the bench seat matched the sickly colour of the carpet and a mural of maniacal-looking leprechauns stared down at her from the opposite wall. The coasters on the table said 'Guinness is good for you'. She lit a cigarette in an effort to mask the smell of spilt beer and urine and had smoked it down to the butt by the time Kate reappeared with a pint in each hand. Jayne stared at the vase of watery lager in front of her and made a note to be more specific with her drinks order.

They made small talk over the first round, sharing cigarettes and travel stories. Jayne bought a second round, another pint for Kate and a bottle of Heineken for herself.

She had Kate pegged for a drink-too-much-and-tell-all kind of girl and she did not disappoint.

'It's not like I want to work specifically for a Christian organisation,' Kate said, setting a third round on the table and raising her voice over the crowd noise. 'I mean, I believe in God and all that, but I don't go to church. I just want to get some experience, you know, to work in international aid.'

'It must be a tough area to get into,' Jayne said, trying to sound sympathetic.

'I reckon.' Kate gulped her beer. 'I mean, you can't get a job unless you've got overseas experience, but how do you get overseas experience when you can't get a job?'

Jayne saw a chance to steer the conversation towards Maryanne Delbeck. 'I suppose that's where volunteering comes in.'

'Huh?'

'People volunteer to work overseas as a stepping-stone to a career in international development.'

'I suppose,' Kate paused to light another cigarette, 'though it doesn't always work that way.'

'What do you mean?'

'We've never sent a single woman to South America who hasn't come back married or pregnant or both.' Kate giggled. 'I'm putting up my hand for the next available posting.'

Jayne forced a smile and tried again. 'How tough is it to get a posting? I mean, do you have to pass some sort of test?'

'Not really. There's an orientation process that everyone has to go through, and a medical.'

'Police check?'

'Rarely. Most host organisations don't require it.'

'So you do the orientation and the medical. Then what happens?'

'You get offered a placement.'

'What if the applicant is not up to scratch?'

'Like what? Crazy or something?'

'Not even crazy. Just inappropriate. What then?'

'Well, if they were really bad, we'd probably just string them along, not offer them anything until they got sick of waiting and tried somewhere else,' Kate said.

'Okay.' Jayne kept her expression neutral. 'What if there's a problem with a volunteer during a placement?'

Kate shrugged. 'YCV's attitude is you either sink or swim. It's part of the cultural immersion experience.'

She must have realised how trite that sounded because she hastened to add, 'YCV doesn't believe in micro-managing relationships. Our job is to match the skills of the volunteer with the needs of the host community. After that, it's up to the respective parties to make things work between them. They're all adults.'

'If someone was having problems would YCV be aware of it?'

'It depends. We'd rely on the volunteer or their host to bring it to our attention.'

'Did Maryanne Delbeck bring anything to your attention?'

Kate seemed surprised at the mention of Maryanne's name. She shook her head.

'What about her hosts?'

'Only after the...I mean, after she...'

'After the alleged suicide,' Jayne offered.

Kate nodded. The topic of conversation seemed to be sobering her up.

'Maryanne's father has asked me to look into the circumstances of her death,' Jayne said.

'Oh?'

Again, her surprise seemed genuine.

'Did you know Maryanne well?'

'I met her a couple of times during her orientation,' Kate said. 'She was a nice person. I was very sorry when she... when she died.'

'Were you surprised?'

'Yes.' Kate swirled the dregs of her beer around in the bottom of her glass and spoke as if she were thinking out loud. 'I *was* surprised. Maryanne didn't seem like the type who'd...'

She paused, flustered, caught saying something she shouldn't.

'I'm speaking from a personal perspective of course,' she said. 'I'm not qualified to comment.'

She drained the last of her beer and placed the empty pint on the table.

'I'm sure Maryanne's father has his reasons, but YCV has nothing to add to what we've already told the Pattaya police and the Australian Embassy.'

'So you're not interested in anything I might turn up?'

'Frankly, I'm going back to three progress reports, two funding applications and a new round of placements for Thailand and Vietnam.'

'Then I'd better not keep you.'

Jayne stood to leave, put her cigarettes into the pocket of her jacket, when a voice behind her said, 'I taught I recognised dose black curls.'

She turned around.

'Hello Declan. How are you? How's Noi?'

'Noi?'

'You know, Thai girl, barely legal—remember?'

Declan grinned. His eyes were amber, but not in an attractive way. As if his skull was full of beer.

'Ach, I was sooch a fool!'

'I won't argue with you there.'

'Aren't you going to introduce me to your friend?' Kate interrupted them, her own bleary eyes locking on Declan's.

'Sure,' Jayne said. 'Kate, this is Declan. Declan this is Kate.'

Jayne inched away as she spoke.

'Kate, I know more about Declan than I wish I did, and Declan, I know less about Kate than I'd like to. But enough about me.'

Neither of them looked at her as she backed out the door.

5

People went to Ekamai only to leave it. Bangkok's Eastern Bus Terminal was a maze of ticket windows, shelters and numbered docking bays, where dozens of buses idled with engines rumbling, air noxious with the smell of diesel fuel and rotting fruit. Despite the diligent cleaning ladies whose grass brooms whisked away litter beneath the feet of thousands of travellers each day, a layer of grime covered every surface, a miasma of dirt hung in the air. Sad-eyed children holding paper cups wandered among the crowds gesturing for food, while their quicker-fingered compatriots filched unguarded purses and wallets. Poor families huddled around red, white and blue striped bags that contained cheap plastic goods, paid for with their life savings, which unscrupulous traders convinced them would sell for a huge profit in their village back home. Flustered tourists rushed from one dock to another in search of their departure point, anxiety mounting at each dead-end. It didn't help that they kept asking people at random for help. Loath to disappoint, the Thais would rather give wrong directions than none at all.

Jayne took pity on a German couple and escorted them to their bus to Rayong, before making her way to the Pattaya berth. On Jim Delbeck's allowance she could have hired a taxi for the trip, but figured she'd try to make some money out of this job.

The frigid temperature inside the bus overcompensated for the humidity of the depot. Jayne chose a window seat towards the middle, took out a jacket and stowed her backpack in the overhead luggage compartment. Her ticket promised on-board entertainment and as the bus pulled out, a video started up on a television mounted above the driver's seat. An American action movie with Thai subtitles. The soundtrack was indecipherable, though that didn't stop the driver from turning up the volume. Jayne tuned out to the din—a skill she'd honed living in Bangkok—and turned her attention to the report into Maryanne Delbeck's death.

According to the Pattaya police, Maryanne's body was found at the foot of the Bayview Hotel's White Wing in the early hours of the morning of Monday 30 September 1996. She appeared to have fallen fourteen storeys from the rooftop terrace to the lawn of the hotel garden. The police were called by the hotel night guard who'd come across the body during a routine inspection. The guard had not seen the accident take place, nor heard anything other than what he thought was a peacock's cry; the exotic birds wandered the gardens of a nearby resort. The report noted for the record that he was a former soldier with a spotless record. Death was confirmed by the police medical officer at the scene, the corpse identified by the hotel receptionist. Maryanne had been staying on the premises for three months. The deceased's room was subsequently cordoned off. Police found nothing there other than personal effects.

The Scientific Crime Detection Division found no evidence of foul play at the scene. There was a swimming pool on the rooftop terrace, but there was nothing to suggest Maryanne had been in or near the pool prior to her death. The safety barrier surrounding the rooftop area—a metre-high wall of painted concrete and iron—was undamaged, and it was not possible to say whether she'd climbed, fallen or been pushed over it based on traces of paint on her feet and clothes.

The rooftop bar was closed for service after ten o'clock at night, though the terrace remained accessible via the main elevator and a goods lift. Estimated time of death was around one in the morning. Police interviewed hotel staff, but no one noticed the lift ascending to the rooftop at that late hour. Nor did they see anything suspicious on the night.

The autopsy report outlined multiple skull and spinal fractures and internal organ damage, and concluded 'the deceased's injuries are consistent with a fall from a height commensurate with the fourteen storey building at the base of which the body was found. Death was most likely instantaneous.'

That thought gave Jayne some comfort as she skimmed through the photographs of Maryanne's broken and bloodied body. She'd landed on her back. Her hands were raised at either side of her face, a sleeping child pose at odds with the pool of blood at the back of her head and the violent twist of her legs. She wore simple cotton pants and a T-shirt and her feet were bare.

The daily newspapers in Thailand were filled with gruesome images like these, ostensibly to remind all good Buddhists of the impermanence of the flesh. However, it felt voyeuristic to Jayne. She put the photos back in their envelope and returned to the report.

With the physical evidence inconclusive and in the absence

of a note or confession, the finding of suicide appeared to have hinged on the testimony of Maryanne Delbeck's colleagues at the New Life Children's Centre where she'd worked as a volunteer. The centre was an orphanage for babies and children who'd been abandoned, relinquished, or admitted into care by families who couldn't afford to keep them. Children eligible for inter-country adoption were housed in their own facility and foreign volunteers engaged to acclimatise them to being around Westerners before their adoptive families arrived to claim them. Maryanne had been assigned to two babies, the first adopted out two months before her death, the second due to be adopted out the week after.

Maryanne's colleagues said she'd seemed unwell in the weeks leading up to her death. Fellow volunteers said she'd complained of headaches and seemed tired all the time. One described her as 'distracted'. Frank Harding, the centre's resident foreign adviser, said Maryanne had become 'increasingly tense and depressed' during her five months in Thailand. He speculated 'she was unable to cope with the level of human despair and degradation she witnessed day-to-day during her placement in Pattaya.'

The crucial testimony came from Doctor Somsri Kaysorn, the specialist medical consultant to the centre. Unbeknownst to either her family or colleagues, Maryanne had regular appointments with Doctor Somsri at his private practice for more than two months prior to her death. Doctor Somsri had diagnosed clinical depression, prescribed antidepressants and conducted therapeutic counselling.

The autopsy found no traces of drugs of any kind in Maryanne's bloodstream. When asked about this, Doctor Somsri maintained that had she taken the prescribed medication, Maryanne's suicidal impulses would have been kept in check.

Jayne flicked back to the autopsy report and noted there was no trace of alcohol in Maryanne's bloodstream either. Nothing. Not even paracetamol for the headaches.

She looked up from her reading and gazed through the tinted window of the bus. There was little countryside between Bangkok and Pattaya, the urban sprawl of the city extended into the new estates and industrial zones all the way to the coast. The highway was thick with fast moving traffic. Ahead of the bus in the adjacent lane was a utility truck loaded with hessian sacks of rice that bulged over the sides of the tray like a paunch overhanging a pair of tight jeans. A motorcyclist tailed the truck, helmet on his handlebars, baseball cap on his head. Other than the odd, amusing use of English—a condominium called 'Happy World', the 'Nanny Pink' fashion boutique, the 'Life Style Shop' selling pedestal toilets—there wasn't much to look at. Not Thailand at its finest.

The other finding of note in the police report was that only a few days before her death, Maryanne had emptied her Thai bank account, withdrawing the equivalent of around three thousand Australian dollars. Bank statements appended to the report showed a history of regular deposits into the account: small amounts in fortnightly payments suggesting a volunteer stipend; larger monthly instalments sent by international transfer, which increased over time and probably came from Jim Delbeck. There was no way of knowing what Maryanne had done with the money, though the chief investigating officer concluded her actions supported the suicide theory 'as the deceased probably felt she had no further use for the funds'. It struck Jayne that if this were the case, Maryanne would have closed the account altogether. Or was she too suicidal to bother with such banal tasks?

She made a note of the anomaly and swapped the police report for the envelope Jim Delbeck had given her. In stark contrast to the forensic images was a head-and-shoulders photo of Maryanne. She had the same guileless smile on her face as she did in *The Bangkok Post*, the air of a person without a care in the world. It was hard to reconcile this image with that of a young volunteer depressed to the point of being suicidal.

Nor was there any sign of depression in Maryanne's letters home to her family. In one of the earliest dated 10 June 1996, Maryanne described her work as 'so satisfying'.

I'm working one-on-one with a little girl called Sobha, though one of my tasks is to get her used to her new name, Sophie, she wrote. *I'm preparing her for life with her adoptive parents, who are coming from the USA to collect her in about six weeks. She's just under a year old and I'm teaching her how to say mummy, daddy, that sort of thing.*

Jayne checked the dates of Maryanne's letters against the doctor's report. Was it significant that her first visit to Doctor Somsri roughly coincided with the departure of Sobha/Sophie to live with her adoptive parents?

Jayne leafed through the photocopied letters.

Sophie's new parents, Mike and Deborah, came for her today, Maryanne wrote to her mother on 19 July. *They were so happy, it was fantastic! Of course, Sophie couldn't really know what was going on, but I like to think I prepared her well. She didn't cry when Deborah picked her up, but let herself be held and cuddled. It helped that Deborah was wearing a string of brightly coloured beads: Sophie loved them. She's totally adorable and I'll miss her. But she's gone to a lovely family, and it feels great to have helped make that happen.*

While Maryanne undoubtedly kept things from her parents—just as Jayne sanitised her experiences in her own letters home—it didn't make sense for her to put on a brave face in this instance. She seemed genuinely happy about the outcome for Sophie.

Jayne read through the rest of the letters and conceded that Jim Delbeck had a point: Maryanne's correspondence was uniformly upbeat. She came across as cheery, her confidence verging on conceit. There was nothing to suggest depression, let alone suicidal tendencies.

Maryanne wrote once a fortnight for the first two months, tapering off to once every three or four weeks thereafter. The only negative inference Jayne could find was in a letter dated 5 August.

I feel sorry for the ones who can't be adopted out, Maryanne wrote. *It's quite common here for poor families to hand over their kids to be raised in an institution. But they're not considered orphans so they can't be put up for adoption. It seems so unfair. It's not as if their families visit them regularly. Some never come back for them at all.*

Even in this case, Maryanne focused on the positives. *They're not all lost causes and we've had a few cases where successful counselling has resulted in a parent or parents putting their child up for adoption. The specialist adviser, Frank Harding, is really good. He's American but he speaks Thai fluently and he's been in Pattaya a long time. Because he knows both Thailand and the USA, he can be honest with the poorer mothers and families about where their child would be better off.*

That's a matter of opinion, Jayne thought.

I really like what I do now, but I'm thinking of asking Frank if I can work with the boarders, Maryanne concluded in a letter on 23 August. *I'd like to try and help make a difference to these kids, and my teacher says it would be a great way to improve my Thai language skills.*

Hardly the words of someone unable to cope.

The Australian Embassy's investigator noted this apparent contradiction, though after re-interviewing Doctor Somsri and staff and volunteers at the New Life Children's Centre, he stood by the Pattaya police report findings. His report included a photocopy of a prescription for antidepressants issued to Maryanne Delbeck six weeks before her death. There were also photocopies of pages from the doctor's appointment diary showing the frequency of Maryanne's visits. The consultant noted that depression was an insidious illness, the effects of which Maryanne could well have kept hidden from her loved ones, particularly given the distance between them.

Jayne scanned back over the letters for any irregularities she might have missed. There were letters addressed to her mother and father, others to her mother alone, none addressed only to her father, but that didn't necessarily mean anything. Passing mention of the brother, Ian, but less concern for his wellbeing than for 'Mitzu the Shiatsu' to whom Maryanne sent love at the end of each letter. She wasn't unique in preferring the company of a dog to a sibling.

The letters were matter-of-fact rather than intimate. There were occasional references to friends in Pattaya but nothing specific and little about the place itself. In short, a G-rated account of her adventures in Thailand. Jayne wondered if there were an R-rated version somewhere. A journal perhaps. Maryanne struck her as the type to keep a diary, but there was no mention of one in any of the reports.

Jayne understood Jim Delbeck's frustration. The finding of suicide appeared to come down to the opinion of a doctor over a father.

She stared again through the bus window. She doubted she'd learn anything new by interviewing the same people for a third time. If there were fresh light to be shed on the case, it would have to come from somewhere else. She went over the case again in her head, searching for gaps, until she remembered a throwaway line in one of Maryanne's letters.

My teacher says it would be a great way to improve my Thai language skills.

Maryanne was studying Thai. There was no mention of anyone having interviewed her Thai teacher. It might not amount to much, but it was a start.

The noise from the video cut out abruptly as the driver announced their arrival at the Pattaya Bus Station. Jayne fended off the taxi drivers and hotel touts and headed to North Pattaya Road to hail a *songthaew*, literally 'two rows'. Pattaya's chief form of public transport was a utility truck, its tray lined with parallel bench seats and sheltered by a canvas awning. Jayne checked the direction the driver was headed and climbed on board. There were six farang men and three Thai women in the vehicle, one bouncing a chubby infant on her lap. Jayne took a seat at the end of the bench on the right side where she had a view out the back.

The *songthaew* headed west along a road lined with billboards plugging beer, shampoo, petrol, mobile phones and 'Tiffany's: The Original Transvestite Cabaret Show New Extravaganza'. Turning left at a roundabout with a dolphin fountain at its centre, they cruised south along the coast road, following the curve of Pattaya Bay. The *songthaew* pulled over to let off the Thai woman and her baby. Jayne got her first good look at the beach. She took in a grubby strip of sand dotted with coconut palms and large-leafed *hu khang* trees. Tourists lazed on wooden sun lounges beneath umbrellas that stretched as far as she could see. Vendors trawled the sand with baskets of fruit on their heads, sarongs draped over their arms, and seafood grilling in metal bowls dangling from poles across their shoulders. A sinewy Thai woman massaged the back of a fleshy blonde in a leopard print bikini. Her companion was having her toenails painted. The whine of distant jet-skis could be heard above the idling *songthaew* engine.

They took off again and Jayne turned her attention to the opposite side of the road, a stretch of open-fronted beer bars, guesthouses, hotels and go-go clubs with a 7-Eleven every fifty paces. The bars had names that ranged from corny—Happy Friend, Lovely Corner, We Are The World Beer Bar—to bawdy. Among the latter, Jayne liked Shaggers for its simplicity. Despite the mid-afternoon sun, the bars were more crowded than the beach, and Jayne noted with a wry smile that where Thai women were concerned, the beach was for covering up, the bars for bikinis.

The trip continued through Central Pattaya past more beer bars, a dive centre, a couple of shopping plazas. Two more farang men descended at Soi Pattayaland 2, aka 'Boyz Town', the town's busiest gay zone, before the *songthaew* turned left into South Pattaya Road and headed away from the beach. Jayne lost her bearings for a few minutes as they zigzagged up the cliff, but caught sight of the Bayview Hotel and pressed the button on the roof to bring the *songthaew* to a stop.

A young Thai woman in high-cut denim shorts, pink singlet and diamante-studded sunglasses watched Jayne get out. In one of those moments when Jayne wished she couldn't speak the language, the woman turned to her friend and in a voice loud enough to be heard over the engine asked, 'What do you think a fat farang like her is looking for in Pattaya?'

6

Jayne could see why Maryanne chose the Bayview Hotel. It was a cliff-top sanctuary dividing the sleaze of Pattaya in the north from Jomtien in the south, a quieter stretch billed as 'family oriented' with a gay beach at one end and a large Russian presence at the other.

The hotel had two distinct sections: the White Wing, a modern tower of 'deluxe' and 'superior' rooms; and the Green Wing, an older, low-rise guesthouse with a dozen 'standard' rooms. Judging from the liberal use of Formica and round feature windows, Jayne dated the Green Wing circa 1960; the White Wing was still so new the paintwork had barely begun to blister.

The Green Wing was not so much surrounded as encroached upon by a tropical garden: the rooms smelled of damp, liana vines crept through the air-vents, and palms jostled against the balcony railings like Triffids. The White Wing by contrast was surrounded by a belt of neat lawn, interrupted only by two large umbrella trees that survived the renovation.

Jayne knew from her file notes that Maryanne had rented a room in the Green Wing after a short-lived experiment in a flat on her own. *The apartment was in what they call a condo,* she wrote home to her parents. *All the neighbours were sleazy European men with much younger Thai girlfriends (or boyfriends!). I came home one night and found a guy trying to break in my door. He said the landlord had sent him to check the security system, but I didn't believe him. I packed up my things on the spot and moved into the hotel where I am now. It's so much safer for me here, more secure. Plus I was getting really run down because work is so exhausting and I couldn't be bothered cooking for myself. But the hotel has a 24-hour kitchen and breakfast is included in the room rate. What do you think? Will you cover the extra?*

This explained the increase in the monthly payments into Maryanne's account.

The police report mentioned that although Maryanne wasn't staying in the White Wing, as a guest she had access to all hotel facilities including the tower's rooftop bar and swimming pool. Hotel staff interviewed by police couldn't say how often Maryanne had made use of these facilities, though it was considered odd that she should be there when the bar and pool were closed.

Jayne booked into an upper storey room in the Green Wing. It crossed her mind that this might well have been Maryanne's room. The Thais would consider it haunted and gladly let it to a godless farang. Good thing she wasn't superstitious.

The simple room contained a queen-sized bed with side tables and reading lamps bolted onto the wall at one end, a unit with a built-in desk, TV, bar fridge, wardrobe and mirror at the other. The en suite bathroom to the left of the entrance was so small you could have a shower, brush your teeth and use the toilet all at the same time. On the far side of the room, glass doors led to a balcony containing two white plastic chairs and a matching table. A glass ashtray rested precariously on the railing.

Jayne unpacked her clothes and placed the paperwork on the desk but didn't linger. Armed with cigarettes, wallet, mobile phone and a notebook, she headed back out to the main road in search of a *songthaew* to take her into Central Pattaya.

Following the direction of the traffic, she walked west along Soi 7 towards the beach. The beer bars were stacked side-by-side and piled on top of one another like speakers at a stadium concert, each playing a different tune. The result was a cacophony of whining Thai pop, booming slow rock and the clang of Thai boxing music, all competing to the point of distortion. Jayne fled to Soi 8, but it was more of the same. The cluttered footpaths forced her on to the road, where she careened into a pile of sand. She stopped to shake out the grit in her sandals, the traffic fumes made her eyes water. She'd planned to explore the district for a while, but soaking up the atmosphere made her feel like she needed a shower.

She headed back to the main drag and waved down another *songthaew*. It was nearing dusk. Neon signs and fairy-lights flickered around the entrances to the bars and restaurants. From the dolphin fountain she continued north, pressing the button to descend at one of the *soi*, or secondary roads, that ran west of Thanon Naklua. She avoided a hole in the road and the spider-web of electrical wires inside it and skirted around a pile of bitumen chunks. She might as well never have left Bangkok.

The New Life Children's Centre was in a gated compound halfway along the soi. In typical Thai fashion, the gate was elaborate wrought iron painted gold, intended to make a good impression. Jayne peered through the railings. Inside was an assortment of freestanding buildings labelled in Thai and English—Administration, Orphanage, Clinic—connected by plant-lined paths and surrounded by manicured lawns. There was a large crucifix on the outer wall of the orphanage. The place looked orderly and welcoming, though a sign on the front gate in Thai and English advised visitors were not admitted without an appointment. Jayne jotted down the phone number. Attached to the gatepost was a perspex box containing pamphlets in English entitled 'Give A Child A New Life: Volunteer Now'. Jayne slipped one into her pocket.

A security guard in a navy uniform with a loop of red braid over one shoulder approached from inside the compound. The logo on his sleeve said 'Steel Man Inc'. A contractor. Jayne asked for directions to the other part of the centre. He sent her further along the soi, down a laneway on the left, straight ahead at a dog's leg intersection to another compound on the right.

This also had a gate, though not as elaborate and painted blue, with a sign in Thai only. Behind the gate the buildings looked ill at ease. They reminded Jayne of classrooms she'd taught in during a student placement in outer-metropolitan Melbourne: intended as temporary but never replaced, the portables huddled on the landscape like squatters in constant fear of eviction. Here each building differed as if they'd been added in stages, the office newer than either the clinic or the building marked *Satharn Liang Dek*, 'Nursery'. The pathways connecting the buildings were unadorned, but a yellow and red striped awning sheltered the path between the clinic and nursery.

As she watched, a nurse emerged cradling a crying infant. Jayne could hear the woman hushing the baby as she hurried to the clinic. She was dressed completely in white, from the perky cap on her head to the pristine sandshoes on her feet. She even wore white stockings.

Moments later, another two women came out of the nursery. Judging by their clothing—both wore singlets, one in flared jeans, the other in a denim miniskirt—they were not staff. One carried what Jayne assumed was an imitation Louis Vuitton tote bag, the other, Dolce e Gabbana.

The women were headed towards the gate when two men—an older farang and a Thai security guard—stepped out from behind a building into the women's path. The farang man wore a crucifix around his neck large enough to make out at a distance of more than ten metres. Jayne guessed this was Frank Harding, the centre's expatriate adviser.

She was too far away to understand what they were saying, but the women's body language suggested the exchange was unwelcome. The one with the D&G tote smiled but clutched her bag tight. The other didn't fold her arms so much as hug herself. The conversation was tense and brief. Jayne noticed that the security guard continued to block their path after the women clearly motioned to leave. From where she stood, it looked like a shakedown.

Jayne ducked back down the laneway to the soi. By the time the women emerged, they were both talking on mobile phones, too distracted to notice her. On impulse, she followed them.

7

Mayuree tried to take her son out of the centre every Sunday. Ever since he was born she treated it as their special day. Sometimes working two jobs—cleaning by day, bar work at night—caught up with her and she'd sleep through her alarm and into the afternoon, until it was too late to do much more than drop by on her way to work and steal a sleepy kiss. But on this occasion she and Wen had succeeded in spending Sunday with their boys.

They'd picked up Kob and Moo mid-morning and brought them back to their shared apartment. They spent time marvelling at how fast the boys were growing. They fed them rice soup and lay alongside them watching as they napped. In the cool of the late afternoon, they took the boys to a quiet, shady part of Naklua beach and let them play in the sand.

It broke Mayuree's heart to leave Kob in an institution. But once Sumet left, she had little choice. For the first few weeks she tried pretending that the centre could substitute for her brother's care. Where once she'd left Kob with Sumet, she took the boy to the nursery each afternoon and picked him up the next morning on her way home from the bar.

Not having Sumet to look after the baby during the day meant taking Kob with her on her cleaning jobs. Fighting exhaustion, she would carry him in a sling on her back while she scrubbed other people's houses. Sometimes she let him lie on a cool, tiled floor, where he swatted at dust-mites caught in beams of sunlight. But as he became more mobile, squirming to be released from the sling, rolling from one side of the room to the other, grabbing at rags, brooms, floor cleaner and bleach, Mayuree was forced to reconsider the arrangement. By necessity, Kob ended up spending more time in the institution, less time with her.

As she took pains to explain to Khun Frank, the counsellor at the centre, it didn't mean she loved Kob less. It's just that her options were limited.

Khun Frank asked her about family support. She wanted to tell him they'd had the perfect arrangement: her brother looked after the baby while she worked to save enough money to get them home to Kanchanaburi. But Sumet had insisted that he could raise money, too—enough to take them further from Pattaya than back to the western province they came from. Poor, sweet, dumb Sumet.

As for her parents, Mayuree pretended she had none, though in truth, she could no more endure long-distance separation from Kob than she could subject him to their disapproval.

Mayuree's native province of Kanchanaburi was known amongst Thais for its national parks and border skirmishes with Burma. Other tourists visited because Kanchanaburi was where the Japanese Imperial Army forced farang prisoners to build the train line to Burma. This 'Death Railway' passed over a bridge on the Kwae River not far from where Mayuree grew up. There was a film about the bridge, which Mayuree had never managed to sit through without falling asleep. That didn't stop her selling the video alongside bottled water, soap and batteries to tourists who came into her parents' store.

Her mother later regretted encouraging her daughter to interact with farangs. She blamed herself for setting in train the events that led to her daughter's disgrace and the birth of a black-skinned bastard grandson—a mother's punishment for having put the family's business interests ahead of Mayuree's honour.

In fact, the farangs in Kanchanaburi were mostly sad-looking old men and polite backpackers, who praised Mayuree's schoolgirl English, never argued about prices and did nothing to prepare her for the sort of foreigners she encountered in Pattaya. But there was no point arguing with her mother. *Mae* saw Kob not as the beautiful baby he was, but as a penalty, a curse. Unlike *Mae*, Sumet was deeply fond of Kob and had tried to make a difference for his sister and his nephew; but he'd been too ambitious. *Euam ded dok fah*—reaching for flowers in the sky.

Mayuree wanted peace and stability for her son. She also wanted to raise him to think highly of himself, to have pride. She wondered at times if it was too much to expect.

Mayuree missed Kanchanaburi. She missed the Erawan Falls that looked like the sacred three-headed elephant. She missed communal bathing in the shallow pools, the old ladies scrubbing their grandchildren while the young girls took turns to shampoo each other's hair. She missed swimming, fully-clothed, with her brother and cousins in the deeper pools where tiny fish nipped at their toes and water cascaded over their necks. She missed their picnics on the rocks, eating barbecued chicken on bamboo skewers, rolling sticky rice into bite-sized balls, shooing the monkeys that tried to steal their fried bananas.

She wanted her son to know these pleasures and the quiet and gentle pace of life on a river. It was a far cry from their life in Pattaya. She wished she could transport him by water instead of by road, lull him to sleep in a rocking long-tail boat instead of a makeshift hammock in her cramped one-room apartment above a pharmacy. But she couldn't take him home to Kanchanaburi until she could hold her head up high enough to protect him with her shadow.

It was to this end that Mayuree worked two jobs. Her plan was to save until she had enough to buy a small business in Kan'buri, a place on the river towards the famous bridge not far from the railway station. She would open a beer bar—she'd worked in the industry long enough to learn a thing or two about running such a business—a low-key place with a pool table at the back and a terrace overlooking the water. She would fill the terrace with plants—gem flowers, a thorny *poi sian* in a dragon pot for luck—and serve cold beer and spicy Thai snacks. She would employ one or two staff to help her and pay them a decent wage. There would be no need for commissions and nothing for sale but food and drink. Music would play low in the background and the volume on the television, if she decided to put one in, would be turned right down. She and Kob would live above the bar. She'd invite her cousin's daughter to live with them and send her to school when she wasn't taking care of the baby.

Mayuree invested her savings in stocks and shares, making use of what she'd learned as an undergraduate in Bangkok: she'd completed two years of a financial management degree with pleasing results, before falling for the wrong kind of man and having her world turned upside down. She calculated that if she worked hard, notwithstanding any unexpected outlays, she'd have enough for a deposit in just over a year's time, within a month or so of Kob's second birthday. She might have saved faster had she continued to work in the go-go club—Wen earned more than her on a weekly basis—but after Kob was born, Mayuree couldn't face it any more. At the beer bar, she earned a basic wage plus commission if she reached her sales quota. If not, she could always dance for tips. It was a chore, but at least she kept her underwear on.

They were running late for work by the time she and Wen brought the boys back to the centre. Kob had fallen asleep sitting up on the motorcycle taxi between Mayuree and the driver, and she carefully transferred him to her shoulder, paid the fare and rang the bell at the gate. Wen bounced a grizzling Moo on her hip. Mayuree pressed the bell again. Chaowalit shuffled into view, saw them standing there, and slowed his pace.

'Kor thort ka,' she implored him, 'Please hurry, older brother. We get fined if we're late for work.'

Chaowalit said nothing, continued to saunter. When he finally unlocked the gate, the women brushed past, ignoring his sarcastic bow.

'Asshole,' Mayuree murmured.

The centre staff were setting out the evening meal for the older children as Mayuree and Wen bustled in. With a nod, they took their sons through to the sleeping area. The boys had standard issue cots that Mayuree and Wen tried to make special with linen and soft toys. But their gifts were swallowed up in the institution.

Mayuree kissed her son's forehead, lay him on his side and patted his bottom a few times. As he dozed, she took the fluffy green frog that was his favourite from her tote bag and placed it under his arm. She put a new set of clothes in the pillowcase at the foot of the cot, and turned back to *hom kaem*—sniff-kiss—his cheek.

'See you soon, my precious boy,' she whispered.

Wen had managed to settle Moo. The two women retraced their steps and headed for the gate, but to Mayuree's dismay, found their path blocked by Chaowalit and Frank the farang counsellor.

'Sisters, I wonder if I could have a word,' he began.

Mayuree forced a tight smile. '*Kor thort na ka*, Khun Frank, but we are running late for work.'

'Ah yes, work,' the farang said.

Chaowalit sniggered, playing his usual role as Khun Frank's standover man. Mayuree ignored him.

'So if you'll excuse us,' she said.

'Perhaps sisters you've had time to consider the proposal I put to you last time we spoke,' Frank continued.

Wen made a move to speak but Mayuree cut her off.

'We've considered the proposal, yes,' she said, 'but we're happy with the current arrangement. Thank you for your concern. Now, please—'

'*Sia jai*,' he said, 'I'm disappointed to hear that. The choice is yours. Perhaps we can talk again sometime soon?'

Mayuree smiled again and gave him a *wai*. Wen followed suit. But Chaowalit's bulk still blocked their path.

'Please let us pass, older brother,' Mayuree said through gritted teeth.

The security guard puffed out his chest and leered at them, before ambling off to open the gate.

'*Pop kan mai*,' Frank called after them. 'Till next time.'

Not if I can help it, Mayuree thought.

68

8

Jayne hailed a motorcycle taxi to tail the *songthaew* taking the two women back towards the coast road. The woman in jeans descended first and as she was the one who did all the talking at the centre, Jayne decided to stick with her.

The woman entered the Coconut Club, one in a strip of open-fronted bars overlooking Pattaya Bay, and disappeared behind a petition. Jayne took a seat. Behind the bar a young man wearing an orange hibiscus flower behind his ear, a perfect match for the motif on his Hawaiian shirt, carved fruit into *lai thai*, decorative leaves and flowers. He put aside a lotus bud sculpted in watermelon to take Jayne's order.

At one end of the bar sat a group of young Australians, a party of British tourists at the other. There was a table of puffy-looking men with thick Eastern European accents and bags of leather goods at their feet, and two very blonde types reading a travel guide in what looked like Swedish. A tiny stage in the far corner of the bar with a pole from floor to ceiling suggested things might hot up as the night wore on.

Jayne took her beer to a table by the bar. In the time it took for her to smoke a cigarette the barman finished his lotus and started transforming a *man kaew*—a white root vegetable she didn't know the name of in English—into a frangipani blossom. The woman resurfaced. She'd swapped her T-shirt for a bikini top made to look like coconut shells and her jeans for a grass skirt. A second woman, similarly clad, followed from behind the partition, pausing to touch up her lipstick in the mirrored surface of a beer tap, while the first went to work on the customers.

These were expert hostesses. They flirted, flattered, kept the drinks flowing and the conversation lively. They challenged patrons to drinking games, applauding those who drained their glasses, sipping demurely from their own drinks. They laughed at bad jokes and feigned innocence in the face of bawdy innuendo. Time spent chatting with lonely guys paid off in large, grateful tips. However, the main game was to get customers to drink more, and faster, for longer.

They didn't count on Jayne being a money-spinner in this regard, which was short-sighted on their part but par for the course. Being a farang woman rendered Jayne invisible to both Thai staff and farang patrons in a place like the Coconut Club. Once it had bothered her but she'd grown used to it, learned to turn it to her advantage.

When the woman from the Children's Centre finally approached to clear her empty bottle, Jayne seized the chance to strike up a conversation.

'Busy night, sister?'

The woman looked up, noticing her for the first time. 'Huh?'

'You seem to be having a busy night.'

Confusion gave way to astonishment, then delight. *'Put thai dai mai?'*

Jayne nodded.

'Hah!' The woman clapped her hands together. 'Jin,

come here,' she said, summoning her companion. 'You won't believe it. This farang speaks Thai!'

Jayne was used to this, too.

'*Jing jing reu*, Mayuree?' Jin said joining them. 'Really?'

Mayuree nodded at Jayne. 'Go on, show her.'

Jayne's Thai was good, but decorum required her to be modest. '*Put ngoo-ngoo, pla-pla*,' she said, literally 'speak snake-snake fish-fish', meaning just the basics.

Mayuree and Jin whooped with laughter.

'Not true,' Mayuree said. 'You speak just like a Thai person.'

'Not as well as you both speak English,' Jayne countered. 'I heard you talking to the customers.'

'*Put ngoo-ngoo, pla-pla*,' Jin giggled. 'My teacher is a farang volunteer.'

'A volunteer?' Jayne sensed an opening. 'I thought I might work as a volunteer in Pattaya, too. Only thing is, I can't work out whether I should teach English or work at this orphanage.'

She took the pamphlet out of her bag and held it out to the Thai women. The photo on the front showed a group of young adults cuddling babies and small children in front of a distinctive set of gold gates.

'*Mai roo*,' Jin shrugged and returned to the bar.

Mayuree looked from the pamphlet to Jayne and back again and frowned.

'Teach English,' she said.

She turned to follow Jin, but hesitated.

'Actually, it would be good to have a volunteer who speaks Thai in there, provided she...'

She sat down at Jayne's table and leaned close.

'I have a son, Kob. He's eleven months old. My friend

Wen has a boy the same age called Moo. Our boys are living in the nursery in that centre—' she gestured at the pamphlet '—but only until we're able to look after them ourselves.'

'As a volunteer, would I get to spend time with your children?'

Mayuree shook her head. 'The farang volunteers work with babies and toddlers who are going to be adopted into Western countries. That's not our boys. Not ever, no matter how hard they try.'

'What do you mean, no matter how hard they try?'

Mayuree looked over her shoulder. 'Sorry, can't talk now. Got to get back to work.' She nodded towards the table of Eastern Europeans. 'It was nice meeting you—?'

'Jayne,' she said with a *wai*. 'I hope to see you again.'

'If you do end up volunteering at the orphanage,' Mayuree said as she backed away, 'check in on Kob and Moo for us. Remember they're in with the boarders, not the orphans, okay?'

Jayne nodded, left a large tip under a coaster on her table, and set off in search of somewhere to eat and collect her thoughts. Her conversation with Mayuree made her think there might be value in a little undercover work at the New Life Children's Centre.

9

Jayne was waiting outside the Santiphap Accounting office, sipping a plastic bag of iced coffee, when Police Major General Wichit's nephew Chai arrived. He'd been expecting her and ushered her into a private office with a computer and printer. She took a seat and set about producing a fictitious resume that listed among her previous positions several childcare jobs in Australia and one in Thailand.

The idea came to her the night before whilst reading the pamphlet from the New Life Children's Centre. 'Our Centre welcomes enthusiastic volunteers to assist in acclimatising orphans to the customs and languages of adoptive parents overseas through our intensive one-on-one pre-departure program. Volunteers are also welcome to assist with fund-raising, gardening, cleaning and administrative duties.' No way was Jayne going to volunteer for cleaning or gardening— tasks she went out of her way to avoid at the best of times— and fundraising and administration weren't really her forte. That left childcare, and it seemed appropriate for her to follow in Maryanne's footsteps.

As well as falsifying her employment history, Jayne selected the Presbyterian Ladies College in Melbourne as her alma mater and lopped nine years off her age, citing the date of birth on the fake student ID card she'd bought on Khao San Road, which made her a sprightly twenty-five.

She took a compact mirror from her daypack and peered into it. Trying to pass for twenty-five was pushing it. Years of self-neglect were taking their toll. The whites of her eyes looked jaundiced and she had the beginning of crow's feet. But there was no trace of grey in her black curls, and thanks to a decent night's sleep her freckled skin looked healthy enough. She applied a light coat of mascara, pinched her cheeks and restored the mirror to her bag.

Next step was to write herself a glowing character reference, describing how her 'strong Christian values' were evident in her 'attention to the wellbeing of the children in her care' and her 'high standards of personal conduct'. Then she called Police Major General Wichit.

'Can I use you as a referee? I need a Thai person who'll say I did a good job of looking after his children.'

As soon as the words were out of her mouth, she realised her gaffe.

'It's a cover story,' she added quickly. 'I'm pretending I have experience looking after *small* children.'

'*Mai pen rai*,' Wichit said, the ubiquitous Thai phrase meaning 'it doesn't matter', even when it did. 'Give them my mobile number to ensure they reach me directly.'

He sounded fine, but Jayne could have kicked herself. Looking after Wichit's children—at least his daughter—was precisely what she *had* done. She didn't want to insult Wichit by implying that he needed reminding of his debt to her. The Police Major General was a powerful ally and she wanted to stay in his good books. She had been in the bad books of a Thai cop once before and had no desire to relive that.

She added Wichit's name and mobile number to her reference, printed it out and sealed it in an envelope. The condensation from her bag of iced coffee had formed a puddle on the desk. Chai put a stop to her attempt to wipe it up and despatched the *mae ban* to take over. Jayne thanked him for his hospitality and made her way to the New Life Children's Centre brandishing her application.

She'd dressed conservatively for the occasion: sky blue T-shirt, knee-length grey denim skirt and flat sandals. As a finishing touch, she slipped a silver crucifix on a leather thong around her neck. She'd bought it to go undercover as a Christian missionary in a dangerous red-light district of Chiang Mai, and it had sat tarnishing in her toiletries bag until she'd plucked it out and polished it that morning. Although Jayne wasn't religious, she hoped that if God did exist, He wasn't offended by her habit of impersonating His followers.

It was ten thirty when she entered the gold-gated compound and headed for the administration building. At the reception desk, a young Thai woman with long, frosted pink fingernails tapped at a computer keyboard. In keeping with her cover story, Jayne didn't let on that she spoke Thai. She said she wanted to volunteer at the centre and was told to take a seat.

The walls of the reception area were decorated with posters of puppies and kittens sitting in baskets, entangled in brightly coloured balls of wool, propped up in toy cars, or tucked into prams wearing ribbons around their necks. The popularity of these images knew no bounds amongst the Thais, though urban myth had it the animals were actually dead, stuffed and posed for the photos.

'Hello, I'm Frank Harding.'

Jayne turned and stood up. She recognised the foreigner from the previous day. He had the colouring of a calico cat, patches of grey, black and ginger on white, but his bushy eyebrows and large nose made him look like a bird of prey. He wore his conspicuous crucifix over a white short-sleeved shirt, grey slacks and loafers.

'I'm Jayne.'

She extended her hand. Frank pressed it between both of his and caressed rather than shook it. She noticed his eyes lock on the cross around her neck.

'Great meeting you. Miss Lah—' he nodded at the receptionist '—says you're interested in volunteer work.'

'That's right,' she began. 'I've brought my CV—'

'Oh, let's get to know each other first,' Frank said. 'Why don't I show you around?'

'That'd be great.'

'*Phom mee tula, ja chai wela praman samsip nahtee krup*,' he said to Miss Lah, literally, 'I have business that will take about thirty minutes.' His Thai was businesslike, grammatically correct.

'Wow, you speak Thai!'

'It's a God-given talent,' he said. 'You?'

'I wish. I'm one of those people with *no* talent for languages,' she lied.

'I'm sure you have other skills. Everyone has something they're good at.'

That'd be drinking, smoking and inappropriate relation-ships, Jayne thought, as she followed him into the building.

'The New Life Children's Centre is an orphanage that processes adoption applications on behalf of the Thai government,' Frank began. 'Do you know how the adoption system works in Thailand?'

She shook her head.

'All applications have to go through the social welfare department, but some organisations, like ours, are authorised to process applications on the government's behalf.'

He opened a door, stepped aside to let her through. The room was subdivided by low partitions like a call centre. Each cubicle contained a desk, phone, filing cabinets and a staff member preoccupied with paperwork. Mostly Thais, from what Jayne could gather.

'This section—' Frank gestured to one half of the room '—processes adoption requests from overseas, matches prospective parents with a baby or child in our care and submits the information to the authorities for approval. While the basic criteria for prospective adoptive parents is stipulated under Thai law, our centre prioritises applications from Christian couples in the United States, Europe and Australia.'

'Christian couples,' Jayne repeated, keeping her voice neutral. 'And the Thais don't object, this being a Buddhist country?'

'Now that's an easy mistake to make,' Frank said in a tone that suggested he might pat her on the head. 'True, Buddhism is the dominant religion. But Thailand is a *secular* country, and the children in our care are being adopted into countries where Christianity is the dominant religion. My Thai colleagues agree it's in the child's best interests to be brought up as a member of the dominant religion to ensure they are better integrated and less marginalised.'

'Hmm,' she murmured, thinking that while Maryanne Delbeck might not have been a religious fanatic, she sure worked for one. Jayne would need to watch her step.

'On the other side of the room is investigations. Here

77

we do family traces and background checks when a child is found abandoned or comes to us with missing paperwork. Birth certificate, proof of relinquishment, maternal death certificate—these documents are necessary for the child to be legally available for adoption.'

'And if you can't trace the documents?'

'The process is outlined in the law. If all possible lines of inquiry have been exhausted and a thorough investigation has failed to produce results, the child can be recognised as abandoned and made eligible for adoption.'

'A lengthy process.'

'It is,' Frank said, 'but we can't be too careful. The system has been open to abuses in the past and we need to be able to reassure both the adoptive parents and the Thai government that the child is legally available before we admit them into the adoption process.'

Frank led her back outside.

'The role of our foreign volunteers is to work one-on-one with a child whose file has been allocated to adoptive parents overseas to prepare them for their new life. They need to get used to foreigners, learn their language. Some are old enough to learn songs and even start to read and write.'

The chatter of children's voices grew louder as they approached the orphanage building.

'See for yourself.'

The door opened on to a large foyer converted into a communal play space, the floor crawling with babies and children. Foreign volunteers—mostly women—sat amongst them. Frank gestured for Jayne to enter.

She caught snatches of conversation as they walked around the room.

British accent, middle-aged woman, helping a small boy with a puzzle: 'You can do it—clever boy! Now let's try...'

Australian accent, student type, talking to a pot-bellied girl wielding a coloured pencil and a piece of paper: 'What are you going to draw next?'

German, pushing sixty, admiring her charge as she dressed him in clothes so new they still had the tags on them: '*Zeig mal Liebchen. Oh, siehst Du aber fein aus...*'

Young man—Korean or Japanese—captivating a group of toddlers with his animated reading: 'The Good Samaritan took pity on the poor man...'

She glanced at the titles on the bookshelf behind him. Classic fairytales from the Brothers Grimm and Hans Christian Andersen, some hard cover picture books and an impressive collection of Bible stories.

A baby started howling. In a practised gesture, the German woman scooped him up, placed him over her shoulder and patted his back. The baby gurgled.

At a signal from Frank, Jayne retraced her steps. She noticed dormitory-style bedrooms off both sides of the main room, mosquito nets bunched up on ropes over the sleeping mats that lined the floor. The Australian girl smiled and nodded as Jayne passed.

Frank's office, marked 'Special Adviser', was in the administration building. He removed the chain from his neck to unlock his door, the key secreted behind the crucifix. Frank's desk was against one wall beneath a map of Thailand. The office also contained a small sitting area. Frank pulled up a rattan chair and invited Jayne to take a seat on the couch. On the wall above Jayne's head was a picture of a kitten dangling from a bucket beneath the words, 'Hang in there'.

She handed over her resume but Frank gave it only a cursory glance.

'I'm sure your credentials are fine,' he said, putting it to one side.

Jayne thought Frank was staring at her breasts, but his focus was her crucifix.

'Tell me, Jayne, what is it that *motivates* you—' he invested the word with great significance '—to work as a volunteer?'

'Well, I want to help people in need, to make a difference, and to do that in a way that's consistent with my values.'

'Ah,' Frank nodded.

'And even more so than Bangkok, Pattaya strikes me as a place desperately in need of God's work, if you know what I mean.'

The increasing tempo of Frank's nods told Jayne she was on track.

'The wages of sin must take a terrible toll on the women here, and their children, too. And if I could make a difference to just one person…Well, as Saint Luke says, "Joy shall be in Heaven over one sinner that repenteth, more than over ninety-nine just persons, which need no repentance".'

This was her coup de grace, memorised that morning from the Gideon Bible in her hotel room.

'Praise the Lord,' Frank said.

Jayne bowed her head with what she hoped came across as humility and bit her lip.

'You'd be a perfect addition to our volunteer team.'

'Oh, I'm so pleased—'

'First, please don't take this the wrong way, but I need to ask you, Jayne: how would you describe your state of mind?'

'My state of mind?'

'Your mental health.'

'I'm sorry. I'm not sure what you mean.'

Frank left his chair and sat on the couch beside her, so close their knees were almost touching.

'Would you describe yourself as a person who is easily depressed?'

'No,' she said slowly. 'Why?'

'Because this place can really test your faith and I need to be sure you're up to it.'

Jayne hesitated. 'It's because of that other girl, isn't it? The one who killed herself.'

Frank raised his eyebrows.

'I'm from Australia. The story was in all the papers. Don't worry,' she hastened to add, 'I'm coming into this with my eyes open.'

To Jayne's alarm, Frank reached over, took her hands in his and bowed his head.

'Let us pray,' he said.

Jayne let her hands go limp in Frank's clammy grasp as he gave thanks for 'delivering Jayne unto our organisation'. He added a prayer for the repose of the soul of Maryanne Delbeck, and finished with an entreaty to continue to bless their work. In Jayne's history of job interviews, this was without doubt the weirdest.

They agreed she would start the following morning.

'I have one last question before I go,' Jayne said. 'What happens to the children who don't meet the criteria for adoption?'

Frank glanced at his watch. 'Come and I'll show you.'

He led her back out the golden gates, where a different guard from the previous day saluted as they passed. Jayne was careful not to let on that she knew the way and made sure Frank reached the blue gates first.

A muscular man in a navy blue uniform, New Life Children's Centre logo on his chest pocket, sat on a white plastic chair just outside the compound reading that morning's edition of *Thai Rath*. A blue tiger tattoo stretched along his inner right arm. This man Jayne recognised—the tough guy from the previous evening. He looked even tougher up close, his dark face pockmarked with scars.

He leapt to his feet when Frank approached.

'*Sawadee krup, nong,*' Frank said to the man as he unlocked the gate. 'This is Mister Chaowalit,' he added in English. 'He's the guard and handyman for this part of the centre.' He turned back to Chaowalit. '*Sabai dee mai?*'

'*Sabai dee,*' Chaowalit said to him. '*Farang khon nee put thai dai mai?*'

He was asking if she spoke Thai. Frank shook his head and Jayne pricked up her ears.

'There's a problem—' Chaowalit said, but Frank cut him off.

'I don't have time now,' he said in Thai. 'I won't be long with her and then we'll meet, okay?'

Chaowalit scowled but stepped aside.

'This section of the centre is for children whose parents place them in institutional care but don't consent to them being adopted out. We call these kids boarders to distinguish them from orphans.'

He led Jayne into the nursery. It had much the same layout as the orphanage, but with fewer toys and no foreign volunteers. The smaller babies dozed or wriggled around on grass mats. Older children—Jayne guessed around age nine or ten—played with the younger ones. The Thai carers were dressed like nurses. One sat on a chair mending a mosquito net.

'Most of these children come from families too poor to educate, house or even feed them. So they send them to the centre,' Frank said. 'Many of the parents are itinerant workers with irregular income and no stability. We become the keepers of the children's birth certificates, vaccination records, even school reports.'

'Why don't the parents give them up for adoption?'

'Different reasons. Many intend to maintain family ties. Others count on a change of luck putting them in a position to care for the child. This is particularly common among the...ah...working girls in Pattaya. They think marrying a rich Westerner will solve all their problems. It doesn't occur to them their future husband might not look too kindly on raising another man's child. Nor do they consider whether such an arrangement would be in the child's best interests—'

He stopped mid-sentence.

'Forgive me, Jayne. Once I'm up on my high horse, I get a little carried away.'

She gave him a polite smile.

'The sad fact is that most of these children are abandoned. They'll remain in our care until they finish middle high school, at which point we are obliged by law to release them to fend for themselves.'

Jayne recalled the words in Maryanne Delbeck's letter home. *It seems so unfair. It's not as if their families visit them all the time. Some never come back for them at all.*

'It seems so unfair,' she echoed.

'Tragic, really.' Frank gestured around the room. 'Many would be perfect for adoption. Thai girls and half-ca—I mean, *mixed race*—babies are particularly sought after.

And as you can see, we have a lot of the latter here, both Eurasian and Afro-Asian.'

A tinny rendition of Beethoven's 'Ode to joy' sounded from Frank's shirt pocket. He took out his mobile phone and glanced at the screen.

'Excuse me,' he said to Jayne. 'Feel free to have a look around.'

She wandered into the main room. The children might not have as much stuff as the orphans, but they looked well fed and cared for. On the plus side, their bookshelves were free of Bible stories.

She watched one of the older girls encouraging an infant to walk.

'Come on Dollar, you can do it,' the girl coaxed.

Jayne smiled. It was trendy among Thai people to give a child an English *cheu len* or nickname and not uncommon, as in Dollar's case, to choose words rather than actual names.

'Look, watch how Kob does it!'

The girl pointed towards a little boy who stood upright using the edge of a chair for balance. He was what the Thais called *look kreung*, literally 'half-child' but meaning half-Thai. With dark skin and corkscrew curls, high cheekbones and almond-shaped eyes, he looked like something from a utopian society where humans were designed to be beautiful. Jayne wondered if this Kob was Mayuree's son.

Casting her eye around the room, Jayne spotted a few more *look kreung*, or what Frank referred to as Eurasian and Afro-Asian. She supposed these were the offspring of the working girls.

'Can you wipe Moo's nose?' A Thai staff member gestured to a boy at Jayne's feet.

She almost fished a tissue out of her bag before remembering she wasn't supposed to understand Thai.

'Sorry?' she shrugged.

The nurse made a wiping gesture and pointed again at the child.

Jayne nodded, suppressed a shudder and squashed the slug of snot beneath the child's nose.

Frank reappeared.

'Already putting you to work I see.'

'Just trying to be helpful,' she said, holding out the used tissue.

'There's a trash can just outside the door.' Frank motioned for her to follow him.

'This section is only down the lane from the orphanage, but the two facilities are separated by a yawning chasm when it comes to opportunity,' he sighed.

Jayne threw away the tissue and held out her hand. 'Thanks for the tour. I guess I'll see you in the morning.'

'Not necessarily. Nurse Connie and the others will put you through your orientation. If you need me, I have offices in both parts of the centre. I'm usually in one or the other.'

'So you work with the boarders, too?'

'There are sometimes opportunities to counsel families to reconsider their decision and relinquish the child for adoption. It's part of my role at the centre to pursue those opportunities. As I said, many of the children would be ideal for adoption and we have such a long waiting list of suitable applicants.'

'Do you ever have foreign volunteers working in this section?'

The mild curiosity underlining the question surged when Frank blanched in response.

'We tried it once but decided it wasn't in the children's best interests.'

And there was Jayne's answer: Maryanne had been granted her wish to work with the boarders.

IO

Frank Harding glanced at the framed photo as he placed his mobile phone on the desk. Him with his brothers, Kevin and Sid, taken just before Kevin left for Nicaragua. Frank was not the only Harding with a missionary calling. Kevin was working to repair the damage done by years of socialism, while Sid was doing the Lord's work on the island of Mindanao in the Southern Philippines.

Like Sid, Frank's calling had brought him to Asia, though Thailand was not his original destination. Five years earlier, Frank was posted to Laos under the auspices of Charitable Care, part of a consortium formed to bring relief to drought-affected areas of southern Laos. His mission was reconnaissance, to explore opportunities for evangelism through Charitable Care's work in food security and famine relief.

Frank was amongst those who volunteered to carry supplies into villages that could only be reached on foot. Ten people participated in the two-day trek, each carrying what they insisted on calling 'fifteen kilos' of supplies—it was thirty-three pounds where Frank came from—plus water for personal use. When they finally reached their destination,

Frank unloaded not the rice his colleagues assumed he was carrying, but thirty-three pounds of Bibles.

He knew he was doing the right thing, bringing something that would sustain the villagers through far more than a single drought. But his colleagues did not see it that way, even when he pointed out that the translation was in the relevant village language. A French doctor, clearly with communist leanings, resorted to name-calling and harassment.

'What does it matter that the Bibles are in the local language?' the man sneered. 'The villagers cannot read, you *imbécile*.'

He said the word in French, but there was no mistaking what he meant. Frank refused to be baited.

'Does it occur to you that the reason they cannot read is because they don't have inspirational reading materials?' Frank said calmly. 'Surely there's no stronger motivation for them to learn than the word of God.'

The Frenchman shook his head and muttered something under his breath, adding in a louder voice, '*Alors*, they are good for one thing.'

He took a Bible from the pile at Frank's feet and handed it to the village headman.

'*Sahai, soup yah, bo*?' he said, addressing the man as 'comrade'.

Frank watched in disgust as the headman tore out a page, dipped into a leather tobacco pouch at his waist, and proceeded to roll a cigarette. He handed the Holy Book around for the other men in the village to do likewise. Their laughter was still ringing in his ears as Frank turned and walked away.

When they returned to the Lao capital Vientiane, he was

summoned to the Ministry of the Interior and charged with crimes against Lao culture. Frank was baffled. He'd only wanted to save the villagers who, in their pagan ignorance, were destined for eternal damnation. And for this he was deported. He suspected the Frenchman of turning him in, but reminded himself that vengeance was the Lord's area of expertise.

The deportation turned out to be a blessing in disguise as it brought Frank to Pattaya. And if ever there was a place in need of the Lord's redeeming light, it was Pattaya and its twin town of Jomtien, Thailand's own Sodom and Gomorrah. People of means came here expressly to gratify their basest desires, preying on the weakness of the poor, the ignorant and the avaricious. A place where the Devil spent his holidays. A place where Frank could make a real difference.

At the same time, after the anti-American paranoia of Laos, there were aspects of life in Pattaya he welcomed: familiar food, convenience stores, modern communications. His grounding in Lao made it easy for him to learn Thai— they were closely related languages—and he applied himself diligently to his studies.

Frank also made a careful study of Pattaya's sex industry in the spirit of 'know thine enemy'. Different sources suggested there were anywhere between six thousand and twenty thousand Thais working in the sex industry in Pattaya, including girls and boys as young as ten years old. His own observations put the figure towards the higher end of the spectrum. In addition to brothels, prostitution operated out of nightclubs, discotheques, beer bars, massage parlours, karaoke clubs, garden restaurants, short-time hotels, even barber shops and hairdressing salons.

The prostitutes—he'd never warmed to the politically correct term 'commercial sex workers'—in the low-end brothels tended to be among the poorest and least educated, earning as little as one American dollar per 'session', the euphemism researchers used to refer to the exchange of sexual favours for money. They were often in bonded labour, their meagre earnings going to the brothel owner to pay off their debt.

Prostitutes in the middle and higher ends of the market tended to be better off, receiving a base salary in addition to commissions and fees that could amount to as much as one hundred dollars per session. They were morally impoverished: with higher levels of education and working under less compulsion, these were women who should have known better—who had choices.

Frank supplemented his desk-based research with fieldwork. Posing as a tourist, he visited a go-go bar where women danced stark naked around poles on a stage while patrons ogled them. A topless woman young enough to be his daughter grabbed at his crotch and rubbed hard tiny breasts across his face. Caught off-guard, Frank was revolted as much by his spontaneous erection as he was by the girl's lewdness. He left quickly, muttering invocations to restore his self-control. Frank had chosen a celibate life, and no teenage whore would jeopardise that.

Worse than the go-go bars were the 'live shows' where women squeezed ping-pong balls from their private parts like they were laying eggs. Or inserted all kinds of objects inside themselves: bananas, fire-spitting sparklers, even razor blades. He'd once seen a woman squat over a birthday cake and blow out the candles with her vagina. It disgusted Frank not only that people treated such profanity as a spectator sport, but that the women—many of them mothers, judging by their stretch marks and caesarean scars—allowed themselves to be so degraded.

Pattaya thrived on degradation. They could blame it on the Americans based in Thailand during the Vietnam War—Pattaya was a sleepy little fishing village until the GIs started using it as an R&R port—but the Thais could put an end to that whenever they wanted. The war had been over for more than twenty years. Instead, they continued to hitch the town's economy to human depravity. The local authorities staged periodic crackdowns on prostitution and vice. And every now and then a billboard went up promoting Pattaya's 'exciting diving destinations' or Jomtien's 'family-friendly beaches'. It was all just for show—another tawdry Pattaya performance.

In the five years since Frank had arrived, Pattaya had only gotten worse. There was nothing that couldn't be bought or sold, no limit to the lengths that people would go to for a buck.

Frank needed to figure out how he could turn this to his advantage—the ends always justified the means when it came to saving souls—and to that end, he scoured the town for a workplace suited to his skills and mission. He'd worked briefly as an army chaplain, but spent most of his working life in the US as a pastoral care worker attached to an inner-city public hospital in Detroit where he specialised in family counselling and foster care placements.

The New Life Children's Centre was the answer to his prayers. The Thai director had been looking for a qualified foreigner to assist in processing inter-country adoption requests and preparing the children for life with their new families. Frank was employed in the role of special adviser and, as the only foreigner on staff, given licence to develop the program.

The pre-departure program that paired individual babies with foreign volunteers was Frank's brainchild, as was the idea to use church networks to recruit volunteers. His work on the adoption program was deeply satisfying, his achievements measurable in the number of children he helped shepherd out of Pattaya. His only frustration was that the New Life Children's Centre could not meet the increasing demand for babies eligible for overseas adoption.

And then the Lord sent him Constance.

They met after a church service. Connie, as she liked to be called, was a nurse-midwife from Hong Kong who had worked throughout Asia, including a stretch in a slum near the US Naval Base at Subic Bay in the Philippines. She'd come to Thailand to take up a job in the maternity ward at the City Hospital. As the least expensive health facility, City Hospital was where most pregnant prostitutes went to deliver their babies.

'My role in the clinic in Subic Bay,' she told Frank, 'was to counsel pregnant women against illegal *abortion*—' she dropped her voice, as if the word itself was too terrible to mention '—and support them to give birth and adopt the baby out.'

For Frank, it was the missing piece of the puzzle.

The New Life Children's Centre had an existing relationship with the City Hospital. Babies found abandoned at the hospital entrance or in the car park were brought to the centre following medical clearance. Frank sought to strengthen links between the two organisations. Connie alerted him to the possibility of counselling women while they were still in the maternity ward and encouraging them to relinquish their newborns. Those who persisted in keeping their babies were referred to a new mothers' clinic at the New Life Centre, not so much to help them care for their babies as to keep them in Frank's sights. Almost invariably the women failed to cope with the demands of motherhood, and the new mothers' clinic became a conduit for babies to be placed in the centre's institutional care facility.

It wasn't enough for Frank. His mission was conversions. Not in the first instance from Buddhism to Christianity—though that remained the ultimate goal—but to convert babies and toddlers languishing in institutional care into orphans eligible for inter-country adoption.

Frank initiated a range of methods to increase the conversion rate. First there was the hospital-based counselling program; the poorer and younger the woman, the more likely she could be convinced to relinquish the child. Secondly, Frank made sure the new mothers at the clinic were given a full tour of the facilities; they got to see the orphans being looked after by foreign volunteers and could envisage the opportunities this afforded them. Thirdly, Chaowalit, the eyes and ears of the place, alerted Frank when any boarders were visited by family members, so Frank could take the opportunity to work on them. He had a similar arrangement with Ittiphol on the centre's investigation team, who let Frank know when an abandoned child's family had been located and could benefit from his counselling.

With the steady influx of converts from boarders to orphans, Frank experimented with deploying a volunteer into the boarding house facility to begin acclimatising the children to foreigners before they officially entered the pre-departure program. Maryanne Delbeck had been the first to put up her hand.

Frank sighed at the thought of Maryanne. He opened his filing cabinet and took out her personnel file. At the front were a copy of *The Bangkok Post* article into her death, a file note on his meeting with the Australian Embassy consultant, and a letter of condolence from the Young Christian Volunteers.

Time had not dulled Frank's grief. He held himself partly to blame for the loss. How could it have escaped his notice that she was clinically depressed? It took Doctor Somsri to point it out to him *after* her death. Of course, he corroborated Somsri's account for the purposes of the investigation. It was the only face-saving thing to do. But it would always sadden him that he'd failed to see what was wrong in time to save Maryanne from committing such a grave sin. She'd seemed like such a bright, spirited young thing.

Frank was more vigilant about the wellbeing of his volunteers these days. That was Maryanne's legacy. While it wouldn't save her soul from the fires of Hell, it was something positive to remember her by.

His phone rang. He restored the Delbeck file to its place in the cabinet and closed the drawer.

'Frank Harding, hello.'

'We've got a problem,' a voice said in Thai.

'What is it Doctor Somsri?' he answered politely.

'Seems your midwife friend overdid the painkillers.'

'I'm sorry, I don't understand.'

'Girl you saw last night,' Somsri said, 'sixteen-year-old from Kalasin. She didn't make it.'

'Didn't make it?' Frank crossed himself. 'I'm sorry to hear that.'

'Sorry doesn't cut it with the people I answer to,'

Somsri said. 'They said to tell you there are penalties for incompetence.'

Frank bristled at his tone.

'But—'

'Body to dispose of, cops to be compensated, forensics paid to lose blood-test results. Someone's got to pay for all of that.'

Frank clenched his fist around his crucifix. The people behind Doctor Somsri had wealth beyond Frank's imagination. This was not about the money.

'Surely your superiors are aware of what a delicate operation we run here,' he began.

'As far as they're concerned, if you can't do the job right, they'll find someone else who can,' Somsri said.

'You can't mean—'

'I know how hard it would be to replace someone with your skills,' he added, his tone softening, 'but that's not how they see it, Khun Frank. We have no choice. We have to make amends. Anything on the books we could expedite?'

Frank hesitated. On the rare occasions he stepped outside legal boundaries to speed up adoption cases, it was because the best interests of the child were being served, not because of the money. Frank wasn't naïve. He knew Somsri answered to people higher up the chain of command who treated their overseas adoption service as a profit-making enterprise. Nothing ever happened in Thailand without high-level patronage. Frank didn't dwell on it, sleeping sound in the knowledge that his own intentions were pure.

'There is one,' he said, 'a boy. I've already matched him to a couple in the US. I'm sure if I can work on the mother just a little longer—'

'No time,' Somsri said, 'unless you want *them* to work on the mother.'

Frank heard the echo of a laugh in the background. He shivered.

'Reassure your superiors that won't be necessary,' he said, keeping his voice steady. 'We'll take care of it.'

'Yes, we will,' Somsri said.

Frank's hands were shaking. He took a deep breath.

'It's in the best interests of the child,' he murmured to himself.

11

As Mayuree's *songthaew* pulled into the kerb, a motorbike slowed alongside her. She clutched her bag to her chest but relaxed when she saw her friend Wen descend from the pillion seat.

They exchanged a smile.

'On time for work this evening,' Wen said.

'Making up for yesterday,' Mayuree answered. 'What brings you to my part of town?'

'Late shift,' Wen said, yawning. 'Thought I'd stop by for a chat. *Okay na*?'

'*Ja*,' Mayuree nodded. 'It's still early.'

They walked towards the Coconut Club. Wen teetered in her stilettos and clutched Mayuree's arm to regain her balance.

'You all right?'

'Just tired,' Wen said. 'The boss is putting pressure on us to work double shifts or take a cut. He reckons there's another crackdown going on.'

'In the middle of high tourist season? I doubt it.'

'Think about it, sister. Now's when everyone makes more money. The cops know it, and they want a piece of the action. That's what my boss says.'

'You're so gullible,' Mayuree said. 'It's just an excuse to keep more of the profit for himself.'

'I've been getting forty-five per cent,' Wen said. 'He wants to cut it to forty.'

'That's not fair and you know it. You should be earning at least fifty per cent.'

'Easy for you to say. You're out of the main game. These days we're competing with Russian girls for the good jobs. Russian girls. In Thailand. The world's going crazy.'

She shook her head.

'Tell me about it,' Mayuree said, nodding towards the bar.

The Russian men from the day before had colonised the same table, this time with several surly young women in tow who might have been their daughters or their mistresses. It was hard to tell as all Russian women seemed to dress the same: tight, short and shiny. The air around the table was thick with cigarette smoke. Next to them a young farang man with a yellow hammer and sickle on his red T-shirt was chatting up a Thai girl in a strapless gold dress.

Not for the first time, Mayuree was thankful to be out of the main game, as Wen put it. Working in the beer bar meant less take-home pay, but she had a regular salary that didn't require navigating the agendas of bosses, clients, competitors and police. Best of all she got to go home alone and safe, not in the arms of some stranger.

'The boss says everyone has to take a cut and if we don't accept forty, he won't have enough to pay off the police and they'll shut the place down,' Wen said, sitting down at the bar.

'*Jing reu?*' Mayuree called from behind the partition. 'You really think it's serious?'

'I don't know for sure. I don't want to lose my job.'

'Do you have to stay at that place?'

'I'm not like you,' Wen said as Mayuree rejoined her and began wiping down the bar. 'I've got debts.'

Mayuree took a good look at her friend. Wen was an attractive woman, but the work was taking its toll. There were shadows under her eyes and her skin was drawn. She'd lost weight and beads of sweat glistened above her upper lip, despite the mild evening weather.

'Well, as long it's not because you're doing anything stupid,' Mayuree said.

'What's that supposed to mean?'

'You know.'

Wen shrugged.

'I take a bit of *ya ma* now and again, but only when I can barely stay awake. It puts you in the mood, too, and let's face it, given some of the dog-hearted guys that walk through the door, that can only be a good thing.'

Mayuree smiled but her heart ached for Wen. She knew a lot of the girls took 'horse medicine' to get through the long hours. The more unscrupulous bar owners encouraged it. Once a girl got hooked, she was easier to push around.

The real danger with *ya ma* was it made you feel invincible, made you take risks. Like letting a client go bareback because he was prepared to pay more, looked nice and said he really liked you. And in your drug-addled state you think, maybe this is it. Maybe my life's about to change. And it does, but not in the way you hoped.

'More beer here!'

The command, issued from the Russian table, snapped Mayuree back to the present.

She placed her hand on Wen's arm. 'I'll ask around. See

if there's any word on a police crackdown. That way you'll know if there's room to negotiate.'

Wen nodded, managed a tired smile.

'And look after yourself,' Mayuree muttered, beaming at the Russians as she headed for their table. 'For your son's sake, if not your own.'

'Do you think the Russians could spare a cigarette?' Wen called after her.

'I don't know about the Russians but I can,' Jayne said, sidling up to the Thai woman at the bar.

Jayne had returned to the Coconut Club, counting on the rapport she'd established the previous night to help her circumvent the usual wait for drinks. She recognised Mayuree's companion from the New Life Centre and held out her packet of *Krung Thip*.

'I'm Jayne,' she added. 'Your friend can vouch for me.' She waved at Mayuree, who raised her eyebrows in greeting.

'I'm Wen,' the woman said, still wary.

She looked from the packet of cigarettes to Jayne and back again. Jayne got the message, summoned the barman and ordered a packet of Marlboro Lights. Wen perked up and accepted the new offering. Jayne leaned forward to light it for her.

'You're Mayuree's flatmate.'

Wen looked surprised. 'Yes.'

'Mayuree was telling me you both have sons about the same age, right?'

'That's right,' Wen said as Mayuree joined them.

Mayuree lifted two jugs on to the counter, placed them under adjacent beer taps, set them pouring. 'She's okay,' she said to Wen. 'Same as last time Jayne?'

She nodded and Mayuree, still keeping one hand on the jugs, passed over a bottle of Singha beer in a stubby holder.

'Thanks,' Jayne said. 'I think I saw your boys today.'

'Really? How was my—'

'What was he doing—'

They both spoke at once. Jayne held up her hands.

'I'm not sure they were your boys,' she said. 'What do they look like?'

'My Moo has exactly the same pig-nose as his father,' Wen said.

'My Kob has ears like an elephant,' Mayuree added, tilting the beer jugs under the taps.

'Kob has such beautiful eyes,' Wen said, 'whereas my poor Moo has small eyes and they aren't even a nice colour.'

'But your Moo has such lovely pale skin,' Mayuree protested. 'My poor Kob is black as a sea gypsy.'

Jayne knew such banter was designed to keep jealous spirits at bay, the same reason they gave their babies unflattering nicknames like Moo meaning 'pig' and Kob meaning 'frog'. She smiled to think of the horrified looks that would greet mothers in Australia who spoke so disparagingly of their offspring.

'True, Kob's skin *is* very black,' Wen said.

Mayuree smiled, knowing she'd won.

'WHERE IS THE BEER?' a voice thundered. One of the Russians had risen to his feet.

Mayuree took a jug in each hand and conjured up a smile. 'Coming now, Sir,' she said. 'And yours will be the first one I pour as I can see you are a very hot man.'

This seemed to mollify the Russian who resumed his seat.

Jayne and Wen watched as Mayuree worked her magic. They couldn't hear the conversation above the boy band crooning over the in-house stereo system, but they could see her chatting and laughing. She patted one patron playfully on the upper arm, wagged her finger at another. Within minutes she had the erstwhile pushy man grinning like a puppy and even the surly girls were having trouble maintaining their scowls.

'Do you work nearby?' Jayne asked Wen.

'Further south,' she said. 'Club called Monkey Business.'

'I don't know it.'

'On The Strip,' Wen said, stubbing out her cigarette so hard it broke in two. 'I hate it. But I've got bills to pay and a kid to raise. At least, I *want* to raise him, only sometimes I wonder if that's really what's best.'

'Of course it is,' Jayne said. 'You're his mother.'

Wen smiled at her for the first time since they'd met.

'Thanks,' she said, 'that's very kind of you.'

Jayne shrugged, drank her beer.

'So, did we establish whether it was our boys you saw today?'

Mayuree returned to the bar, picking up the conversation where she left off.

'Not quite,' said Jayne. 'The Kob I saw was almost walking. And Moo had a runny nose.'

'It sounds like my Kob,' Mayuree said. 'He's just started pulling himself up on to the furniture.'

'And it sounds like my Moo, too,' Wen said. 'He had the sniffles on Sunday. Are you going to be looking after them?'

'No, they only let volunteers work with the orphans,' Jayne said.

'They let Maryanne—' Mayuree began but stopped

short. 'It's good they keep things separate between the orphans and boarders.'

'Maryanne?' Jayne said. 'The Australian girl? Did you know her?'

'I met her once or twice,' Mayuree said, wiping down the bar. 'She volunteered at the centre when I used to take Kob there for check-ups before I...before he started staying there overnight.'

Jayne got the impression there was more to the story, but this was not the time to pursue it. The bar was filling up, Wen was ready to leave and Jayne needed to psych herself up for her first day at the orphanage. She settled her bill and pressed the Marlboros on Wen.

As she walked down the street from the bar, she scribbled a reminder to follow up with Mayuree about Maryanne and almost tripped over a sandwich board advertising a computer school. She took it as a sign and dialled Rajiv's number.

12

Alicia asked her husband to repeat himself.

'Our case has been expedited,' Leroy said. 'They want us to fly over now. Tonight if possible.'

'How come?'

'I don't know.'

He rubbed his hand over the stubble on his scalp. He'd been out of the Marines five years but still wore the buzz cut.

'They said the timeline they gave us was a worst-case scenario. Seems our application advanced faster than expected.'

'From months to days?'

'I don't understand it either, honey. Maybe my military record counted for somethin'. Who knows?'

He crossed the kitchen and encircled her in his great arms. 'It's what we dreamed of.' He kissed her forehead.

Alicia raised her head to look at him. 'It all seems so sudden.'

Leroy ran his fingers through her long, black hair. 'It's been ten years, honey.'

How could she forget?

They'd hoped for a child from the moment they married. A honeymoon baby, Leroy declared. By the time their second wedding anniversary came around, they were concerned enough to consult a minister and a doctor. But neither the prayers of the local Baptist congregation nor expert medical advice seemed to help. Still childless after four years, concern turned to panic and they started fertility treatment.

Alicia did everything she could. She joined prayer groups. She left a job she liked because it wasn't compatible with the treatment. She gave up coffee and chilli because she read they increased the risk of miscarriage. She substituted wild, spontaneous sex with carefully timed acts of intercourse to maximise the chance of conception. Back in the days when they could still joke about it, Leroy said she did the Pope proud, the way she reserved sex for procreation.

Then they stopped having sex altogether. Fertilisation took place 'in vitro' and conception via the intervention of medical experts. Alicia gave up every last vestige of pleasure. Still there was no baby.

For six years she subjected herself to mood-altering drugs and invasive medical procedures, followed by two weeks of symptoms—swollen breasts, hunger pangs, fatigue, irritability—that in a cruel twist could signify either pre-menstrual tension or pregnancy. In her case, never the latter.

Everywhere she looked, other women were pregnant, breastfeeding, pushing babies in prams. Alicia stared at them with such envy she learned what it meant to put the evil eye on someone. She couldn't bear to be around friends with children. 'They gloat,' she told Leroy, who said she was paranoid. What would he know? He had work to take his mind off what was going on around them. Alicia caught the pitying looks and read their implications. Hers was the story told to make others feel better when they were having a run of bad luck. 'So you've been trying to get pregnant for over a year? That's not so long. I know someone who's been trying for *six* years and not even IVF seems to be working for her, poor thing.'

It took thousands of dollars and twenty-seven failed attempts before they finally faced the painful truth that they'd never have a biological child. Even surrogacy was ruled out. For reasons they didn't understand, God had decided this would be their cross to bear.

Alicia couldn't imagine how painful it would be to lose a child, when losing the idea of a child hurt this much. There was no public ritual to acknowledge the loss, no sympathy cards from family and friends. It was a death with no body to weep over but her own.

Then Leroy came up with a proposal: why not adopt a baby from overseas?

Domestic adoptions in the US were fraught. Assuming you could get access to a relinquished baby that wasn't crack addicted, sooner or later, likely as not, you'd have to deal with family of origin issues. It was more cut and dried with inter-country adoptions. You registered with a local accredited agency affiliated with an orphanage overseas. The US agency made sure you met the requirements as adopting parents and the foreign agency matched your file to a baby or child in their care. Once the paperwork was in order and the child given a clean bill of health, he or she would be issued with a passport and an immigration visa for the US. You could even state a preference for a boy or girl.

'Boy,' Alicia had said without thinking. 'But from which country?'

'Thailand,' Leroy said.

Alicia smiled.

Thailand was where they'd met. Leroy was docked in Pattaya on R&R when Alicia stopped off on her way to Koh Samet. Alicia didn't make it to Koh Samet until they returned to Thailand a year later for their honeymoon. Back then they thought nothing would ever be stronger than their faith and the desire they felt for each other. It seemed fitting that in going back there they might find the one other person they longed for.

A six- to twelve-month wait to adopt a baby seemed like nothing compared to what they'd been through, but it was less than three months since they'd received the photo of the then seven-month-old baby boy who'd been chosen for them. Alicia already thought of him as Jesse.

'You're not gettin' cold feet are you?' Leroy said.

'No, of course not,' she said. 'It's just I want him so much, it scares me. I couldn't bear it if anything went wrong.'

'How could anything go wrong?' Leroy said. 'We've done all the right things, honey. We've just had a lucky break is all. And after all we've been through, ain't it time we got lucky?'

'It isn't about luck, my love,' Alicia said. 'We prayed for this and at last our prayers have been answered.'

She fingered the ruby-studded crucifix on the chain around her neck, a tenth wedding anniversary gift from her husband.

'God wants us to have this baby.'

'Of course he does,' Leroy said, kissing her again on the top of her head. 'Now, you want to start packing while I get on the phone to the travel agent?'

13

For Jayne the appeal of staying in a hotel was to have a coffee and the daily newspaper delivered before she even got out of bed. So it came as a double blow to find the coffee at the Bayview undrinkable and the newspaper not one of the national dailies but the weekly *Pattaya Mail*. Being the kind to read the side of a cereal packet if nothing else was available, she gave it her full attention. Amidst the advertisements for skin whitening and tightening, cosmetic dental surgery, real estate investment opportunities and steakhouses, she found an article about the body of a sixteen-year-old prostitute found in a laneway in Central Pattaya. The girl had recently given birth. Though there was no sign of the baby, theory was she'd abandoned it at the City Hospital where a newborn baby girl was found the previous day.

'This is the third case of its kind in the past year in which the death of a young woman has coincided with the abandonment of a newborn,' she read. 'Findings of suicide were reached in both previous cases. Is Pattaya facing an epidemic of pregnant teenagers abandoning their babies and dying for shame and lack of medical care?'

Jayne thought of Frank Harding preaching about working girls and their babies. Would he believe it was in the best interests of the child for the mother to abandon her baby and die? She wasn't game to ask.

Jayne was met at the gate of the centre by a woman in a nurse's uniform. She was a head shorter than Jayne with a body like a pigeon, high bust and round belly tapering to narrow hips and thin legs. Her hair was styled in a matronly bun, though judging by her complexion Jayne guessed she was less than forty.

'I'm Sister Constance,' she said, holding out a limp hand, 'though you can call me Connie. Mister Frank asked me to show you around and brief you on your responsibilities.'

'Thanks,' Jayne began. 'So where are you from?'

'Hong Kong,' Connie said. 'Please save any other questions till the end.'

She turned on the heel of her white sandshoe expecting Jayne to follow.

'The New Life Children's Centre was established in 1981,' Connie said, as if addressing a group tour. 'The orphanage has facilities for forty children. The ratio of carers to children is one to five, not counting volunteers. This is one of the highest staff-child ratios in Thailand.'

She gestured towards a couple of buildings Jayne had not been inside on her tour with Frank. 'The clinic is staffed by nurses and a doctor.'

'Is that where you work?' Jayne said.

Connie frowned. 'I work as a nurse-midwife at City Hospital, and when I'm not on duty there, I work here in the new mothers' clinic. The centre also has access to a specialist medical practitioner. The children receive routine vaccinations and are tested for HIV and hepatitis as a pre-adoption requirement.'

Jayne couldn't help herself. 'What's the other building?'

'Laundry,' Connie snapped, continuing along the path. 'This is the main part of the orphanage.'

She opened the door. There was little of the activity Jayne had seen in the playroom the previous day. A toddler wandered around with one sock on his foot, the other on his hand. A slightly older child lay on her stomach in the reading corner leafing through a picture book.

'They must still be finishing breakfast,' Connie said.

She led Jayne through the door to where an eating area fronted on to a galley kitchen. The children sat on plastic mats on the floor eating rice porridge, the older ones feeding themselves, the babies being fed by the Thai staff and a couple of volunteers Jayne recognised from the previous day. She waved a collective greeting.

'We have about thirty children here at the moment, all of whom have been allocated to adoptive parents, except the newest, Nok. She only came to us two days ago. Most of their mothers—' Connie swept her hand over the children '—were probably prostitutes. The fathers?—Who knows. Europeans, Americans, Australians. Men who come here as sex tourists—' she lowered her voice as if to protect the children '—and fiercely deny paternity when confronted with the aftermath of their holiday.'

There was an edge to Connie's voice: she took this stuff personally. 'I mean, look at little Phet there.' She gestured at a toddler with straight, auburn hair, almond-shaped eyes and a splash of freckles across his nose. 'You can't tell me his father was Thai.'

Jayne shifted her weight from one foot to the other.

'Now it's time we got you across your work. Mister Frank thought given your background and your *passion* was the word he used, you'd be willing to assist the staff and volunteers with personal care of the children, at least for the first week or two, while we think about assigning you a one-on-one.'

'Personal care?' Jayne asked.

'Yes, you know, bathing, toileting, changing nappies—or do you call them diapers in Australia?'

'Nappies,' Jayne mumbled.

Connie glanced at her watch. 'You're going to have to excuse me. If you have any questions, Dang here has the best English.'

She nodded at a Thai woman in a pale blue uniform, who smiled as she spooned rice porridge into the mouth of the baby on her lap.

'But—' Jayne began to protest.

'Yes?' Connie said.

There was no point.

'I finish at five, right?'

'That's right,' Connie said, already halfway out the door. 'You can work out your break times with the other volunteers while the children are sleeping.'

Jayne forced a smile and squatted down on her haunches so she was eye level with the crowd in the kitchen. 'I'm Jayne from Australia.'

'Hilde from Germany.' The older woman from the previous day. 'And my little *Nesthäkchen*—' she cuddled the boy on her lap '—is Kai, soon to be Rolfe.'

'*Nesthäkchen?*'

'It means the baby who is much younger than the one before in the family,' the student type said. 'Sweet, isn't it.

I'm Dianne, by the way. Also from Australia. You came through yesterday, right?'

Jayne nodded.

'And this is Sin,' Dianne said, patting the girl next to her. 'Short for Cinderella.'

'Is that what her adoptive parents call her?'

'No,' Dianne laughed. 'Sin's her Thai name. Her adoptive parents think it's so cute, they're going to keep it. Kind of. She'll be Cynthia.'

'And you?' Jayne raised her eyebrows to the Thai staff, most of whom giggled and looked away.

'My name Dang,' said the woman in blue stepping forward and giving her a *wai*.

'Connie says you're going to help out with personal care,' Dianne piped up. 'That's such a relief 'cause Marion— she's the English lady—*hates* changing nappies. Thinks she's going to get cholera or something. And Hilde here gets a rash from the liquid soap we use to disinfect our hands.'

'And what about you?'

'Oh, I've got Sin potty trained, haven't I?' she said to the little girl.

Just my luck, Jayne thought. She took a deep breath. 'Where do I start?'

'This one needs changing.'

Hilde thrust a small baby of indeterminate gender towards Jayne. She took the baby and rose awkwardly to her feet.

'Through that door,' Dianne said. 'Perhaps you could bring back some damp cloths to clean up the kids as they finish breakfast?'

Jayne made her way to a small room marked 'Diaper change'. On the shelves she found disposable nappies, washcloths and anti-rash powder. Though she hadn't changed a nappy since babysitting in her teens, it turned out to be like riding a bike. Within minutes she'd removed the dirty nappy, lobbed it into the bin, wiped and dusted what turned out to be *his* crotch, and fastened the clean nappy into place. The baby gurgled as she washed her hands.

She picked him up again and headed back to the kitchen, pleased with her success, but the bubble burst when she found Hilde had lined up another two.

'Did you remember the face cloths?' Dianne said.

'I'll bring them back next time,' Jayne said, taking one of the infants from Hilde.

'I'll get one of the Thai staff to help you,' Dianne said. '*Pee tam ngan kup khun Jayne, dai mai?*'

It translated as 'Older sister, can you work with Jayne?' A little clumsy, but not a bad effort.

'You speak Thai,' Jayne said.

'Not nearly as much as I'd like.' Dianne waved her hand. 'You should hurry. That baby your holding has a…leakage problem.'

Jayne looked down. Shit was seeping out from under the baby's nappy on to her wrist. She held the child away from her body and made a dash for the change room.

She made the same trek seven more times until all the babies' nappies were changed, faces wiped and hands washed.

'Done,' she said, handing the last of them back to Dang.

'Now we'd better start on the potty trained ones,' Dianne said. 'One of the Thai staff will help you.'

It dawned on Jayne that she'd volunteered to spend entire days, maybe weeks, caring for small children. And she'd chosen this because she thought cleaning or gardening would be too much like hard work. She must have been out of her mind.

By ten o'clock she was exhausted. A couple of other volunteers had joined Hilde and Dianne—Marion, a forty-something Brit, and James the Bible storyteller from Korea—to entertain the children in the playroom, and Jayne seized the chance to take a break. She sat down out of sight in the kitchen. Her handbag hung from a hook on the back of the door and she stared at it, wondering where she could get a decent cup of coffee to team with her first cigarette of the day.

'Time to get snack ready,' said Dang, shuffling into the room in plastic sandals. 'Then we do laundry.'

Jayne struggled to keep her expression neutral. 'Laundry?'

'We wash sheets, towels and clothes. Then we make bottles and lunch. Connie explain, yes?'

Jayne shook her head, now desperate for a smoke. 'Guess she wanted to surprise me,' she muttered, the sarcasm lost on Dang, who gestured towards the change room.

'Come, I show you Jayne. After you do trash a few times, you not notice bad smell anymore.'

14

It was nearing three in the morning when Mayuree descended from the *songthaew* at the corner of her street. It had been a long night, she was exhausted. The backstreets of Naklua were dark. She walked as quickly as her high heels and sore feet allowed. The wad of cash in her bag felt like deadweight. She was carrying her usual fortnightly salary plus two months' pay in advance to invest in shares of a company she'd had her eye on. If her hunch was right, she'd make enough to repay the debt to her boss with interest and still make a killing.

She was anxious to get home and regretted not having sprung for a motorcycle taxi. An engine noise behind her slowed as it drew closer and she turned in the hope of coming across a driver who would take her to her door. To her dismay, it was a cop. He sped up, swerved to block her path, shut off the engine and dismounted.

He put his keys in the chest pocket of a brown shirt so tight it threatened to tear, removed his white helmet and placed it on the motorcycle seat. The moonlight revealed the face of a man in his early twenties with the pout of a spoiled child. The beginning of jowls and a paunch suggested his physical peak had been but a small bump on the downhill road to excess. Even his fingers were turning to fat.

Before Mayuree could make out the name on his badge, he unclipped it and added it to the bulging shirt pocket.

'What's a nice girl like you doing walking the dark streets of Pattaya at this time of night?' he said. 'Show me your papers, *nong*.'

He addressed her as 'younger sister' as a mark of disrespect; she clearly had several years on him.

Mayuree dipped into her bag in search of her identification, but the cop snatched it from her.

'Allow me,' he said, turning his back.

Mayuree held her breath. It wasn't unheard of for police to plant drugs in such situations, especially if they'd had a quiet week and needed a bust to impress the boss.

'Ah hah.'

Mayuree froze.

'What's this I've found?' he said, holding the wad of cash, the ticket to freedom for herself and her baby.

'That's my salary.'

'I see.' He flipped through the bundle of baht notes. 'Nice work if you can get it. I don't even earn that much in a month.'

'I—It's not what I earn in a month,' she said. 'I got an advance.'

'*Really?*' the cop said with exaggerated interest. 'That's a good story, but I don't believe it and I have a better one. I think you derived this income from illegal activities.'

'Sir, no—'

'Everyone knows good Thai girls don't walk around this late at night carrying large amounts of cash. Whereas a *borikan thang phet* would—'

'I'm not a sex worker,' she pleaded. 'I work in a beer bar.'

'—and according to the Anti-Prostitution Law of 1960,' the cop continued, ignoring the interjection, 'those who practise sex work are liable to a fine or jail term.' He shook his head. 'The Governor has ordered the police to crack down on such illegal behaviour. You're going to have to accompany me to the station.'

'But my boss can vouch for me.'

The cop pursed his lips. 'You wouldn't really want to bring your boss into this, would you? You wouldn't want to put him in the position of going up against the word of an officer of the Royal Thai Police Force. I mean, I *saw* you take that money from a rich farang.'

Mayuree's heart sank. 'Please don't do this.'

'And of course I'll have to confiscate the money,' he said, tossing it back and forth from one hand to the other. 'Evidence.'

'No, no, no.'

'What's that? You're not trying to resist arrest are you? Don't want to make things worse for yourself?'

Mayuree bowed her head. 'No sir.'

'I didn't think so.'

He stopped tossing the money, pinched her by the chin and raised her face to his. 'You know, you're not bad looking.'

Tears welled up in the back of her throat, she swallowed hard to keep them at bay. Too late she realised Wen was right about the crackdown.

'Isn't there some way we could avoid a trip to the station?' she murmured.

The cop leered and reached into his back pocket. 'Good thing I happen to be carrying these, *chai mai*?'

He dangled a strip of condoms in her face.

Mayuree suppressed a shudder and forced a smile as the cop handed back her tote bag and gestured to a dark alleyway. She took a deep breath and walked off ahead of him, swaying her hips, conscious of his eyes on her arse.

She couldn't afford to think of herself or Kob or the money. Nothing must distract her from her prime objective: to make the dog-fucking son of a bitch cop come so quickly he wouldn't know what hit him till it was over.

She'd deal with everything else later.

15

Jayne had barely enough energy to stop and eat on her way home from work before collapsing into bed at the unprecedented hour of nine o'clock and sleeping until her alarm went off at six-thirty the next morning. Her upper arms hurt and there was a dull pain her in lower back, the result of the previous day's lifting, carrying and bending over change tables. She was in half a mind to phone in sick, but pride wouldn't let her. She was convinced Frank had given her a shit job—literally—if not as a test then as a reward for her apparent piety. She had to live up to the role he'd given her if she was to ingratiate herself enough to learn more about Maryanne.

She allowed herself time for a breakfast of noodle soup and two cups of coffee at a street-side café, and then paused to savour a cigarette on her way to the centre. She'd cut down since meeting Rajiv, and smoking in the morning made her feel like a naughty schoolgirl. But if the previous day was anything to go by, she'd be hard-pressed to fit in a cigarette break before quitting time and she couldn't survive that long without nicotine.

At the centre, the children were finishing breakfast.

Hilde and Dianne were already playing with their charges. Jayne hung up her bag and knew without being told to start on what she privately coined 'poo patrol', checking each baby's nappy in turn and lining them up to be changed. Next came 'potty patrol', another pride-swallowing exercise of wiping shit from little bottoms.

Without Dianne's prompting, she remembered the face cloths and cleaned up the children before releasing them to play. She helped the Thai staff clear the breakfast things and started on the laundry. While the linen was washing, she helped prepare morning tea and repeated the whole nappy, potty, face-wiping routine, at which point the laundry was ready to be hung out. She volunteered to mix the bottles of infant formula and ended up feeding one to a little girl who, with a Mohawk of black hair and a blue-black smudge of a birthmark on her left cheek, looked like a baby punk.

When lunch was done, she helped sponge down the babies and bathe the older children, and by one o'clock they were all settled for a nap. The Thai staff slept with the children, Hilde and Marion made themselves scarce and James had called in sick, leaving Dianne and Jayne to tidy the playroom.

'*Sabai-sabai*,' Dianne said. 'Peace at last.'

'You speak Thai very well,' Jayne said. 'How long have you been volunteering here?'

'About six months now. I'm supposed to start uni in a few weeks, but I can't decide what I want to do. I mean, my parents want me to do law, and I got the marks to get in, but I really want to study early childhood development.'

Jayne nodded, doing the sums in her head. Six months. That meant Dianne's time at the centre overlapped with Maryanne's by about a month.

'Follow your heart,' Jayne said. 'Life's too short. Just think of what happened to that other Australian girl who was here—what was her name?'

'You mean Maryanne,' Dianne said in a hushed voice. 'But she killed *herself.*'

'You believe that?'

Dianne shrugged. 'I didn't at first. Maryanne didn't seem like the type to do that. She seemed so...cheerful.'

That word again.

'Then Frank sat us down and told us she was seeing a shrink and taking antidepressants, and we had to face the truth. We were all so shocked. I mean, it makes you realise how little you know someone.'

Jayne murmured, wondering what gave Frank Harding such sway. No one seemed to think Maryanne killed herself until Frank convinced them otherwise.

'You were interviewed by the police?'

Dianne nodded.

'So were you and Maryanne close?'

'I only knew her a short time, but we were close, yes. We were the only two Australians here and she helped me get on my feet. You know, it's a lot of work moving countries. You've got to get the right visa, open a bank account, find somewhere to live. There's a guy on staff here who's supposed to help, but all the places he showed me were in, like, high-rise apartment buildings.' Dianne made a face. 'I think his relatives owned most of them.'

'You were lucky to have Maryanne's help,' Jayne said, steering the conversation back on track. 'What about a Thai teacher? I mean, you must have had lessons—I'd like to get some too. Maryanne give you any good tips?'

'She put me on to her teacher, but he left Pattaya just

121

after Maryanne...passed away.'

'Oh?'

'Shame really, he was such a nice guy. Taught high school English in Kanchanaburi but quit his job to come to Pattaya when his sister had a baby. She wasn't married and apparently the parents couldn't handle it. So he came to help her look after the baby. Can you believe it? I don't know about you, but no way would one of my brothers do something like that for me.'

'That's dedication,' Jayne said. 'But he's gone now, right?'

'Right.' Dianne lowered her voice and leaned closer to Jayne. 'If you ask me, I reckon Sumet had feelings for Maryanne.'

'Really? Was she keen on him, too?'

'Oh, I doubt it. I mean, it's not really the done thing for farang women to go out with Thai men. It's usually the other way around.'

Jayne let that pass.

'Did you mention this...what was his name?

'Sumet.'

'Did you mention this Sumet to the police when they interviewed you?'

'I couldn't see the point. It wasn't like there was anything going on between him and Maryanne.'

Jayne found it hard to believe this woman knew anything she didn't broadcast.

'Besides, he was such a nice guy.'

Dianne sighed and Jayne understood. Whatever her thoughts on farang women dating Thai men, Dianne had harboured feelings for Sumet, and she'd kept the object of her affection out of the police report.

'Now he's gone to...?'

'Kanchanaburi.'

'Kanchanaburi, right,' Jayne said. 'So, no chance of having Thai lessons with him. Who else can you recommend?'

Dianne prattled on and Jayne made a show of taking down her new teacher's mobile number as her mind ticked over with possibilities. Was it significant that Maryanne's Thai teacher left town just after she died? Did Sumet have feelings for Maryanne and, if so, were those feelings reciprocated or rebuffed? Was Maryanne the victim of a love affair gone wrong?

All pure speculation but, if nothing else, she'd found a line of inquiry the police hadn't pursued. The only problem was how to find Sumet, and how to raise that prospect with Dianne without generating suspicion.

'Do you reckon I could look Sumet up if I went to Kanchanaburi?' Jayne ventured. 'I was thinking of going there for Thai New Year, you know, to visit the Bridge on the River Kwai and all the sights. My grandfather was a war veteran. It would be great to have a contact there who speaks English.'

Dianne shrugged and leaned forward to brush an imaginary speck from the children's play table.

'I don't have contact details for him.'

'Pity.' Jayne thought for a moment. 'What about the sister? You said he had a sister with a baby here in Pattaya.'

'Don't know what happened to them. For all I know, the baby ended up here.'

She swept her hand across the room.

'Speaking of babies...' Dianne nodded towards the door to the nearest dormitory where a collective snuffling and shuffling was underway. 'We'd better get moving.'

16

Sumet shielded his eyes from the sun as he made his way
down the uneven concrete stairs from Wat Tham Seua
to the base of the hill. The grandiose Tiger Cave Temple
was his mother's idea. Sumet had hoped for a quiet retreat,
but *Mae* insisted on the busy pilgrimage site. He was her
only son and his ordination was the biggest merit-making
opportunity his mother would ever have. It was natural she
rejoiced in seeing her son enter the monkhood to become
thit, a 'fully ripe man'. Little could she know Sumet had
already had enough of manhood to last one lifetime.

He lifted his robes a little as he navigated the steps. He
was still getting used to the restricted movement, though he
welcomed this and all the austerities of monkhood. Ascetic
and celibate was a far cry from the life he'd expected to lead
by now—it was fitting he should suffer.

During the ordination ceremony when he prostrated
himself in homage to his ancestors, he pressed his bare chest
against the hot earth as if it might brand him the coward that
he was. He prayed the elders might slip up as they took turns
to cut a piece of his hair, or that the lotus leaf containing
his shaved locks might be caught by a sudden gust of wind

and fall to the ground in an ill omen. But these things didn't happen. Sumet scratched at the stubble. His eyebrows had been shaved off, too, a practice adopted by Thai monks to distinguish them from the Burmese. Most novices, intending to stay only three months, let their eyebrows grow straight back. Not Sumet.

He passed by the entrance to the Tiger Cave. The hillsides in the area were dotted with caves, and it had been part of the ritual to inform their resident spirits of his intention to become a monk. His family made a big show of it, their voices echoing through the caverns, but Sumet barely spoke. There was one spirit on his shoulder whom no amount of chatter would distract, no Buddhist ordination would appease.

He recited the ten Buddhist precepts as he made his way to Wat Tham Khao Noi on the adjacent ridge. Refrain from killing living beings. Refrain from taking what is not given. Refrain from false speech. Refrain from intoxicants that cause carelessness. Refrain from eating at the forbidden time. Refrain from dancing, singing, music and other entertainment. Refrain from wearing garlands and using perfumes. Refrain from sleeping in high, large or comfortable beds.

He was missing two. What were they?

Refrain from accepting gold and silver.

The words came back to him, sending ice through his veins.

Refrain from adulterous conduct.

Greed and lust: the twin pillars of his misfortune.

'Are you human?'

The monks put this question to him during the ordination ceremony. Sumet knew what was behind it: legend had it a *naga* serpent in disguise tried to become a monk. The Buddha explained that his ordination was impossible as only humans could be ordained. The question struck Sumet with particular poignancy. Was he human? Could someone with a human heart have done what he did?

There was a titter among the crowd of family and friends as they awaited Sumet's answer.

'Are you human?' the monk said again.

'Sumet,' another monk whispered, 'answer yes.'

'Yes, sir,' Sumet said mechanically.

The crowd let out a collective sigh.

'Are you a man?' the monk continued.

Another tough question.

'Yes, sir,' Sumet said.

But not man enough.

'Are you free from debt?' the monk said.

'Yes, sir.'

But I might have been rich.

'Do you have your parents' permission?'

'Yes, sir,' Sumet said.

He could anticipate his mother's lament once she realised he was never leaving the monastery.

What about grandchildren? Who's going to carry on the family traditions, look after the ancestors?

Would Sumet be able to resist pointing out that she had a grandson whom she ignored?

'Are you fully twenty years old?'

'Yes, sir.'

'Are your alms bowl and robes complete?'

'Yes, sir.'

'What is your name?'

'Venerable sir, my name is Sumet...'

Phra Sumet, as he was now known, felt the sun beat down on his shaved head as he climbed the steep staircase to the Little Hill Cave Temple. The Chinese-style pagoda at the summit had seven tiers, and it was to a small octagonal room on the first floor that Sumet ascended.

At its centre was a statue depicting the Buddha during his retreat to the forest—the incarnation for Wednesday afternoon. At the Buddha's feet were an elephant offering a water pot and a monkey holding out a honeycomb.

It was the monkey he came to meditate on, a skinny little figure with hands raised in supplication. To Sumet it looked like a human foetus with a tail.

17

Mayuree slept so deeply that when she woke, she wondered if the horror of the night before was just a terrible dream. She checked her bag. There was no denying it. That cop had robbed her and forced himself on her. The money was gone and she'd have to pay it back. She'd lost ten weeks' salary and would need to work at least three times as long to cover her costs while repaying her debt—longer, as she'd have to borrow money in the meantime, incurring more debt. It would take more than a year to recover lost ground.

Mayuree put her head in her hands, wondering what she could have done in a past life to incur such bad fortune in this one.

For the first time since Kob's birth, she contemplated getting back into the game, sleeping with customers for tips and gifts. She thought of that fat cop shoving his gamy cock in her mouth and knew she couldn't do it.

She ran to the bathroom and dry-retched into the toilet. She rinsed her mouth, doused her face in cold water and stared at her reflection in the mirror above the basin. Her almond-shaped eyes were puffy and bloodshot. Her lips were swollen and the skin around her mouth rubbed sore where the cop had rammed his pelvis against her face. She'd scrubbed him from her skin when she got home and went to bed with wet hair, which now hung down her back in matted strands.

Mayuree picked up her comb and started running it through her hair, but it caught on a knot bringing tears to her eyes. She put the comb back down on the edge of the sink and looked inside the bathroom cabinet behind the mirror. Her gaze fell on the orange tube of sleeping pills Wen took on occasion to counteract the amphetamines. It was half-full. Enough to put her to sleep for good.

She moved the orange tube to one side, found a strip of paracetamol and closed the cupboard. She washed down the painkillers with a glass of water and splashed more water on her hair. Then she smeared her comb with conditioner and went to work straightening out the kinks and untangling the knots, until her hair felt smooth and sleek again.

Mayuree used haemorrhoid cream to shrink the bags under her eyes—a trick Wen had taught her—and massaged whitening cream into her skin. She rubbed lotion all over her body, working it into her elbows, knees and ankles, and finished with a spray of cologne.

Her clothes from the night before were scattered on the floor of the main room that served as bedroom, lounge and eating area. Mayuree bundled these with the rest of the washing into a plastic bag to drop off at the Chinese laundry next door. She pulled on a pair of clean jeans and a blue top, a colour supposedly lucky for those born on a Friday. Then she grabbed her handbag and laundry and headed down the stairs.

She needed to meet with her boss, explore the possibility of working additional shifts to pay off some of the debt in kind. Perhaps she could convince him to increase the frequency of her pole dances. They were good for tips.

Before that, she needed to visit Kob and apologise to him for this latest setback in their plans. It didn't matter that he wouldn't understand. Mayuree needed to see him, to hold him. To know she could still feel love enough to outweigh the hatred and bitterness in her heart. To remind herself how he made it all worthwhile.

She pressed the bell beside the blue gate. Chaowalit ambled into view, registered her standing there, and disappeared again.

'Older brother?' Mayuree called. 'Anyone? Please let me in.'

She checked her watch, waited a full minute, pressed the bell again.

This time it was Frank who appeared in the yard of the compound.

'Khun Frank,' Mayuree called. 'It's me, Kob's mother. Can you let me in? I need to see my son.'

Frank walked over to the gate and opened it, but not enough for her to enter.

'Little sister, I was about to call you. It's about your son.'

A stab of fear ran through Mayuree's body. 'What about my son?'

'Don't panic,' Frank said, 'but we've transferred him to the clinic for tests.'

'Tests? What kind of tests?'

'Medical tests. We're worried about his health. Doctor Somsri thinks there are signs he might have a rare congenital disorder.'

'I don't understand,' Mayuree said, trying to look past

him. 'Where's my son? I need to see my son!'

Frank cleared his throat. 'It's better if Kob is kept in isolation, rather than being exposed to potential infection in his state.'

Mayuree grabbed a fistful of Frank's shirt and threw herself against his chest. 'Please,' she begged, 'please let me see my boy.'

Frank raised his arms in the air and stepped back. The momentum brought them both inside the gate.

'I need to see my son,' Mayuree screamed, pounding her fists on his shirtfront.

Frank took her firmly by the shoulders and held her at arm's length. 'Let me check with the clinic staff.'

He turned and took a few steps towards the main building, punching numbers into a mobile phone as he walked. His spoke too softly for Mayuree to hear, but turned back and nodded.

'You can see him for a few minutes,' he said. 'But don't wake him.'

Mayuree pressed her palms together and raised them to her forehead in a *wai*. 'Thank you so much.'

Kob was in a low-sided perspex cot. He was lying on his stomach with his hands raised either side of his face, wearing nothing but a nappy and a cotton vest. There was colour in his cheeks and his skin was warm to the touch.

'Oh, my poor little boy,' Mayuree murmured.

She stroked the skin of his upper arm. She leaned over, put her face close to the back of his neck and inhaled. Through the antiseptic aroma of the clinic she smelled the unique scent that was Kob.

'I'm so sorry, my darling. I want to take you home but I...'

She hung her head. How could she keep doing this to Kob, promising him a life together only to let him down? How could she keep leaving him in the care of strangers, day after day, struggling to stay awake during what little time they spent together? Maybe Khun Frank was right. Maybe she should give him up.

Mayuree gazed again at her sleeping boy. His fingers were splayed, making his chubby hands look like little brown starfish. She remembered him at the beach on the weekend running handfuls of sand through those fingers, giggling as though it tickled. His mouth was open, lips squashed into a pout, soft pink tongue resting behind six tiny teeth. She lifted one of the black curls on his head. It recoiled like a spring.

She knew his body more intimately than that of any lover, and she loved him more than anything. She could never relinquish him.

She leaned forward so her lips were close to his ear.

'Trust me, my beautiful boy,' she whispered. 'Please be good, get well, and it won't be long before I can take you away from all this and we can be together all the time.'

She ran her hand from the top of his head to the soles of his feet and gave his cheek one final sniff-kiss. 'See you soon, my lovely.'

Mayuree stepped back into the foyer of the clinic where Khun Frank was waiting.

'I won't lie to you,' he said. 'Kob is a sick little boy.'

'I don't understand. He seemed fine on Sunday.'

'We're testing him for a few conditions, one of which can lie dormant then manifest suddenly with grave consequences.'

Mayuree hugged herself. She knew what she had to do.

'Thank you for letting me see my boy,' she said. 'Please, look after him.'

She walked out the gate and down the *soi* to the main road, where she hailed a *songthaew*; the loose change in her bag would pay the fare. She checked her wallet. The cop had left it untouched. She had close to five hundred baht. Enough for what she needed.

Pattaya Bay came into view as the *songthaew* turned on to the beach road. Mayuree would stay on until it turned inland again and reached Wat Chaimongkon on South Pattaya Road. There she would buy garlands of marigolds and jasmine, a bunch of lotus buds, and a platter of fruit to offer the monks. She would light nine incense sticks and leave them standing upright in the earth of a bronze pot, counting on the smoke to carry her petition to the Lord Buddha.

'Make Kob well,' she prayed. 'Keep him safe.'

She would ask nothing for herself.

18

'That was close,' Somsri said.

'Actually, I think it was a blessing the mother showed up like that,' Frank said. 'Now she knows her child is sick.'

'Perhaps.' Somsri ran his tongue over his teeth. 'Chaowalit did well.'

'Yes, it was quick thinking on his part to call me. It bought us the time we needed. Speaking of timing, how long will the child stay under?'

'A few hours yet. The dose I gave him should last long enough to get through the formalities.'

'And the rise in body temperature?'

'We put a lamp over the cot for a few minutes. Just long enough to heat him up a little.'

'Simple but effective.'

The doctor nodded.

'And all the paperwork's in order?'

Somsri nodded again.

'Good, good,' Frank said. 'I'm going to head over to the orphanage and make sure all the volunteers leave on time. You've teed up the meeting with your contact from the Board?'

'Yes, though it will cost more to have him come outside business hours.'

Frank held up one hand. 'Not my jurisdiction,' he said, still smarting from their recent phone conversation. 'It's up to you to handle that.'

He took leave of the doctor and made his way out of the compound. He was content with proceedings, though he felt sullied by the mother's performance. What did that shameless whore think she was doing, throwing herself at him like that? She almost knocked him off his feet. Frank tried to recall if she'd made contact with his skin. The possibility made him shudder.

More than ever, Frank was convinced God had sent him to Pattaya to restore order to chaos. Some women with children were not fit to be mothers. Others fit to be mothers were denied children. It was Frank's duty to right these wrongs.

Jayne was not the maternal type. When her contemporaries married and started having children, one after the other, it seemed they'd all succumbed to an epidemic to which Jayne alone seemed immune. She fled the country and became an expatriate largely because her aspirations when it came to marriage, mortgages and children were so at odds with those of her family and peers. That they were also at odds with the vast majority of Thai people—who always asked how many children she had and looked crestfallen to learn she had none—was beside the point. As a foreigner, she was allowed to be different. What made her a misfit at home added to her exoticism in Thailand.

Her time in the orphanage was doing little to change her mind. The toddlers were amusing, the way they walked like zombies and struggled to speak Thai and English—or German in little Gai/Rolfe's case. But all you could do with a baby was put food in one end and clean up the shit that came out the other.

'Everyone is special', proclaimed the poster on the wall, the slogan emblazoned over a photograph of a penguin colony. 'We are all God's children', advised another that featured an image of a warthog.

They reminded Jayne to keep her uncharitable thoughts to herself and she read them over and over throughout the day when she felt herself at risk of slipping out of character.

She read them again in the late afternoon as she and Dianne paced the playroom, each with an infant over one shoulder, waiting for them to burp. Jayne was carrying the baby with the mohawk, whose name was Ant. Dianne carried the tiny newborn Nok.

'She was abandoned at the hospital a couple of days ago, poor thing,' Dianne told Jayne. 'They say her mother was probably that teenage prostitute whose body was found on the weekend.'

'I know the one you mean, I read about it in the local paper. Poor girl.'

'Oh, she'll be okay,' Dianne said. 'In fact, she's probably much better off. She'll be cared for here for a while and then get adopted overseas into a well-off family.'

I was talking about the mother, Jayne wanted to say, but the penguins and warthogs told her to bite her tongue. She patted Ant on the back a little faster than necessary.

'It's the thing I love about this work,' Dianne continued, cradling Nok's head in her hand. 'It feels good to be part of an organisation devoted to improving children's lives. New Life—the name says it all.'

'Doesn't it,' Jayne said, adding self-consciously, 'Praise the Lord.'

She glanced at the warthog, wondering if she was laying it on a bit thick. He raised an eyebrow but Dianne beamed.

'You know, you're amazing Jayne. Everyone is talking about how you've taken on all the dirty work around here with no complaints. It takes a special person to do that.'

Jayne flushed in spite of herself.

'Frank must think very highly of you.'

'I've hardly seen him.'

'Ah, but as he'll tell you himself, Frank has very good instincts when it comes to people.'

Jayne felt something warm and wet hit her shoulder.

'And he must think you're really special to have trusted this work to you.'

The warm, wet stuff started to trickle down Jayne's back.

'So what are your plans for this evening?' Dianne said. 'There's this new place opened in town that serves fondue. A few of us thought we might try it out.'

She was saved from answering by the appearance of Frank Harding.

'Just dropped by to see how you're all getting on,' he said. 'How're you going, Jayne?'

'Fine,' she said, backing away towards the bathroom. 'Busy.'

He chuckled as if she were joking. 'Dianne keeping you on your toes is she?' He smiled at the volunteer.

'Actually, she's pretty low-maintenance, whereas these babies…I'm sorry, you'll have to excuse me. I need to get cleaned up.'

Frank held up his hand. 'It's good to hear you're settling in.'

'Absolutely,' she said. 'Loving it.'

Baby spew was sliding down Jayne's back, headed for the waistband of her jeans. How had Ant managed to vomit *under* her T-shirt?

'You shouldn't overdo it, especially in the first few weeks.'

'Right,' Jayne nodded.

'Don't feel obliged to stay late.'

'Okay then.'

There was an awkward moment when both of them waited for the other to speak.

'Well then—' Frank said.

'I'll be—' Jayne said at the same time.

'Go on,' Frank said.

'I really need to get cleaned up.'

He glanced at his watch. 'Yes, of course, don't let me keep you.'

It was too late to salvage her jeans. Ant had fallen asleep and Jayne handed her over to one of the Thai staff on her way to the bathroom. She mopped up the vomit as best she could. But the smell clung to her as she headed back to the hotel causing her fellow *songthaew* passengers to screw up their noses and give her a wide berth. They probably thought she'd been drinking.

I should be so lucky, Jayne thought.

Frank Harding had a nerve, counselling her not to work late. Jayne couldn't get out of there fast enough. Fuck the penguins. Fuck the warthogs. And fuck the fondue. The minute she got cleaned up, she was heading out for a beer, a smoke and a game of pool—preferably all at the same time.

138

19

Chaowalit watched the nurse fasten the strings of the baby's top.

'It's a boy, right?' he asked.

'Does it matter?' she snapped.

Chaowalit kept his expression neutral. 'It might. What if I bump into someone who recognises the baby? I'll need to be able to explain that I'm taking *him* or *her* to see a doctor on behalf of my employer—which is true, in a manner of speaking.'

She grunted, reluctant to concede the point. 'Yes, he's a boy, okay?'

'Okay.'

She swaddled the baby in a white muslin cloth and checked under his eyelids before handing him over. The baby had been drugged and didn't stir as Chaowalit placed him inside a striped *phakhama* sling across his chest. He checked his reflection in the mirror on the back of the nursery door.

He'd swapped his navy security guard's uniform for a pale yellow polo shirt, green slacks and black plastic sandals. To anyone passing in the street, he looked like an honest worker—a tailor, perhaps—making his way home at the end of a long day, carrying his baby son. The casual clothes softened the harder lines of his face, making the furrow on his brow seem less intense, the lines around his mouth less pronounced. Experience had prematurely aged Chaowalit, but in the guise of a parent, he looked younger.

He straightened his shoulders and with a nod from the nurse, set out for the orphanage wing. He took a long detour, making the most of what it felt like, albeit briefly, to be *tamada*, to blend in with the crowd.

He sauntered along a *soi* transformed at night into a strip of makeshift cafés. Small blue plastic stools clustered around low tables against the outer wall of an office block. Vendors with cooking carts dished out local specialties: rice noodles with fish balls and *tom yam po taek*, 'broken fish trap soup'. The smells of fish, galangal, lemongrass and basil made Chaowalit's stomach rumble beneath the weight of the baby. With no time for a meal, he satisfied his hunger with a spicy sausage on a stick, before continuing on his way.

A car whizzed past, sounding its horn to clear the way. Chaowalit felt the baby stir. He pulled back the edge of the sling to check on him. A fleeting observer could have mistaken the gesture for affection, but Chaowalit was concerned only that the sedative didn't wear off.

The baby stayed asleep. Chaowalit resumed his walk. He wished they could meet in twenty years' time. He'd like to call in the debt this baby owed him for the service he'd performed. But by then this baby would be a farang, wouldn't even speak Thai.

Son of a whore.

It was one of the worst insults that could be thrown at a person. How much worse, then, when the insult were true?

'You can't escape it, you little bastard,' he whispered to

the baby whose name he didn't know. 'You can try to hide, but shame sticks like shit. They'll smell it on you wherever you go, even inside the temple. Not that you'd wanna live the life of a monk, eh? Fuck that for a joke.'

He leered at the sleeping baby, imagined him taking it all in, hanging on every word.

'There's only one way out, little brother,' he said. 'You gotta leave behind everything you have—your name, your family, your friends—and start again. You gotta find a place where you have no past, only a future. You gotta seize whatever opportunities come your way with both hands because no one else is going to help you. It's every man for himself.'

Chaowalit knew what he was talking about. His father was a nameless john who fucked his mother for money. His mother was dead to him long before the disease that killed her. He'd lived among aunts and cousins in his maternal grandmother's home where he was treated as an unpaid servant, until the day he decided they could all go to hell.

Chaowalit looked up at the billboards over the intersection. A pale man with Chinese features punched the air with his mobile phone. A woman with white skin, Asian eyes, a European nose and ringlets in her hair seemed ecstatic about the tea she was drinking. It was fashionable now to be *look kreung*, a mix of Asian and farang, provided the mix resulted in whiter skin. But Chaowalit's was the wrong mix. His features were big and blunt, not small and refined. His hair was the wrong tint, neither glossy black nor chestnut. More like rat-brown. And his skin was scarred and black as an Isarn farmer, making him a second-class citizen in the eyes of many Thai people.

Without Chaowalit to help him, the baby in his arms would have been destined to suffer the same ignominy.

'You may never know it,' he whispered to the sleeping boy, 'but I'm the best friend you'll ever have.'

20

As a student at the Melbourne College of Advanced Education, Jayne spent a month's teaching placement in a boys' prison, euphemistically called a Youth Training Centre. Classes were voluntary, few boys attended and those who did objected to lessons, agreeing only to play games or use the computers. Jayne spent most of her time, as the inmates did, trying to find ways of overcoming boredom. To this end, she took the boys up on their offer to teach her to play pool, unaware of an unwritten and uniquely Australian rule that a player who fails to sink a single ball is required to 'drop their dacks' and run a lap around the table. Only when she was one shot away from losing did the boys enlighten her, the beefier ones moving to block the exit in case she thought they were joking. The *frisson* of risk lifted her game and while she didn't win, she kept her pants on.

The game proved addictive and over the years she'd honed her skills. She could hold her own against off-duty bar girls at the Woodstock Bar in Bangkok's seedy Nana Plaza and even won on occasion, at her best when she'd drunk just enough alcohol to boost her confidence without diminishing her skills. If she drank too much, which she usually did, her bravado would increase and her skills decrease at the same rate. If she was ever forced to teach maths again, she could use this phenomenon to demonstrate an inverse mathematical relationship, it was that precise.

Jayne decided on the open-sided beachfront bars of Central Pattaya as the place she was mostly likely to get a game of pool without going deaf. She walked along the footpath sussing out the options, when a howling electric guitar called to her from amidst the pedestrian slow rock and R&B. Jimi Hendrix. He beckoned from a bar called B-52, a bamboo shack draped in camouflage webbing with upside-down helicopters painted on the ceiling, chopper blades formed by the ceiling fans. The walls were decorated with American flags and movie posters. *Good Morning Vietnam. Platoon. Born on the Fourth of July. Full Metal Jacket.* A third of the floor space was taken up by an L-shaped bar, bamboo-panelled to match the walls, the short side fronting on to the street, the other lined with barstools with a sea view. The remaining space housed a few tables and chairs clustered around a pool table. The men behind the bar wore camouflage pants and tight black T-shirts, the female staff high-cut khaki shorts and black bikini tops with dog tags around their necks, homage to a war that was over before any of them were born. A chalked-up list offered the eponymous B-52 cocktail and others called 'Tet Offensive', 'Napalm' and 'Agent Orange'.

It was tacky and tasteless and about as far from the New Life Children's Centre as Jayne could imagine. She took a seat at one of the tables where a Heineken Bier ashtray and a Tiger Beer coaster competed for her custom. When a waitress appeared she thumbed her nose at both and order a Singha. She sipped it slowly and sussed out the competition.

Four men whose crew cuts and banter gave them away as US Marines were playing pool. Two black guys sat at one table, a white guy at another, his redheaded companion leaning over the pool table to take a shot. Jayne picked up that they'd recently spent six months in Da Nang searching for the remains of Americans still listed as missing in action from the Vietnam War.

They were finishing their fourth game and Jayne her third beer, when she stepped forward and placed a ten baht coin on the table. This was enough to make the redhead miscue and sink the black.

A waitress stepped forward, pocketed the coin and racked up the balls. Jayne dusted her hands with talc, selected a cue and chalked the tip.

'Which one of you is going to sit out?' she asked the winners.

They frowned at her unexpected accent and she had to repeat herself before the taller of the two raised his hand.

As Jayne leaned forward to break, both men moved into her peripheral vision either side of the table, a ploy designed to put her off.

'Game on,' she murmured to herself, as she smashed the cue ball into the triangular configuration and listened for the plop of a ball falling into a pocket. She heard it twice. A quick count told her she'd sunk one of each.

Jayne surveyed what remained and chose her target, sinking one small ball and then another. She misjudged the next shot but the white ball bounced off the side cushion on to another of her balls and sent it on a trajectory towards the corner. Her opponent gasped when it dropped into the pocket. Jayne feigned nonchalance. Although she missed the next shot, her opponent never recovered his composure and she won the game.

Her next challenger was one of the white guys, who brushed past her with a ''Scuse me, m'am' to take his first shot, which also proved to be his last.

The Goddess of Pool was indeed smiling on her.

The tall black marine was the next to take her on. 'Mitch here ain't as good as me, m'am,' he said, rising from his chair. 'I'm Tommy.'

He shook her hand. His high forehead and prominent cheekbones framed wide innocent eyes, but the dimples either side of his generous lips hinted at mischief. He was—to use the Australian idiom—built like a brick shithouse. His biceps, triceps and other muscle groups Jayne couldn't name strained at the sleeves of his white T-shirt. He looked like he could snap his cue in two and use it as a toothpick.

'That ain't true and you know it,' said Mitch.

'How many balls did you make in that last game, man? Four? Well, you jus' keep an eye on Tommy, here. You'all might learn a thing or two.'

Tommy flashed a dazzling smile at Jayne as she leaned down to take her break. His skill wasn't on par with his cockiness; she won even more convincingly than she had against Mitch.

The other two Marines spoke only to tell her their names, Jerry and Earl, and to challenge her again. She defeated each in turn, at which point they both threw money on their table and left. Mitch and Tommy stayed, challenging Jayne to more games, raising the stakes by playing for drinks.

'What's happenin' man?' Mitch protested as they both took her on at the same time. 'I *gave* you that ball and you didn' make it?'

'Jayne's just too damn good, man,' Tommy countered, winking at her, 'that's how come we's in this predicament.'

Even having a handsome man flirt with her was not enough to break Jayne's concentration. She took a deep breath and won with the following shot. Smiling, Tommy shook his head and insisted on buying her a cocktail.

'Jeez, don't you'all wish Leroy was here to see this,' Mitch chuckled, 'the two of us gettin' our asses whipped by a ch—' he looked sheepishly at Jayne, 'by a *lady*.'

'Leroy's my cousin, m'am,' Tommy added, 'and he reckons that *ladies* can't play pool.'

'Well, tell him to come on down,' Jayne said. 'I'll set him straight.'

'Was a time you'd have found him here with us, m'am,' Tommy said. 'Only him and his wife, they just got themselves a baby. Leroy's a proud daddy now. Ain't nothin' gonna tear him away from his family.'

'What do you mean, *got* a baby?'

'Well, m'am—I mean Jayne—Leroy's wife, Alicia, she couldn't have no kids. So they come to Thailand to adopt. Two nights ago they sent word they was on their way to meet their little boy here in Pattaya. It's jus' luck we was here at the same time.'

'So you went along to the ceremony?'

Tommy picked up his camera and waved it in the air. 'I was the official photographer. We was there jus' before we came here. They gotta wait a few days in Bangkok for the kid's passport, and then they's headin' back to North Carolina.'

'*In my mind I'm goin' to Carolina*,' Mitch started to sing. 'Who was it sung that song?'

'So they've adopted a Thai baby?' Jayne said to Tommy.

'Well, looks like his daddy was one of us, know what I'm sayin'?'

Jayne thought of Kob and the other *look kreung* at the New Life Children's Centre and nodded.

'John Denver?' said Mitch, still humming the song.

'Don McLean,' said Tommy.

'I think you'll find it was James Taylor,' Jayne said.

'Hey, I ain't gonna argue,' Tommy held up his hands. 'You the one on the winnin' streak.'

A waitress set three drinks on their table, bright pink liquid in tall glasses with fruit skewered to the swizzle stick, cocktail umbrellas and coloured straws. Jayne picked up a glass, sniffed and sipped. It tasted like Red Bull, the sugary, caffeinated drink long-haul truck drivers used to wash down their amphetamines.

'What's this?'

'Ah...' Tommy scanned the drinks menu on their table. 'That'd be a Wartime Romance.'

He grinned and actually licked his lips. Jayne gave him a withering look and set the glass back down.

'So,' she said, lighting a cigarette to get the taste of Wartime Romance out of her mouth. 'Which one of you wants to get your ass whipped next?'

It was after midnight when she returned to the Bayview Hotel. She was tipsy and her mouth tasted like cough medicine. But it felt great to have had a night out. Her pool form had never been better. And it didn't hurt being the target of some serious flirtation on Tommy's part.

As she entered her room, she found a message slip just inside the door. 'Rajiv called to you, 21.30'. She felt a twinge of guilt, shook it off. It wasn't as if anything had happened between her and Tommy. For that matter, it wasn't as if much had happened between her and Rajiv either.

She'd allowed Tommy to take her photo before they left the bar—'a pin-up shot for my locker,' he said—and accepted a kiss on the cheek. But she declined his invitation to meet at the same time and place the following evening.

'I'm sorry,' she said, 'but I'm otherwise engaged.'

'Aw man, did you hear that?' Tommy said to Mitch. 'She's *engaged*!'

Jayne smiled at the memory, raised her hand to the cheek Tommy had kissed.

21

Alicia gazed at the baby in her lap. Everything about him seemed miraculous. One arm had escaped his swaddling and he'd flung it across his face as if to shield his eyes from the glare of the streetlights. All through the flight to Bangkok and the taxi ride to Pattaya, Alicia had fought back panic at the thought she might not love this baby, who until now existed only as a photo and a typed description: 'Boy, 11 months old, 8.2 kilograms (18 lb), 74 cm (29 in), brown eyes, black hair, black skin'. She needn't have worried. Alicia loved Jesse from the moment she laid eyes on him. He was warm, brown and soft, and smelled like heaven.

Though they'd only known each other a few hours, he was already her son. She'd have thrown her naked body over cut glass to protect him.

The handover was as lacking in ceremony as a shotgun wedding. There was an English-speaking Thai doctor who vouched for Jesse's health and provided a medical certificate; and an American who gave them the adoption paperwork. Alicia had prepared for an interrogation, but was asked only a few perfunctory questions by a Thai official, before

Jesse was handed to her. No fanfare. One moment her arms were empty, the next they were cradling a child. Her child. Her heart leapt at the first touch, and neither Leroy nor his cousin could coax her into looking up for the photos: she couldn't take her eyes off her boy.

Alicia stroked his soft curls. He'd slept the whole time since they'd collected him, but she supposed this was normal. In his sleep he gripped the finger she placed against the palm of his hand and turned his face towards her, as if he were the one claiming her.

There were a few more layers of bureaucracy to get through before they could take him home. Jesse's passport wouldn't be available until the following afternoon—it would be issued in his Thai name, Theera Meemulthong—and they had to take this and all the other paperwork to the US Embassy in Bangkok so Jesse could be issued with an immigration visa.

Alicia had waited ten years to have a child. Waiting another week or two before they could leave Thailand shouldn't seem like much, but she was done with waiting. She wanted to take him home.

She looked from the baby in her lap to her husband and back again. She hadn't anticipated how it would feel to have a child who, to the uninformed observer, looked like he could be the offspring of one of them but not both. Jesse didn't look like her. He didn't look much like Leroy either, but there was something similar about the shape of their mouths, the way their jaws were set. Would people think Jesse was Leroy's son, the product of a previous relationship, and assume Alicia was his stepmother?

She looked again at her finger in Jesse's fist and leaned forward to smell the top of his head. Plenty of women had children who took after their fathers and bore no resemblance to them. Alicia would love Jesse so fiercely no one would doubt he was her son.

The taxi came to a halt.

'We're here,' Leroy said. 'Need a hand?'

She shook her head. 'I can manage the baby if you get our things.'

He nodded and took out his wallet as the driver opened her door.

Alicia carefully released her seatbelt. She placed the baby against her chest so his head was resting against her shoulder and eased herself out of the air-conditioned car. The sudden change in temperature made her break out in a sweat and she hastened to the foyer of their hotel.

'Good evening sir, madam,' the receptionist said. 'Welcome to the Suriya Hotel. Will you need a cot for your baby?'

Your baby. Music to Alicia's ears.

'That's okay,' she said, 'he'll sleep with us.'

Alicia hadn't discussed this with Leroy. If he'd asked her earlier in the day about a cot, she would've chastised him for not having organised it already. But there was no way Alicia could leave Jesse to sleep alone in a cot. She would hold him all through the night so he would wake up knowing how much he was loved.

Leroy took the room key and they made their way to the elevator. Jesse slumped warm against Alicia's chest. Leroy rustled plastic bags filled with disposable diapers, wipes, infant formula, plastic bottles, teats, pacifiers, creams and lotions. They stepped inside. He pushed the button for the fifth floor and the doors closed. Alicia turned around to face the mirrored wall at the back of the elevator. She touched her husband lightly on the shoulder and Leroy turned around to see her pointing at their reflection. They didn't need to speak. They both knew what the other was thinking. They'd almost lost hope of ever seeing this, but there they were.

A family.

22

Jayne stepped inside the gate to the sound of wailing. She thought at first it was coming from the orphanage and groaned. All she needed after a big night was howling babies on top of the shit and piss. But it wasn't coming from the orphanage and it wasn't a baby crying. These were the gut-wrenching screams of a grown woman and they were coming from inside the administration building.

Jayne saw Mayuree come running out the door and along the path towards the gate, her face contorted with grief. Frank Harding appeared in her wake, but didn't run after her. Mayuree was too distressed to notice Jayne and almost knocked over the guard in her haste to get out.

'What on earth was that about?' Jayne said, staring after her.

Frank's face was grim. 'Her son, one of the boarders, passed away during the night.'

Jayne felt lead in the pit of her stomach, her skin flushed cold then hot in an instant.

'*What*?' she gasped. 'How did it happen?'

Frank glanced at his watch. 'I'm sorry Jayne. I haven't got time to go into this now. You'll appreciate there are things I have to do...'

'Of course.'

'There'll be a briefing in my office at one o'clock. Would you please ask all the volunteers to be there?'

Jayne nodded and headed towards the orphanage in a daze. She couldn't imagine what Mayuree must be going through. How could a little boy who'd seemed healthy when she glimpsed him on Monday be dead by Thursday?

The thought stopped Jayne in her tracks. It didn't make sense. Babies didn't die like this in Thailand, at least not in urban centres like Pattaya whilst in the care of well-funded institutions. Christ, if you could get fondue in Pattaya surely a sick child could get decent healthcare, even if the parents couldn't afford it. Wasn't that why they put their kids into institutions in the first place?

She glanced at her watch. Almost five hours until the briefing. She sighed and opened the door.

A loud cry greeted her, as if the news of Kob's death had filtered through to one of the children. It was Dianne's charge, Sin, protesting at getting dressed.

'Come on,' Dianne said, slipping a sundress over the toddler's head, 'you'll look so pretty in this nice dress. Oh, hi Jayne. How are you this fine morning?'

Clearly she hadn't been apprised of recent developments. Frank had said to ask the volunteers to a briefing. It wasn't her job to tell them why.

'I'm okay.' She fossicked around in her handbag for some painkillers but came up empty handed. 'You don't have any Panadol on you?'

'Oh no, I try not to take drugs,' Dianne said.

They're not drugs, they're *medicine*, Jayne wanted to say. Then she had a thought that helped ease the pain.

'My stomach's a bit off this morning,' she said to Dianne. 'Any chance you could give me a hand and deal with some of the more disgusting nappies?'

The young woman's smile faltered ever so slightly. 'No worries.'

'Thanks,' Jayne smiled.

Mayuree was supposed to be sent to his office at the *other* compound where Doctor Somsri was waiting to inform her of her son's death. Thanks to his easily intimidated receptionist, Frank had to deal with the hysterical woman himself. He'd tried to put his counselling skills to good use. But Mayuree took it badly. She wouldn't listen to what he had to say about Kob going to a better place. She just kept howling and demanding to see the child's body. Frank had never seen a Thai person behave so badly.

In the end he summoned Somsri and let him explain why the child's body had been hastily cremated. He was a doctor and he was Thai. A woman like Mayuree couldn't question his authority.

Perhaps it was a case of once bitten, twice shy— Maryanne Delbeck's legacy—but Frank decided to invite the doctor back to attend the briefing with the volunteers just in case anyone else got emotional.

Somsri was already seated when they filed in: Hilde, Marion, James, Dianne and Jayne. Frank gestured for them to take a seat. Hilde, Dianne and Jayne took the couch, a box of tissues on the coffee table in front of them.

'Most of you know Doctor Somsri,' Frank said, 'our centre's medical consultant. I've asked Doctor Somsri along today in case you have any questions. It's my sad duty to inform you all that one of the boarders passed away last night.'

Hilde and Marion gasped in concert and James crossed himself.

'Which baby?' Dianne asked.

'His name was Kob,' Frank said, 'boy, just under a year old. Been with us about three months.'

'What happened?' said Marion, tearing up.

'The Lord giveth and the Lord taketh away,' Frank said. 'As I tried to explain to the mother, little Kob has gone to a better place.'

'As Jesus said, "Suffer the children to come unto me for theirs is the Kingdom of Heaven."'

Frank gave James an approving nod. Dianne joined Hilde in reaching for tissues to dab their eyes. Jayne bowed her head, keeping her emotions in check.

'It's only human to feel upset,' Frank said. 'But as people of faith we must rejoice in Kob's eternal salvation.'

No one said anything for a moment; the women sniffled.

'How?' Jayne asked. 'How did the baby die?'

Frank gave Somsri his cue.

'Let me try to explain, Khun—?'

'Jayne.'

'Well, Khun Jayne, despite our best efforts, we do lose children placed in our care from time to time. Many are the offspring of uneducated country girls who don't know enough about their bodies to protect themselves from getting pregnant in the first place. They expose their unborn babies to sexually transmissible infections such as syphilis and gonorrhoea, not to mention AIDS, which contributes significantly to increased morbidity and mortality rates in their offspring.'

He leaned forward, smiling in the unique way of Thai

people imparting unpleasant information. 'That is, their babies get sick and die.'

He sat back. Dianne nodded, still sniffling. Jayne said nothing.

'On top of this, by the time some babies reach us, they've been sick for a long time. Their mothers are more likely to take a sick child to a spirit doctor than a hospital. Maybe they visit a drugstore, but this often leads to misdiagnosis and treatment, resulting in iatrogenic complications.'

He leaned forward once more. 'That is, problems caused by the treatment itself.'

Dianne nodded again and clutched Jayne by the hand.

'Kidney failure is the most common. By the time we see the babies, it's often too late to provide anything other than palliative care—to care for them until they die.'

'Excuse me for asking, Doctor,' Jayne said, 'but there's a clinic within the nursery compound. Don't you test and treat all the children there?'

'We do, we do,' Somsri nodded. 'And we often make real progress. But then the family come to visit and insist on taking the child off for a weekend. Suddenly the treatment regime is disrupted and we are worse off than when we started because the child is now at risk of developing drug resistance.'

'Excuse me again, Doctor, but I want to understand correctly. Are these the problems that caused Kob's death?'

'Ah, I have been speaking generally, but now I will be specific.' Somsri leaned forward to address Jayne directly. 'His was a special case. That baby had *sickle-cell anaemia*. It's a condition we see a lot in the offspring of African-Americans. That and AIDS, of course.'

'Is it contagious?' Marion gasped.

'As a precaution, we expedited the cremation of the body,' the doctor said. 'You can rest assured there is no risk of infection to yourself or anyone else associated with the orphanage.'

'Are you sure?'

'I guarantee it. I was called to sign the death certificate and saw to the infection control personally.'

This seemed to mollify the Englishwoman.

Doctor Somsri sat back in his chair, pressed his fingertips together and nodded to Frank.

'I'm sure you'll agree it was fortunate the doctor could join us this afternoon and provide you with his explanation as a medical expert.'

There was a murmur of assent as Somsri rose to his feet. The volunteers stood up as he handed each of them his business card.

'Please don't hesitate to visit me in my consulting rooms if you have any further questions,' he said, 'or any problems with your own health.'

'There is one other thing, Doctor,' Jayne piped up. 'The Australian girl who worked here last year, Maryanne: do you think it was the dying children that got to her? Could that be why she took her own life?'

The question startled Frank, but Somsri took it in his stride.

'No one can be sure. Khun Maryanne had a lot of problems. You, Khun Jayne, strike me as a more mature person. As I say, my door is open if you would like to see me.'

He took leave of them with a *wai*.

Frank turned to the group. He took the hands of Jayne and Marion who were standing either side of him. 'How about we say a prayer?'

They all joined hands and bowed their heads.

'Lord, bless our baby brother Kamolsert,' Frank began.

Kamolsert. So that was Kob's official name, the one the monks had given him, taking into account the day of the week he was born and configuring the vowels and consonants to bring out the best prospects in his horoscope.

But sometimes the monks got it wrong. Jayne knew because her friend Ying, previously known as Sasathorn had petitioned an expert to review the composition of her name, believing a mistake might account for her life's difficulties. After analysing her horoscope, the monk renamed her Nonthathorn, meaning 'a better life'. Though she remained known by her nickname, the change seemed to do her good. Jayne attributed it to the power of positive thinking. She wasn't superstitious enough to believe Kob—Kamolsert Apornsuwanna—might have fared better with a different name.

The briefing with Doctor Somsri did little to answer Jayne's questions. She recognised his name from the police report as the expert witness whose diagnosis of depression was crucial to the finding of Maryanne Delbeck's death as suicide. His tongue was as silver as his hair, and Jayne couldn't help feeling he was trying to confuse rather than enlighten her. One minute he was talking about AIDS, the next some other disease. His explanations seemed to rely more on prejudice than science.

As for that platitudinous, self-righteous prick Frank Harding, the thought that he'd told Mayuree that her son had gone to a better place made Jayne's blood boil. When he took her hand and started to pray, it required a Herculean effort not to slap the condescending smile from his face.

She eluded the rest of the volunteers by pretending to need the bathroom and scuttled out the gate into the laneway for a cigarette. She inhaled deeply and paused to take stock.

Kob hadn't seemed ill when she saw him on Monday and Mayuree had said nothing about him being sick. So what happened? Could his death have been an accident that the centre was trying to cover up? It was possible, but not likely. The childcare facility appeared to be well run, there were few hazards that Jayne could see, and the Thai staff were competent.

Perhaps it was a cot death. But if that was the case, why cremate the body with such haste? In fact, why rush both the autopsy and cremation unless there was something to hide?

Stories circulated in the Thai press from time to time about street children in towns like Pattaya being killed so their vital organs could be harvested and sold to rich, ailing farangs. Likely as not, these were urban myths, expressing the anxiety people felt about the encroachment of Western culture on Thai society, or about the dark side of their own corrupt elites. Besides, whatever her misgivings about Christian evangelists, Jayne couldn't imagine Frank Harding being involved in something as grotesque as organ farming.

She lit a second cigarette with the butt of the first and punched Rajiv's number into her mobile phone. He answered before she had time to exhale.

'Hi Rajiv.'

He liked everything about her, even the sound of her voice.

'How are you?'

'Fine.'

He could tell that she was smoking and wondered if

the children were getting on her nerves. It amused him to imagine Jayne working in an orphanage.

'You don't sound fine.'

'I'm...confused,' she said. 'One of the babies in the orphanage died last night. Actually, he wasn't in the orphanage. He was in another section where poor Thais leave their children to be cared for. I know his mother.'

'Oh my goodness, that's dreadful,' Rajiv said. 'What happened?'

'I don't know. I mean, I'm not sure. You don't happen to know anything about sickle cell anaemia, do you?'

Rajiv thought for a moment. 'You are talking about a blood disorder mostly found in people from parts of sub-Saharan Africa?'

'I think so.'

'A fascinating disease,' he said. 'The sickle cells are abnormally-shaped red blood vessels, which the malaria parasite does not like one little bit. This makes the carrier of sickle-cell disease resistant to malaria.'

'That sounds like a good thing. I thought the disease was fatal.'

'Please wait a moment, Jayne.'

He put down the phone and hurried to the non-fiction section of Uncle's bookstore, where there was a decade-old medical encyclopaedia among the stock. He brought it back to the counter and leafed through to the relevant information.

'"The disease is chronic and lifelong,"' he read over the phone. '"Sufferers can stay well for years, but they are subject to painful spells and risk complications that greatly shorten their life expectancy to just over forty years".'

'Forty years?' Jayne said. 'I knew there was something

suss about all this. There's a doctor here trying to convince me that's what this baby died of—'

'Hold on a moment.' His eyes skimmed down the page as he spoke. 'There's something here about children. It is saying there are potentially lethal complications of sickle-cell disease, which includes strokes in children. Also—and I am quoting—"from the age of birth up to five years, children born with sickle cell disease should take daily doses of folic acid and penicillin to protect them from a range of early childhood illnesses to which they are more prone by virtue of this genetic condition".'

'So it *is* possible the baby could have died from complications of sickle cell disease,' she said.

Rajiv could almost hear her mind ticking through the phone.

'Jayne, you weren't there when the baby died, were you?'

'No, it happened overnight and volunteers only do day shifts.'

'So you weren't working last night.' The words tumbled out before he could stop them. 'Not that it is a problem,' he added quickly. 'It is just that when I couldn't reach you, I'm afraid my imagination got the better of me. I started noticing all the articles in the *Bangkok Post* about criminal activity in Pattaya—the scams and rackets, the foreign gang activity, the tourists getting drugged and robbed. And yet even as I am saying this, I know my Jayne is too clever to be fooled by any local tricksters and—'

'Nice save, Rajiv,' she muttered. 'I was out playing pool. I left my mobile at the hotel by mistake. Sorry to worry you.'

'No, no, *I'm* sorry,' he said.

It was the last thing she needed, him acting like a jealous boyfriend.

'I'm sorry about the baby…passing away.'

'It's not like we were close.'

He waited in case she wanted to add more. She didn't.

'Are you sure you're okay?'

'I'm fine,' she said. 'Just tired. Working with kids is exhausting and the early mornings are nearly killing me.'

Rajiv smiled. That sounded more like the woman he knew.

'There's just one thing bugging me,' she said. 'You said sickle cell disease was a genetic condition, right?'

'That is correct,' Rajiv said, scanning the text. 'You can be an affected or unaffected carrier. If both parents are carriers, the risk of passing it on to the child is one in four.'

'So it's not infectious?'

'Not at all.'

'You can't catch sickle cell disease from someone else, living or dead.'

'No, no, no. That is what I am telling you.'

'So why would they need to destroy the body?' she muttered.

'What do you mean, destroy the body? What are you talking about?'

'Nothing. Look, I have to go. Let's talk soon about when you might come and join me here. And Rajiv?'

'Yes.'

'Thanks for the information. You're a legend.'

Rajiv thought he was far too young, alive and ordinary to be a legend, but he accepted her compliment in the spirit in which it was intended. It gave him the courage to go through with the idea that came to him during the call. He dialled his cousin Rohit who ran a travel agency in Pahurat.

'Greetings, cousin-brother,' he said when Rohit answered. 'What information can you be giving me on buses leaving this afternoon for Pattaya?'

23

Jayne shed her work clothes and headed for what the brochure referred to as the garden pool at the Bayview Hotel. Lake-like and shaded by large trees, it wasn't conducive to swimming so much as floating, frolicking and sipping cocktails from submerged barstools around a central island bar. The pool on the rooftop of the Tower Wing would be quieter, but it was hardly a place where Jayne could relax given its association with Maryanne's death. So she dropped her towel on a white plastic sunlounge and, leaving her sunglasses on, waded through a sea of holiday makers to a quiet spot in the water.

At the bar a man with acne on his back was sipping beer and shooting glances at a couple of topless women sunbathing. An Asian couple next to him—honeymooners, Jayne guessed—took turns at photographing each other drinking the juice of whole green coconuts. Over by the steps, a small Indian-looking girl floated in an inflatable pink ring, protesting at the attempts of a blond man to fish her out of the pool.

The man signalled for help and was joined by an equally fair woman, who succeeded in cajoling the child into her arms. The woman cuddled the child while the man retrieved the ring and ran ahead to get a towel. The child grizzled as they wrapped her in the towel, bundled up their belongings and joined the exodus of families heading back to their rooms as dinnertime approached. They stood out only because the little girl, being so physically different from her parents, was clearly adopted.

Perhaps because she'd spent the previous three days looking after other people's children, Jayne felt a surge of respect for the adoptive parents. At the same time she wondered about their decision to adopt a child so wholly different from themselves. Was it gutsy or showy? Did they even have a choice?

Jayne floated on her back, allowing water to fill her ears and block out the noise. She recalled her conversation with Tommy about his cousin adopting a baby, and Tommy's comment that the child's father 'looked like one of us'. She supposed adoption agencies tried to match parents and children where possible: in Tommy's cousin's case, allocating to an African-American couple a Thai child most likely fathered by an African-American man.

A child like Kob.

Despite her best efforts to unwind, Jayne's mind kicked into overdrive. It was one hell of a coincidence that on the same night Doctor Somsri had pronounced Kob dead from a rare illness, a child matching his description was adopted in Pattaya by an American couple. And if it wasn't a coincidence, then what? Were the staff at the New Life Children's Centre involved in adoption fraud? Could this be linked to Maryanne Delbeck's death? Or was Jayne's mistrust of religious zealots clouding her judgment?

She gave up on the swim, picked up her towel and headed

back to her room. She showered and dressed, all the while turning the case over in her mind. She took her cigarettes, phone and notebook out to the balcony and wrote down everything she remembered about Tommy's cousin Leroy, his wife Alicia, and the adoption. Then she wrote down what was nagging at her: 'No one believes Maryanne was suicidal apart from Doctor Somsri. Doctor Somsri says he cremated Kob's body for infection control, but the disease he says killed Kob isn't infectious. Doctor Somsri is lying.'

She lit a cigarette and called Major General Wichit.

'What is required for foreigners to adopt a Thai baby?' she asked.

'It depends in part on the country.'

'What about the USA?'

'Proof the child has no parents due to the death or disappearance of, abandonment or desertion by, separation from, or loss of both parents,' the Police Major General said, 'or written evidence that any surviving parent has irrevocably released the orphan for emigration and adoption.'

'You sound like you're reading from the manual.'

'I've committed it to memory. You'd be surprised how many tourists drift into my office with the idea that a Thai baby would make the perfect holiday souvenir.'

'Bloody hell,' Jayne muttered in English, adding in a louder voice, 'What does all that mean in terms of paperwork?'

'Baby's birth certificate, maternal death certificate and/or written evidence of relinquishment.'

'Could such documents be forged?'

'The Thai government has strict rules in place to protect children from adoption-related trafficking,' he said. 'Thanks to the work we have done over the past few decades in improving access to institutional care for poor families, we have effectively stamped out baby selling.'

Jayne knew Wichit was obliged to give her the official line, though she doubted he believed it any more than she did.

'*Jing reu?*' she said, a useful Thai expression that could mean either 'is that so' or 'bullshit', depending on the context. 'I'm not talking about baby selling. I'm talking about baby *laundering*: taking children placed in institutional care and transforming them into orphans without consent.'

She paused to let it sink in.

'So, notwithstanding the Thai government's excellent policies and safeguards, is it possible that criminal elements could arrange for the necessary paperwork to be forged?'

Another pause.

'Very difficult,' Wichit said slowly, 'but not impossible. What evidence do you have for this baby laundering?'

'No evidence yet, just a hunch. I'm working on it.'

'Be careful, Jayne. For an operation like that to succeed it would need the support of powerful people with connections both inside and out of official channels. Make sure you don't tread on any toes.'

She liked the way the Police Major General translated English idioms into Thai.

'I'll do my best. One last thing, what sort of time is involved in taking a child out of the country once it's been adopted?'

'Again, it varies. For American citizens, assuming all the paperwork is in order, there's a wait of about a week while the immigration visa is issued.'

'And that can only be done at the US Embassy in Bangkok?'

'Correct.'

'Thank you, sir.'

'*Mai pen rai*,' Wichit said. 'And, Jayne, if you do find any evidence of adoption fraud, I urge you to contact me immediately.'

'Very well, Major General.'

'I mean it,' he said.

Jayne read back over her notes. Conjecture. Guesswork. Pure speculation. She wasn't lying when she told Police Major General Wichit all she had was a hunch. She lit a cigarette and started jotting down ideas for evidence.

Signed confessions from Frank Harding and Doctor Somsri: strike that. Copy of the baby's medical records: might be useful, worth considering, not sure how she'd get her hands on them. Copy of birth and death certificates: perhaps she could get these from Mayuree. Jayne could take a statement from Mayuree, too, about Kob's health prior to his being pronounced dead. Then again, no one would believe the word of a bar girl over Doctor Somsri. And was it fair to involve Mayuree in her investigation when there was still a possibility Kob was in fact dead?

She tapped the ash from her cigarette and closed her notebook labelled 'Maryanne Delbeck Case'. She was working on Jim Delbeck's time. Could she justify pursuing an investigation that seemed tangential, at best, to his daughter's death? She flicked through her earlier notes and found her hastily scrawled reminder to follow up with Mayuree about Maryanne. Finding out what happened to Kob gave her the chance to get close to Mayuree, and she was sure Mayuree knew more about Maryanne than she was letting on.

Jayne took another drag of her cigarette and returned

her thoughts to the conversation with the Marines. Tommy had taken pictures with his camera at the ceremony where Leroy and Alicia collected their baby. If Jayne could get her hands on those photos, at least she'd know if she was on to something.

24

Tommy and Mitch were not at the B-52 Bar. She recognised Jerry and Earl from the previous evening, but they failed to recognise her. She nursed a beer for nearly an hour. When there was still no sign of Tommy and Mitch, Jayne tapped the redhead on the shoulder.

'Hi,' she said. 'Remember me?'

Jerry grunted.

'The other guys who were here last night, Mitch and Tommy, you wouldn't happen to know where they are?'

Both men frowned.

'M'am?'

'The Marines,' she tried again, 'the other guys whose asses I whipped on the pool table? Do you know where I might find them?'

'Darn, you mean Mitch and Tommy!'

He pronounced Mitch as if it had two syllables, and Tommy to rhyme with army.

'Blue Lagoon A-Go-Go.' He jerked his thumb northwards.

'Thanks,' Jayne said.

'Say, m'am, where're you from?' the redhead asked.

'Australia.'

'*Australia?* —Man, you got the strangest German accent I ever heard.'

Jayne mulled over this surreal exchange as she went in search of the go-go bar. She hoped for her country's sake the redheaded Marine was never at the receiving end of an order to bomb *Austria*.

The brisk walk to the Blue Lagoon was enough to make Jayne break out in a sweat. To the left of the entrance was a stage the size of a card-table where a dancer wearing a strategically draped lei of silk flowers and a grass micro-miniskirt was admiring her moves in a full-length mirror framed with plastic shells. Jayne peered around the woman's legs to check her reflection.

Her red face and messy hair put her at a disadvantage, given what she had planned. She couldn't explain her investigation to Tommy and Mitch. Leroy was Tommy's cousin and she doubted they'd conspire against him. She'd have to try and rekindle Tommy's interest of the previous evening and, when his guard was down, get her hands on his photos. What it might take to have him drop his guard made her nervous.

For once Jayne welcomed the icy blast of air-conditioning. She paused in the doorway, allowing the sweat to evaporate and the heat subside while she scanned the crowd for Tommy and Mitch.

She saw them but they didn't see her, distracted by their drinking companions: two Thai women wearing the same costume as the go-go dancer at the door, only with smaller leis and skimpier grass skirts. More women, some topless, danced on stages in each corner of the room, mirrors capturing their every angle. Jayne could always pick the newcomers as the ones who made an effort to look erotic. The old hands just looked bored.

Tommy and Mitch had a bottle of Johnnie Walker Red Label whisky, a bucket of ice and a collection of mixers in the middle of their table. Their hostesses took turns to top up their highball glasses after each sip and at the rate they were going, the whisky wouldn't last the hour.

Jayne summoned Tommy's companion over and offered the woman one thousand baht of Jim Delbeck's money to change places with her. The waitress raised her eyebrows, shrugged and accepted the money without comment. Jayne strolled over to the table. Tommy's eyes lit up when he saw her.

'When you didn't show up at the B-52 Bar I thought you'd left town,' she said, taking a seat and nodding at Mitch. 'Now I see you got a better offer. Am I that expendable?'

She held her cigarette towards Tommy in a way she hoped made her look more *femme fatale* than wanker.

'No m'am,' Tommy said, flicking open his Zippo.

'It's no big deal.' She drew back on her cigarette and blew the smoke over his head. 'Just don't call me m'am, okay.'

Tommy grinned and signalled for a waitress to bring a fresh glass. He poured three fingers of whisky.

'Coke?'

'Soda.'

He added ice, handed it to Jayne, leaned close. 'I hope it's not too strong for you.'

His breath in her ear raised the hairs on the back of her neck. Role-playing was Jayne's favourite part of detective work, but on this occasion she wasn't sure what she was playing with.

She leaned back and inhaled deeply on her cigarette.

'So, have you printed that picture of me for your locker yet?'

'Yes m—Jayne. I got it here. You'all want to see it?'

Tommy unzipped his brown leather money belt and took out an envelope of photos. Jayne was relieved: this meant she didn't have to steal his camera.

'Can I see?'

'Jus' you wait a minute.' Tommy shuffled through the prints. 'Here it is.'

Jayne usually didn't like pictures of herself but this wasn't a bad shot. Leaning against the pool table with a winning grin on her face, pool cue in one hand and cocktail in the other, she looked locker-worthy.

'What else have you got in there?' she nodded at the rest of the photos.

'Oh, nuthin,' Tommy said, 'nuthin' interesting.'

Jayne sensed his discomfort and it piqued her curiosity. 'Have you got a picture of your ship?' She leaned towards him.

'Yes m'am—I mean, Jayne.'

He leafed through the pile again but held it too close to his chest for Jayne to see.

'There you go: my home away from home.'

'It's big, isn't it.' she said, then realising how pathetic that sounded, quickly added, 'So what exactly is your mission in Thailand?'

'Oh, this is jus' a social call for me, though Mitch here's been working with Full Accounting.'

'What's that?'

'The Joint Task Force. You know, bringing them home, all the MIAs and POWs. From Vietnam. Laos, too.'

Jayne nodded, although she struggled to see how they could really believe US soldiers were still being held prisoner in Southeast Asia more than twenty years after the war. Had everyone in America seen too many Chuck Norris movies?

'So you here for much longer?' she said, still eyeing the packet of photos.

'We ship out tomorrow.'

To her dismay, Tommy stuffed the envelope back into his money belt. He put his hand on her thigh and nodded at the shot of the frigate she was still holding.

'Why don' you keep that one there as a souvenir.'

He licked his lips, just as he'd done the night before. Jayne drank a large gulp of whisky and reached for another cigarette. Tommy took the opportunity to lean over and kiss her lightly on the mouth. His lips felt like velvet pillows. Jayne returned the kiss, drawing it out while she felt for Tommy's money belt. He tasted of scotch and Coke. Warm, sweet and bad for you. The money belt was zipped shut.

Tommy's lips moved from her mouth to her ear. 'Let's get outta here,' he whispered.

'W-what about the bill?'

Things were moving too fast. She'd planned to pick up where the bar girl left off, get Tommy and Mitch so drunk they got careless with their belongings, steal the photos, make her getaway. Tommy had other plans.

'This one's on Mitch,' he said, nodding to his companion who high-fived him with the hand that wasn't up his consort's grass skirt.

'Your place or mine?' Tommy said, putting his arm around Jayne's waist.

'Yours.'

Her stomach fluttered with whisky, nerves, lust. Tommy's

arm felt like steel as he led her off the beach road and down a *soi* to the sort of guesthouse that rented more rooms by the hour than by the night.

He steered them into an elevator. As the doors closed, he took both Jayne's breasts in his hands, squeezed and kissed her. She broke into a renewed sweat and tried to plot an escape route. When the elevator doors opened on to the first floor, they spilled into the corridor. Tommy clamped Jayne to him with one arm, his free hand unzipping his money belt and fishing for his room key. He opened the door and carried Jayne inside.

She felt him unclip his money belt, heard it drop to the floor. Next he slithered out of his T-shirt and started unbuttoning her blouse. She could see his cock straining at the crotch of his jeans. He saw her notice and ground his pelvis against hers, while kissing the side of her neck. When his hands slid under her bra and pinched her nipples, she gasped and pulled away.

'What's up, honey? Tommy jus' a little too fast for you'all. I'm sorry.'

He took her hand and pulled her back close to him, planting kisses in a line from her exposed shoulder to her ear.

Jayne failed to suppress a moan.

'No i-i-t's not that,' she stammered. 'It's j-just that I really need a shower. I'm all hot and sweaty and—'

'Don' you be worryin' yourself about that.' Tommy inhaled deeply against her neck to prove his point.

She pulled away again. 'Tommy, sweetie.' She took his face in her hands. 'I know it's a hang-up, but it would make me feel so much more *relaxed* if I could have a shower. Please?'

Tommy shrugged. 'Okay, okay, honey, whatever. Why don' we take a shower together?'

'Great.'

Jayne wracked her brain for a way to stall him. Tommy took off his jeans and started on her belt.

'Ah, Tommy, I—I need to do something *private* first.'

'What's that?'

He undid her belt buckle.

'It's to do with...um...contraception.'

'Don't you worry none about that. I got rubbers.' He reached into his jeans back pocket. 'US Army issue.'

'That's great,' she said, kissing the closely cropped hair on the crown of his head as he fumbled with the button on her jeans. 'But I use a diaphragm as an added precaution.'

Tommy looked up from his work with raised eyebrows. 'Why don' you'all just go on the pill?'

Because then guys think they don't have to bother with condoms.

'Makes me sick,' she said.

He squatted back on his haunches and shook his head. Nothing like talk of contraception to dampen a man's ardour.

'Why don't you get started,' Jayne said, 'run the shower for us and get in. I'll only be a couple of minutes.'

To her relief, Tommy nodded and headed for the bathroom.

'Don' be long now, honey,' he called over his shoulder.

Jayne snatched the money belt from the floor, whisked out the photos and stuffed them into the waistband of her jeans. She didn't stop to do up her belt or blouse, but clutched her handbag to her chest for cover. As soon as she heard Tommy step under the running water, she headed for the door.

'Just a minute,' she called.

She took the stairs, pausing when she got outside to fasten her buttons. A mistake.

'Hey!'

She raised her head to see Mitch with his Thai companion from Blue Lagoon coming down the *soi* towards her.

Jayne ran around the first corner she came to. A blind alley. Not a wise move. She ducked into the portico of what looked like a warehouse and pressed her back against the door. It gave way against her weight, sending her tumbling inside arse first. She sprung to her feet and spun around to face a stage lined with thirty-odd Thai beauties, resplendent in gowns, big hair, tiaras and high-gloss lipstick. Apart from two portable bench seats, the space in front of them was empty. The whole room was flooded with harsh fluorescent light, leaving nowhere to hide.

Smiles thawed in the wake of Jayne's incursion. Hands were raised to open mouths. One woman sneered as if Jayne was something distasteful she'd found on the sole of her jewel-encrusted stiletto heel. Another swooned with the theatricality of a soap opera actress.

The exaggerated femininity gave them away. This was a pageant for *kratoey*, Thailand's infamous 'ladyboys'. *Kratoey* could be scathing misogynists, especially en masse like this. Jayne had to think fast.

'Younger sisters,' she said with a *wai*, 'my name is Jayne. There's a tall, dark, handsome Marine chasing me and I don't want anything to do with him. I need to hide fast. Can you help me?'

There was a moment's stunned silence as they took in Jayne's ability to speak Thai, her flattering form of address and the implications of her predicament. Then the room burst into a flurry of activity.

Under the direction of their leader—she was the tallest and the only one in red—the beauty queens rearranged themselves in a group formation. Those with the highest splits up the sides of their dresses sat up front in mermaid pose. Others shuffled as fast as their straight skirts would allow and stood behind them. A bench was spirited up from the floor to form a middle row.

'Girls with broadest shoulders,' the leader barked, 'get into the second row. That means you, Jojo. Quickly.'

'But *Ajarn* Thanya—'

'Don't argue,' the one addressed as Teacher Thanya snapped. 'Move closer together. Now you, farang—'

'It's Jayne,' she piped up.

'Get behind the middle row.'

Jayne did as she was told, plunging into a fug of perfume and hairspray.

'Girls at the back on each end, step back a little. That's it. Khun Jayne, crouch down.'

The directive put Jayne's eyes at arse-level. She wondered how many of those sculpted curves were 'surgically enhanced', as the magazine ads put it.

'Duck as low as you can,' Thanya said.

At that moment the door burst open and Jayne heard Tommy's voice. Mitch must have set him on her tail.

'Where are you, you little—?' he began. 'What the—?'

'*Sawadee ka*,' Thanya said, the bark in her voice giving way to a purr.

Jayne felt a rustle of skirts around her as the group bowed in unison. She squatted down on her heels.

'Can we help you?' Thanya said in English.

'I don't know, m'am,' Tommy said, still angry. 'Any of you seen a white girl, about five-eight, dark curly hair, Australian?'

'*Australian?*' Thanya said. 'I've never heard of an Australian girl trying to compete in a Thai beauty contest, have you?'

'No, m'am,' Tommy said. 'But—'

'Thai girls are so much more beautiful than Australian girls that it wouldn't be fair,' she added. 'Don't you agree?'

Yeah, yeah, rub it in, Jayne thought, brushing a stray feather from her face.

'Yes, m'am,' Tommy said. 'But—'

'So maybe you see a Thai girl you like better than the farang you came in looking for.'

'Well, sure but—'

Jayne heard him hesitate, imagined him weighing up his options. Should he pursue Jayne as a matter of pride? Or was he better off cutting his losses and forgetting about her in the arms of one of these beauties? She supposed she should feel flattered that he even gave it a second thought.

'Or maybe you'd rather keep looking for your Australian friend.' Thanya tapped her toe on the concrete floor.

'No, m'am,' Tommy said. 'It's just that you ladies look so lovely an' all. I can't possibly choose...'

What a charmer, Jayne thought, her legs starting to cramp.

'Count me out,' murmured one in Thai. 'Chocolate is bad for my figure.'

A whoop of laughter was silenced when Thanya cleared her throat.

'Perhaps you like me to choose for you?'

'M'am, that sure would help me out.'

Jayne smiled. Thanya had played Tommy perfectly.

'Rasmi?' she called.

Jayne craned her head to see which set of stockinged legs stepped forward. They were long and slender, the muscular side of shapely, tottering on gold stilettos and encased in a figure-hugging skirt of purple and gold silk, split to mid-thigh at the back.

Tommy let out his breath with a whistle.

'*Sawadee ka*,' Jayne heard Rasmi say, imagined her bowing low.

'*Sawadee ka* to you, too, m'am,' Tommy said, using a form of address in Thai reserved for women and *kratoey*, sending another titter through the group.

'Hush,' Thanya said. 'I'm sure Rasmi will take your mind off the loss of your Australian friend,' she said to Tommy.

'Yes m'am.'

He sounded so eager, Jayne almost felt embarrassed for him.

Rasmi might have been going away for months, the way she took leave, hugging each person in the group and wishing them all *chowk dee*. Just when Jayne thought her legs would give out, Rasmi finally escorted Tommy from the building.

There was a collective pause while everyone waited to be sure they'd gone, followed by a burst of shrieks, gasps and chatter.

'Oh my god, did you see his ass,' one started.

'Ooh, and those broad shoulders—so manly,' said another.

'Thick neck,' said a third, 'not so good.'

Jayne stood and stretched her legs.

'I bet he's got a huge cock,' the first one added.

'Is that why you were running away, girlfriend—too hot for you to handle?'

This from a *kratoey* with hands on her hips and a nasty smile.

Jayne felt the gaze of the group. The easy way out was to say yes, the Marine was too hot for her, let the *kratoey* have another laugh at her expense, and get the hell out of there. But she felt an irrational urge to impress them.

'Actually, I'm a private detective,' she said. 'I stole something from that Marine—evidence for a case I'm working on.'

To her satisfaction, this sent a new buzz through the group.

'Ooh, how exciting!' said one, clapping her hands.

'Are you a good enough detective to find me a husband?' said Jojo, clasping her hands to her bosom, which seemed to deflate a little under the pressure.

'Are you kidding, no detective's *that* good,' another weighed in.

'That Marine's in for quite a night,' Thanya said, fiddling with the tiny crystal chandelier that hung from her earlobe.

'What do you mean?' Jayne asked.

'Well, he's already had his pocket picked once. And now he's gone home with Rasmi who has a special talent for separating her admirers from their hard-earned cash using only her natural charms and a little sleeping medicine applied to a part of the body any red-blooded man would find hard not to lick.'

Jayne raised her eyebrows. Stories about sex workers in Pattaya who drugged and robbed their clients were weekly fodder for the Thai tabloids. Most infamous was a *kratoey* alleged to administer sedatives by rubbing them on her breasts, dubbed by the press as the 'thief with tainted nipples'. Up to now Jayne thought it was just another urban myth.

'She never gets reported,' Thanya said. 'She leaves a note saying she has their contact details and some compromising photos that her sister will send by post addressed to the lady of the house if anything ever happens to her. No one's ever dared call her bluff.'

Jayne smiled and shook her head. 'If only I'd known. Next time I need something pilfered, I'm calling Rasmi.'

A couple of the *kratoey* giggled but Jayne could see that her interest value was wearing off.

'Sisters, I'm very grateful for your help. I won't keep you any longer from your rehearsal.'

'A good thing, too,' Thanya clapped her hands again and gestured for the girls to get back in line. 'We have too much to do. Finalise the music. Fix the lighting. Choreograph the parades.'

'What's the occasion?' Jayne said.

'You know the Tiffany Cabaret?'

Jayne recalled the billboard on the outskirts of town.

'Well, we're rehearsing for the inaugural Miss Tiffany Universe contest,' Thanya said. 'It will be spectacular, breathtaking. Not just the greatest show in Pattaya—it's going to be bigger than Miss Thailand.'

Jayne expected this to be met with more howls of laughter but the *kratoey* were straight-faced. Thanya tilted her chin high enough to make her earrings tinkle.

'The winner of Miss Tiffany Universe will qualify to compete in the Miss Queen of the Universe pageant in America,' she said. 'You should come, Khun Jayne.'

'When is it?'

'End of May.'

Jayne counted on being back in Bangkok long before then, but nodded politely.

'I'll certainly try.'

She gave Thanya a *wai* and bowed to the rest of her unlikely bodyguards as they resumed their line across the stage. The strains of Whitney Houston singing 'I'm every woman' could be heard from a hidden sound system and several of the beauty queens lip-synched along. As she let herself out the back door, Jayne remembered another term for Thailand's third sex: *nang faa chamlaeng*, 'angels in disguise'.

She hailed a *songthaew*, took a seat at the end of the bench, and pulled Tommy's photos from the waistband of her jeans. They were a little crumpled from the ordeal, but otherwise undamaged. She examined them by the passing light of neon signs and street lamps. Mitch and Tommy on surf-skis; having massages on the beach; drinking cocktails in coconut shells; posing thumbs-up, with go-go dancers behind them, beside them, on top of them. The women wore nothing but strained smiles.

Jayne's face burned to think she not only kissed Tommy, she almost enjoyed it. She spat out the back of the car and willed Rasmi to fleece him for all he was worth.

The photos of an African-American couple—presumably Leroy and his wife—with an infant stood in stark contrast. The woman held the child with palpable tenderness, her head bowed low like a Byzantine Madonna. Jayne couldn't see the baby's face. On the wall in the background were framed certificates, degrees and qualifications with official seals.

There were several more family shots—the man looking up, grinning nervously, the woman transfixed by the baby— one of Tommy and Mitch with the new family, and one with Frank and Doctor Somsri standing either side of Leroy and Alicia. Then finally a close-up of the child.

The *songthaew* turned and headed up the hill towards Jayne's hotel. There were few streetlights on this stretch and Jayne strained to get a good look at the picture. It wasn't until the car pulled over to let her off that she had enough light to see. His eyes were closed and his chin partly obscured by a blanket, but Jayne was sure of it.

The little boy Tommy's cousin had adopted was Mayuree's son Kob.

25

Wen had already moved out. Mayuree cleaned the apartment in her wake and packed the little that remained in a red, white and blue striped plastic bag. A few clothes, her old college textbooks, a bunch of letters. She found a photo of Sumet and Kob taken on a visit to the Elephant Village and slipped it into her handbag together with Kob's stuffed frog and the small wooden box wrapped in white cloth, which contained his ashes. She took out her phone and contemplated calling her brother. She couldn't do it. Not yet.

She gave Wen all Kob's clothes, knowing she'd sell them to a second-hand dealer rather than risk having his bad luck rub off on Moo. Mayuree gave her all her own work clothes, shoes, cosmetics and perfume, too. Wen promised to keep these things for her but Mayuree insisted she get rid of them. While she might not know what was in store for her, she had no intention of ever returning to Pattaya.

Mayuree's hair hung limp in an unkempt ponytail. Not a trace of makeup remained on her face and her skin was dry. The sleeping tablets Doctor Somsri had given her made her feel groggy and parched but she kept taking them to dull the pain. What little joy there was in Mayuree's life had died with Kob. Not even her boss's decision to cancel her debt in light of her misfortune could raise Mayuree's spirits. She'd welcome such debt ten times over if it would bring back her son.

Mayuree closed the door to her flat and slipped the key under it. She made her way downstairs to the street and hailed a motorcycle taxi to take her to the bus depot. As the driver revved the engine, she eased herself on to the pillion seat and balanced the bag on her lap.

Doctor Somsri's drugs didn't stop her head from aching with the pressure of unshed tears. She wished she could cry. Crying might allow her to cleanse her son's spirit since she had been denied the chance to wash his dead body.

Mayuree didn't understand why her son had been cremated with such haste. The doctor had said something about a risk of infection. Surely they could have allowed her to see his body in the hospital. Even from a distance. Even from behind plate-glass. She'd asked them about this, too.

'Too distressing,' the doctor had said.

Too distressing? What could be more distressing than losing her son, other than losing him and not being able to say goodbye?

She had let Kob down in life. There was no denying it. She should never have brought him with her to Pattaya. It was crazy to think she and Sumet could have sustained the arrangement they had. She should have left Kob with her parents in Kanchanaburi. They might have disapproved of him, but they would have kept him alive.

She'd let him down in death, too. Unable to arrange the rites to ensure a peaceful transition to the next life, his soul would be left wandering, a *phi lok* in an endless search for the comfort and care she'd failed to give him.

Mayuree gathered up the bag in her lap and threw it to the side of the road. The bag split as it hit the ground, scattering her things in the dust.

The motorcycle driver swerved and slowed. 'Woah, sister, you need me to stop?' he called over his shoulder.

'No, keep going.'

Who was she kidding? She might leave all her possessions behind, take a bus to the other end of the country, go back to college, change her name, and make a new life for herself. But she would never leave Pattaya behind. There would always be something holding her here.

She wanted to kill herself, but that was selfish, and selfishness had killed her son. To go on living without him— that was how she would atone for the mess she'd made of her life and for the life denied her son. Only this was punishment enough.

She would return to her parents' place in Kanchanaburi and offer herself to them as a servant. She would serve them diligently and without complaint, welcoming any opportunity to humble herself. No task would be too menial, no abuse too degrading. She would work until her hands were red raw and her hair matted with sweat and dust. Until her knees were calloused, her shoulders stooped, and no movement was without pain. Until her skin was as black as her son's had been.

Mayuree would offer up every sacrifice for the sake of her son and take every opportunity to make merit for him. On holy days she would crawl up the pilgrim's path to the top of the Tiger Cave Temple and pray alongside her brother for the spirits to show mercy. Not for herself, but for Kob, so his ghost might find a place to rest.

26

Rajiv was sitting in an armchair in the hotel lobby reading a newspaper when Jayne walked in. Her pounding heart skipped a beat at the sight of him and she ducked behind a pillar to catch her breath and collect her thoughts.

She wasn't expecting him. As far as she knew, they hadn't set a date for when he might join her. Now that he was here, Jayne wanted nothing more than to take Rajiv by the hand, lead him up to her room and screw him senseless. She ached for it, primed by Tommy's kisses and the whole sleazy fuck-fest that was Pattaya.

But how could she even be thinking about sex when she had proof Kob was alive? Jayne needed to find Mayuree above all else. She also needed time to think about the implications of her discovery. She was sure some sort of baby laundering racket was going on. Frank Harding and Doctor Somsri were involved, but who else at the New Life Children's Centre was in on it? What about the stern Connie, or perky Dianne? The other staff and volunteers? Was adoption fraud behind Maryanne Delbeck's death?

Jayne glanced at Rajiv. He stared at the same page, not reading at all.

She pressed her back against the pillar. There was no choice: she had to find Mayuree. She checked her watch—it was already after ten—and there was no telling how long Rajiv had been waiting for her. She'd been gone nearly three hours.

She massaged her forehead, feeling the grime of dust, sweat and makeup beneath her touch. Perhaps there was a third option—the proverbial 'middle path' aspired to by all good Thai Buddhists—that might enable her to do the right thing by Mayuree without losing Rajiv.

She caught sight of her reflection in a nearby mirror, mercifully angled where Rajiv could not see her. With hair coiled into snakes and eyes rimmed with smudged mascara she looked like a Gorgon. All traces of her so-called kiss-proof lipstick were gone, and there was dirt under her fingernails. Her clothes were a crumpled mess. Her asymmetrically buttoned blouse was a dead giveaway that she'd dressed in a rush.

Using her pack as a shield, Jayne straightened her buttons. She cleaned her face as best she could with a tissue and spit and restored her lipstick. The serpentine hair was still a problem, but that could be accounted for by the combined effects of sea air and *songthaew* rides. She took a deep breath, willed herself not to blush and stepped out from behind the pillar.

'Sorry I'm late.'

Rajiv leapt to his feet, *Bangkok Post* falling to the floor. 'Hello, Jayne, I wasn't sure...that is, I didn't know...' He ran his fingers through his hair and looked from her to the newspaper and back again.

'I can't tell you how happy I am to see you,' she said.

He relaxed visibly.

'Well, I *can*,' she corrected herself. 'But do you mind if I do it on the road?'

Rajiv wasn't sure what sort of reception to expect, but it didn't involve being dragged out in the middle of the night, clambering into the back of a *songthaew*, and going off in search of a Thai woman. He couldn't believe his luck: he was out with Jayne on a case.

First stop was a bar on the seafront, one in a row of similar shacks where foreign men drank beer until they went red in the face, then put their arms around each other and sang songs. Rajiv saw it all the time on Khao San Road. It was commonplace for Indian men to walk down the street holding hands but Western men seemed to need to drink a lot of alcohol before they would touch each other and then they couldn't stop. Rajiv viewed them from the doorway while Jayne went inside. She wasn't gone long.

'She's not there,' Jayne said. 'Her colleague said she resigned to return home to the countryside. We need to move fast.'

'Do you know where she lives?'

'No, but I know someone who does.'

'This is what you call following a lead, yes?'

She smiled, her face lit by the neon signs of the beer bars and hotels that lined the beach road. 'It's about a ten minute walk.'

They headed south, the beach on their right. Streetlights illuminated the coconut palms, thatched umbrellas and sunlounges, deserted apart from a few Thai tourists making the most of the dark to take in the sea air.

'So who are we looking for?' he asked.

'I'm looking for the mother of the baby who died, the

one they said had sickle cell anaemia.'

'The one you told me about over the phone.'

'Yes, only…Look Rajiv, I'm going to have to swear you to secrecy on something, okay?'

He wiggled his head.

'I mean it,' Jayne said. 'Not a word to anyone.'

'On my honour.'

She stopped walking and placed a hand on his arm. Although unlikely anyone would overhear given the blaring pop music coming from the bars, she leaned over and whispered in his ear.

'The baby isn't dead. He was stolen from his mother and adopted out to an American couple. His death was faked.'

Rajiv let out his breath with a whistle. 'How did you find out about this?'

'The usual combination of good detective work and blind luck. Mayuree needs to know her baby is still alive.'

'Of course,' Rajiv said. 'Where is the baby now?'

'I'm not sure, but I'll be making a few calls to Bangkok first thing tomorrow morning to find out.'

An early start wasn't exactly what Rajiv was hoping for, but he told himself to go with the flow. 'So how are you going to find the mother?'

'Her flatmate works at a club on The Strip.'

'The Strip?'

'Pattaya's wild side,' Jayne said. 'We're coming up to it now.'

They'd reached a busy crossroads. The sea view was engulfed by a row of tightly packed buildings, go-go bars, clubs and karaoke as far as the eye could see. The air smelled of stale beer, rotten fruit and room deodoriser. The Strip must have been what cousin Rohit had in mind when he referred to Pattaya as 'Patpong by the sea'.

It was less risqué than Rajiv had imagined. In a boxing-ring-cum-bar, two men wearing billowing satin shorts, boxing gloves and white ropes around their biceps kicked and punched to jingling music and loud cheers from spectators. There was a row of seafood restaurants with their edible aquariums of fish, lobsters, crabs and abalone. A pub. Lots of bars.

They passed a placed called Magic A Go-Go with a sign boasting 'Only European Women on the First Floor'. Rajiv looked up to see a blonde in a coffee-coloured negligee gyrating inside a glassed-in corner of the building. He almost tripped over a Thai woman in a bikini top and miniskirt standing on the path holding a sign 'Henhouse A Go-Go: Many New Chicks To Choose This Week'. Jostling for attention next to her was a man in a three-piece suit and tie; his sign read 'Live Sex Show Upstairs – Lady and Man – Lady and Lady – Lady and Snake'.

He grabbed Jayne's arm. 'Did you see that?' He tilted his head at the tout.

She paused to look over her shoulder. 'Yeah, bizarre,' she said. 'That suit must be really hot.'

They passed more venues with names like Winner Bar, Lucky Score, Fortunate Son. Looking at the people around him, Rajiv figured a few of them could do with some luck. Many were older Western men with leathery skin whose unbuttoned shirts exposed grey chest hairs. There were younger men, too, wearing buzz cuts and singlets to show off newly inked tattoos of tigers and dragons. A man with a red beard and a big belly walked by wearing a T-shirt that said 'No money, no honey'; as he had a 'honey' on his arm, Rajiv guessed he must have money. An elderly farang brushed past him, talking and gesticulating at two tourist police in black uniforms and matching berets.

To Rajiv's surprise, there were couples and even families promenading, too: an Indian couple with a crying baby, an aging Thai transsexual carrying a sleeping boy. A pale man whose facial features looked ironed flat bought a yellow rose, kissed it, and handed it to his consort, a burly blonde whose pantsuit matched the colour of the flower. She flushed with pleasure and kissed her paramour once on each cheek.

It all seemed so good natured—nothing like the brothel districts of New Dehli—though it was noisy as a camel fair. Every venue played a different song. Rajiv heard snatches of The Eagles, Bob Marley, Bon Jovi, Bryan Adams, 'The Macarena'. A live rock band competed with an Elvis impersonator and people singing karaoke in what sounded like Russian.

His nostrils caught a waft of aromatic smoke. It came from a large concrete spirit house surrounded by tubs of smouldering incense, ropes of jasmine and some three-dozen opened bottles of red Mirinda, a white straw poking out of each. The thought that South Pattaya's resident land spirit was a hyperactive child high on sugary soft drink seemed apt to Rajiv. He marvelled that even in a place this profane, the residents found sacred space. This much they had in common with their counterparts in India.

A firm hand to his solar plexus stopped him in his tracks. He looked down at long fingers tapering to glittery gold nails. The nails were adhered to the hands of a heavily made-up ladyboy, with beaded earrings dripping to shoulder-level and a top so low-cut her nipples were showing. Rajiv had a healthy fear of *hijras*—in India, the cross-dressing eunuchs could curse you if you angered them—and accepted the brochure she thrust at him. The ladyboy released him. Rajiv glanced at the cover—something about a cabaret show—and disposed of it as soon as he could.

Just as he wondered when it would end, Jayne stopped and gestured towards a bar across the road, an empty stage at its centre surrounded by tables and chairs. Out front a woman in cut-off jeans and a T-shirt way too small for her wore a sandwich board that said 'Monkey Business – Draft Beer 55 B – Lady Drink 99 B – No Cover Charge'.

Jayne turned to face him.

'So Rajiv, how do you feel about buying a lady a drink?'

If he were honest, the thought of it made him sick. 'Are you asking me to do this to assist you with the case?' he asked.

'Sure, you can be my own personal Doctor Watson.'

'I don't recall this being the kind of duty Sherlock Holmes ever required of his Doctor Watson.'

'True,' Jayne said. 'But *my* Doctor Watson gets to have much more fun than Holmes's ever did.'

She was treating it like a game. She wasn't to know she'd touched a raw nerve.

'What exactly are you wanting me to do?' Rajiv said.

'Take a table close to the street and when a waitress comes over order a drink and ask for Miss Wen. When she joins you, order a drink for her, too, and start a conversation. I'll pretend to catch sight of you through the crowd and will come over.'

'Why don't you just talk to Wen directly?'

'Trust me,' Jayne said, 'it's easier this way. Wen gets paid for her time and we avoid creating suspicion.'

'Very well,' he said. 'But what do I talk to her about?'

'Don't worry about it. She's a professional. She'll take care of the conversation.'

He shifted his weight from one foot to the other.

'Are you sure you're up for this?' Jayne said.

Rajiv shrugged. 'I just need a cigarette before I get started.'

She handed him the packet. 'I'll be with you in twenty minutes.'

She disappeared into the crowd.

Rajiv lit a smoke and took a deep drag, fortifying himself with the thought that Pattaya's Strip was nothing like New Delhi's GB Road with its hardware stores at street level and its squalid *kothas* upstairs. Besides, he wasn't a paying customer looking to satisfy his curiosity or urges; he was just masquerading as one. But it was all too much for his poor conscience. The memory he'd tried to suppress came rushing back.

The steep stone staircase smelled of garbage. Rajiv followed the woman, whose deep pink lipstick matched the colour of her *salwar kameez*, to the brothel on the second floor. He had chosen her for her voluptuous breasts and because she looked like a woman who could teach him something.

She opened the door on a dimly lit room with few furnishings apart from a bed and a couple of low tables. She gestured towards a washroom off to one side that smelled of camphor, walls stained black with mould. There was a worn cake of soap and a small towel on the edge of a chipped basin and Rajiv guessed he should undress and wash himself. He put his underwear back on and carried his clothes out in a pile.

The woman lay on the bed, naked from the waist down, her *kameez* straining to cover her breasts. The prospect of fondling those breasts was enough to make him hard, but he was too embarrassed to ask the woman to remove her shirt. She tried to engage him in conversation, but Rajiv was too nervous for small talk. He placed his clothes on the floor, slipped out of his underpants and rolled a rubber condom down the length of his eager penis. He gestured for the woman to turn over so her back was to him. She waited for him on her hands and knees, arching her back to tilt her arse towards him.

He knelt behind her on the bed and pushed himself inside her. He didn't even have time to grope for her breasts. With a few short thrusts, he felt his body quiver and explode.

He slumped forward over the woman, still propped on her hands and knees, panting more from surprise than exertion. He reached for her breasts, but the woman did not linger. She squirmed out from under him, pointed to a brass pot by the bedside table and disappeared into the washroom. Rajiv understood he was to put money in the pot, get dressed and get out.

He was fastening his belt buckle when the woman reappeared, frowning to indicate he should move faster.

He headed for the door when he thought he heard the woman crying. When he turned back, he saw her lift something from the darkest corner of the room and cradle it in her arms. It wailed like a kitten—Rajiv wanted to believe that's what it was—but he couldn't deny what he saw. He got his wish and saw the prostitute's naked breast—as she offered it to her crying baby.

To his shame this remained Rajiv's one, inglorious experience of sexual intercourse in twenty-eight years.

Jayne watched Rajiv linger over his cigarette, worried she was pushing him too far. He seemed nervous, though that was to his credit: clearly he didn't make a habit of chatting up sex workers.

She was relieved when he finally stubbed out his smoke and sauntered over to the bar where Wen worked. Jayne chose a table where she could keep an eye on him, putting her alongside a Thai boxing ring. She checked her watch and, much as she would've liked a beer, ordered lemonade.

The in-house sound system was playing Madonna, though not loudly enough to drown out the strains of 'Can't live if livin' is without you' coming from the karaoke bar next door. It was a dreadful rendition but the singer was politely applauded all the same. In the *muay thai* ring, a sweaty Thai boxer posed with a podgy shirtless tourist, pretending for the photographs that the farang had beaten him up. Not for the first time Jayne was struck by how accommodating Thai people were. The crowd that paraded along The Strip was a far cry from humanity at its finest, yet everyone was made to feel welcome. Pattaya might not be Jayne's style but she understood its appeal.

Rajiv had followed her instructions to the letter and sat at the front of the bar, Wen by his side with her hand on his knee.

'Rajiv!' Jayne called out as she walked towards him.

'Ramesh,' he corrected her.

'Ramesh?' She stifled a grin. 'Of course, my mistake. How *are* you?'

'I'm fine. Won't you join us?'

'Thank you.'

'This is Wen—' Rajiv began.

'*Roo jak kan laew,*' Jayne greeted Wen with a wai as she took a seat. 'It's okay Raj—Ramesh, Wen and I know each other,' she added in English before returning to Thai. 'How are you, sister?'

'I'm fine, Khun Jayne.'

She didn't look it.

'And your little boy?'

'He's fine, too.' She lowered her voice. 'I'm sending him away from here. He's going to stay with my relatives in Si Saket.'

'You're worried after what happened to Mayuree's baby.'

Wen looked around as if someone might be listening.

'It's okay,' Jayne said. 'I understand. Wen, I need to find Mayuree urgently. Can you help me, give me your address in Pattaya?'

'I will write down the address where we lived,' Wen said, 'but I don't think Mayuree will be there. She should be on her way home to Kanchanaburi by now.'

Jayne handed her a pen and paper. 'Kanchanaburi— that's where she's from?'

Wen nodded as she wrote.

'Do you have an address for her there, too?'

Wen shook her head and handed back the paper and pen. 'I'm sorry. You could ask Mister Frank. He has the addresses of all our families.'

'Thanks,' Jayne said. 'I have one other question. Was Mayuree close to Maryanne, the volunteer who worked at the orphanage last year, the one who passed away?'

Wen frowned. 'Why do you keep asking about Maryanne?'

It had been an innocent question, but she'd hit a raw nerve. Jayne improvised.

'We were friends in Australia,' she said.

Wen raised her eyebrows. 'So you know about Sumet.'

Jayne had heard that name before. 'Her Thai teacher?'

Wen nodded, eyebrows raised, waiting for more.

Jayne wracked her brain. What was it Dianne had said about Sumet? He'd come to Pattaya because his sister had a baby. And before that he'd been a high school teacher... Where was it...?

Kanchanaburi.

'And Mayuree's brother, right?'

Wen exhaled as though she'd been holding her breath.

'How could I have forgotten,' Jayne said, waving her hand as though Wen had told her nothing she didn't already know.

When Jayne asked Mayuree if she knew Maryanne, she hadn't mentioned the link with her brother. What was it about Sumet that made the women around him—first Dianne, now Mayuree—so protective?

There was more Jayne wanted to ask, but she didn't know where to start, and Wen was getting edgy, alternately biting her fingernail and looking over her shoulder.

'Sister, here's my number in case you need it.' She handed Wen a card and rose to her feet. Rajiv leapt up beside her. 'Thanks for your time. Now, do you mind if I take your friend here away with me?'

Wen shrugged, gave them a half-hearted *wai* and scuttled off to join the throng around the stage where the pole dancing had started to the tune of 'I want to break free' by Queen.

'*Ramesh?*' Jayne poked Rajiv in the ribs as they made their way back along The Strip. 'What was all that about?'

He squirmed out of her reach and flashed his dimples. 'I thought I should be having an alias, you know, while I am on the case.'

'Couldn't you have picked something a little more exotic?'

'Like what?'

'I don't know, like Bruce.'

Rajiv grinned.

'Speaking of the case, I'm going to try this address for Mayuree. Are you up for it because if not, you can go back to the hotel and I can meet you—'

Rajiv raised his hand. 'I'm your Doctor Watson, remember? I go where you go.'

He thought for a moment. 'Actually it might be more accurate to say I am the Charles Butler to your Kathy Mallory.'

The reference was to characters in the novels of Carol O'Connell, whose book Jayne was looking for the first time she met Rajiv. It was flattering enough to think he'd read it. Better still, Charles Butler was besotted by Mallory.

'I'm not sure that's an appropriate analogy,' she countered, 'given Charles's love for Mallory was unrequited.'

They met each other's gaze and again Jayne fought the desire to drop everything and hotfoot it back to her hotel. Instead—she re-checked Wen's note—they were headed in the opposite direction, north to Naklua.

27

The neon sign on top of the building said 'RUGSTORE', the letter D broken long ago, but the glowing green cross identified it as a pharmacy. The shop was closed for the night. Mayuree's flat was up a narrow flight of stairs at the back. No light showed in the gap under the door and Jayne's knock went unanswered. She took a penlight from her bag and got down on her hands and knees.

'What are you doing?' Rajiv whispered.

'Routine check.' She shone the torch under the door. 'That looks promising.'

'What is it?'

'Not sure. Pass me a stick or something.'

He found a bent fork. 'Will this do?'

'Perfect.'

Jayne slid the handle of the fork under the door. There was a soft clink of metal on metal. She pulled out the fork with a key dangling from its tines. She rose to her feet, unlocked the door and felt inside for the light-switch.

Rajiv raised his eyebrows. 'Impressive.'

'Not really,' she replied as a fluorescent tube sputtered on. 'Mayuree had to leave the key somewhere, and this—'

she nodded at the door '—you need the key to lock. So it had to be nearby.'

'There's a real art to this detective work, isn't it?'

'And luck, don't forget. Mayuree might have left the key with the shop-owners downstairs. You coming in?'

He looked over his shoulder. 'No, I will be keeping watch out here.'

Jayne shrugged, slipped off her shoes and entered a small, harsh-lit room with a tiny bathroom off to one side. A single window overlooked a nest of electrical cables tinged green by the light of the drugstore sign. At first glance, the place looked rundown and neglected. A mouldy bulge near the ceiling hinted at a leak in the roof and floor tiles rattled beneath Jayne's feet. But someone had worked hard to make the best of it. The view might be dull but the window was spotless, the walls bore no sign of the scum you'd expect with a leaking roof, and the floor tiles though loose were clean and smooth. On the cupboards that ran the length of one wall she could make out the silhouettes of ducks and rabbits where stickers had been removed.

She searched the cupboards in the main room and the bathroom cabinet, opening and closing all doors and drawers, checking for loose panels.

'What are you looking for?' Rajiv called.

'Something with Mayuree's Kanchanaburi address on it. I think we're out of luck. If this was a crime scene, forensics would struggle.'

'So what now?' he said as she joined him.

'I'm not sure. Wen said everyone's details were kept on file at the centre. I don't know who I can trust to ask and I don't want to raise suspicions by asking the wrong person.'

'Does this mean we are coming to a dead end?'

'Not yet. There's always the option of breaking in—'

'You want to do *another* burglary tonight?'

'Technically, this wasn't a burglary. We didn't *take* anything. In fact, you'd be hard pressed to call it a break and enter—we used the key.'

'Jayne, it's nearly midnight!'

She checked her watch. No wonder Rajiv sounded impatient.

'I'm sorry about this, but I didn't know you were coming and I've got a job to do...' She tried again. 'Look, I understand if you want to go back ahead of me, but I have to see this through. I hope it won't take much longer but I can't promise anything.'

Rajiv wiggled his head. 'I'm staying with you.'

She leaned forward to kiss him but he backed away.

'We don't have time for that,' he said. 'We are having another break-in to organise, remember?'

She told herself he was right: she shouldn't let herself get distracted when there was still work to be done. But first Tommy had abandoned her for Rasmi and now Rajiv didn't want to kiss her. She was starting to take it personally.

Neither of them spoke during the journey. The excitement Rajiv felt was giving way to exhaustion and resentment. He couldn't go back to the hotel and wait for her even if he wanted to: without Jayne to vouch for him, he'd never be allowed into her room, and taking his own room would defeat the purpose.

He'd have brooded for longer but the walk along the dark laneway to the orphanage got his heart pumping, the same thrilling sensation that made him follow Jayne on this wild goose chase in the first place. Rajiv was hooked. He knew it. Perhaps Jayne knew it, too.

The blue metal gate was unlocked.

'Curious,' Jayne whispered.

She pushed it open, took Rajiv by the hand, and led him across the darkened compound to an office building. There were signs a guard was around—a bottle of Red Bull and a copy of a Thai newspaper on the plastic chair by the entrance—but no guard in sight. Jayne pulled at the front door. It was open. They slipped inside.

'Stay close,' Jayne whispered as she flashed her penlight around the foyer.

They stopped outside an office marked with a sign in Thai that Rajiv couldn't decipher. Jayne tried the handle.

'Is it locked?'

'Not for long.'

She took out a credit card and with one brisk swipe they were in. Rajiv was astonished.

'How did you do that?' he hissed as she closed the door behind them.

'Shoddy builders.'

He frowned.

'The doorframes are made of unbroken aluminium strips. You can think you've locked the door but you've only locked the handle. The door can't be locked unless there's a hole to slot the bolt into. Get it?'

'Is there anything you can't break into?'

'The filing cabinet's a problem. Frank wears the key around his neck and if I break in, he's going to know it.'

She rifled through the desk drawer and the penholder beside the computer. Nothing. She felt around the back of the filing cabinet. Still nothing.

'No spare in the usual places.'

She looked from the computer to Rajiv and back again. 'I'll have to force the lock—unless I can get what I need from the computer.'

Rajiv raised his eyebrows. 'I'll be your assistant, not your accomplice.'

He sounded more peeved than intended, but he was tired.

'Fair enough,' Jayne said. 'I'll do the actual work. You just talk me though it, okay?'

Rajiv wiggled his head.

'Keep your hands in your pockets so you don't leave any fingerprints, right?'

He didn't know if she was teasing him or not. He slung his thumbs through the belt loops on his jeans.

'First, turn it on,' he said.

Jayne gave him a sarcastic smile and switched on the computer, which rumbled into life like an old car engine protesting a gear change. After running through DOS, a prompt appeared requesting a password.

'Shit,' Jayne said.

Rajiv leaned over her shoulder to look at the screen. 'Most people are choosing familiar passwords, such as their name, date of birth, that kind of thing. They are usually quite easy to guess. Most people do not realise—'

While he was still speaking, Jayne typed F-R-A-N-K.

'No!' Rajiv hissed, but it was too late.

She'd hit the 'enter' key. The computer protested with a loud beep and 'Incorrect password' flashed up on the screen.

'Be careful. You will only be having three attempts. After that the computer guesses that someone is trying to break in and is shutting itself down for protection.'

'So what next?'

'The password is usually something easy to remember, perhaps something the person can see from where they are sitting.'

They looked at the wall above the desk: inane animal posters and a map of Thailand, Pattaya marked with a gold star.

'Try Pattaya,' Rajiv said.

Jayne typed it in. The error message reappeared on the screen. 'Shit.'

She leaned back in the chair, put her hands behind her head and stared at the ceiling. Rajiv glanced from his watch to the door and back again.

'I've got it! It's so obvious.'

Rajiv put a hand on her arm. 'I must be warning you, Jayne, if this doesn't work, not only will the computer be shutting itself down but the next time someone turns it on, they will know it has been tampered with.'

'In which case we bust the locks on the filing cabinet and make it look like there was a robbery,' she said. 'But that won't be necessary.'

'I certainly hope not.'

Rajiv watched over her shoulder as Jayne typed 'J-E-S-U-S'. They held their breath. The computer screen went black for a moment before flashing back to life and churning through the start-up functions. They sighed with relief.

'What's the quickest way to find a file?' she asked.

Resisting the urge to take over, Rajiv talked her through the search function. The computer was archaic, the hard drive whirring and clunking as it scanned the files. Finally, they had a hit on 'Mayuree', a document listing her places of work and the services she used at the centre, but no home address. They tried searching for Kamolsert, waiting another noisy minute before they hit paydirt.

'Sixteen stroke two Thanon Mae Nam Kwae,' Jayne read aloud. 'That's it.'

She scribbled it down on a scrap of paper, stuffed it in her pocket and was halfway to the door when Rajiv said, 'Don't forget to shut down the computer.'

'Do it for me?'

Rajiv hesitated. He hadn't touched a thing and turning off the computer meant leaving his fingerprints on the keyboard. Was it a test of his loyalty? Or was he being paranoid?

'No problem,' he said.

Blocking her view of the keyboard with his body, he pulled his sleeve down over his hand and shut it down. He was about to head for the door when Jayne grabbed him by the wrist and yanked him to the floor.

'Don't move,' she said. 'Someone's coming.'

28

Chaowalit lingered in the street, leering at the girl selling dried squid from a *rot khen* on the corner. He liked that she used matching pink pegs to hang the stiff squid from the lines on her push-cart. The elastic bands she used to fasten her take-away bags were pink, too. He liked to watch her tenderise the squid through the mangle: it showed the muscles in her forearms and made sweat bead above her upper lip. As he bit into his salty *pla meuk*, he imagined he could taste that sweat.

Of course, the girl barely noticed him.

To watch her work the mangle, Chaowalit ordered extra squid and sold the surplus at a marked-up rate to the nurses at the centre. He had more mobility than most of his colleagues on the late shift and used it to his advantage, handling orders for food and other goods, and occasionally, in collusion with the night-shift nurses, off-loading surplus medicines.

His role as guard was largely symbolic: his employers didn't hesitate to send him off-site for more than an hour at a time when there was a baby to be despatched. Once he summoned the nerve to question Mister Frank about this.

'I thank you for your concern, brother Chaowalit,'

Mister Frank said, 'but I trust in the Lord to watch over us.'

Chaowalit supposed the risk of theft or property damage was low, given their quiet location. Besides there wasn't much worth stealing; he'd looked into it. The good stuff was kept at the other compound where security was outsourced to a private company and the guards rotated on an eight-hourly basis.

Chaowalit wasn't complaining. The job was pretty easy and the sideline business gave him more power than any security company flunky.

He carried his bags of squid back to his post, locking the gate behind him. He took a fortifying mouthful of *Krating Deng* and resumed his post. The moon was on the wane, just as it was the night the farang girl died.

He still couldn't figure out exactly how it happened. He'd meant to set the girl straight, not send her over the edge.

He knew she liked him. She flirted with him, even when she was seeing Sumet. But Sumet couldn't protect her the way Chaowalit could. And he'd gone along with Sumet's ridiculous plan to show her that. Her response was not what they'd expected.

Chaowalit shook his head to dislodge the memory and reached beneath his chair for a second bottle also labelled Red Bull but filled with Mekong whisky. He took long gulps, feeling the fire in his belly. He bit his dried squid and this time imagined he could taste the push-cart vendor's tender cunt. The more he thought about it, the stiffer his cock grew until he couldn't sit still.

Putting aside the squid, holding on to the bottle, Chaowalit veered around to the back of the building and unzipped his pants.

*

'Someone's coming all right,' Jayne said, peering through a gap beneath the blind. 'It's the guard.'

'Get away from the window,' Rajiv whispered.

'I don't think his mind is on the job,' she chuckled. 'He's having a wank.'

'What?'

'You know, playing with himself, jerking off.'

'Oh dear.'

The masturbating guard didn't shock Rajiv so much as Jayne's nonchalance.

'We should get out of here while he's got his hands full, so to speak,' she said. 'Let's go.'

They heard the guard moan as they crawled out of the office and closed the door. Jayne paused briefly at the abandoned guard post then signalled for Rajiv to follow.

They sprinted across the open compound to the gate only to find it padlocked.

'Shit,' Jayne swore. 'We'll have to climb over.'

Rajiv's eyes widened but he nodded, scaled the gate, swung his lanky legs over the top and dropped to the ground on the other side like a cat.

'You've done this before,' Jayne whispered.

Rajiv nodded. It was true. The same could not be said for Jayne. Lacking his dexterity and height, it was an awkward climb for her. She managed to get to the top and had one leg over when there was a shout from the compound. They looked up to see a guard running in her direction. Rajiv's heart sank.

'Hide,' Jayne hissed, 'I'll handle this.'

As he slipped into the shadows, Rajiv heard her call out. He angled his watch to check the time and sighed.

*

Jayne was about to launch into an explanation when she remembered that as far as Chaowalit was concerned, she couldn't speak Thai. She adopted her best guesthouse English.

'Hello, where you go? I call you. I not ring bell because I not want to wake babies.'

Chaowalit had been running towards the gate, baton drawn, but slowed to a shuffle when he saw Jayne straddling the gate. She had one leg either side of a row of metal spikes, her weight resting on her hands. A slip-up would split her in two.

'You help me down?' she added.

Chaowalit took pleasure in her predicament. He stopped and, smirking, took much longer than was necessary to restore the baton to his belt. He muttered an expletive and shuffled closer.

'What you doing?' he growled.

Jayne bit back *none of your business*, and wracked her brain for a plausible excuse.

'I no have ATM card. Maybe I lose here when I meet Mister Frank.'

Chaowalit frowned.

'I lose ATM card,' she said in a louder voice. 'I think here.'

It would be easier if she could free her hands to make gestures, but she couldn't let go of the gate.

'No have money,' she pleaded. 'Need money...'

She finally hit on a word he recognised. Chaowalit reached and helped her down.

'Thank you,' she said through gritted teeth.

She drew a small rectangle in the air with her fingers. 'Need to find card for bank machine.' She pointed to the administration building.

Before he could respond, Jayne made a beeline for the entrance, eager to put some distance between them. She slipped back into the foyer and pretended to pick something up off the floor whilst fishing through her wallet for her card. She stood up and turned to leave, almost crashing into Chaowalit, hot on her heels.

'Found it—' she waved the card at him. 'Lucky me!'

'Lucky,' Chaowalit agreed with an unpleasant smile.

Jayne turned towards the gate but Chaowalit grabbed her by the wrist. She caught a whiff of alcohol on his breath.

'You want I tell Mister Frank you come here?'

'Take your hands off me,' Jayne said firmly.

'You want I tell Mister Frank you come here?' he repeated, tightening his grip.

She shook her head, more annoyed than frightened.

'Then what you give me?'

He had her in a bind. If she offered him money, he'd know she was lying about not having any. What else did she have? He was too strong for her to fight and, assuming she could rouse him, Rajiv would be no match for Chaowalit either.

'Open the gate,' she said, nodding towards the entrance.

'What you give me?' He tugged at her wrist, probably with the same hand he'd used to pull his cock.

'Listen pal,' she said in her best Thai slang. 'You let me go now and I won't report you to Mister Frank for jerking off behind the admin building and being drunk on the job, okay?'

Chaowalit released his grip. 'Older sister, you speak Thai,' he said, shocked enough to use the polite form.

'That's right, little brother. Let's make that our secret, okay? Now it's late. Please, open the gate.'

Chaowalit nodded and stepped forward to remove the padlock. He seemed dazed.

'Mister Frank doesn't need to know we've seen each other at all tonight,' she said.

Chaowalit closed the gate, restored the padlock. Instead of returning to his post, he stared after her. Jayne willed herself to turn and smile, but she was seething. Chaowalit now knew she spoke Thai, that made her vulnerable. She'd need to watch her back.

'*Chowk dee nong Chaowalit,*' she shouted over her shoulder, hoping both to dismiss the guard and attract Rajiv's attention.

She scanned the street and caught sight of his lanky frame pacing across the *soi,* impatience in his gait. She'd set out hours earlier determined to find Mayuree without alienating Rajiv. But she'd failed on both counts and it was nearly two in the morning.

She joined Rajiv on the corner and hailed a *songthaew.* They barely spoke on the way back to the hotel, Rajiv fading before her eyes. Jayne half-carried him to the reception desk, where the concierge handed over her room key, no doubt used to guests' tendencies for sudden couplings.

Jayne steered Rajiv through the door. He disappeared into the bathroom. After a few minutes, he re-emerged with damp hair, wearing nothing but a white towel slung low over his hips. Jayne noted the curve of his pelvic bone, slender waist, navel encircled by wiry black hair that tapered into a narrow line and disappeared beneath the towel like a question mark.

Yes, she wanted to answer, *whatever the question.*

He looked at the double bed, registering it for the first time. 'Do you want me to sleep on the floor?'

The question threw her. 'No, of course not.'

'Thank you,' he said. 'You have my word that I will not molest you in the night.'

He kissed her gently on the forehead.

'But—'

'Jayne, I'm exhausted.'

She blushed at the thought her lust was so transparent. 'Me too,' she lied, her body pumped with adrenaline. 'I'm sorry about tonight.'

'Don't be worrying about it,' Rajiv said through a yawn.

'I'll make it up to you.'

He murmured something as Jayne turned to the bathroom. Reflected in the mirror, she saw Rajiv remove the towel from his waist and slip on a pair of white drawstring pants before collapsing into bed. He was asleep before his head hit the pillow.

To be on the safe side Jayne locked the bathroom door behind her so she could come in private.

29

Max gazed at the smooth brown back in bed beside him. His name, Oud, was the Thai equivalent of 'oink'. But there was nothing porcine about this lover, a featherweight *muay thai* boxer, with not an inch of fat on him. Even his arse was solid muscle. Max doubted they had much of a future together. He was too old for workouts at the gym, and sooner or later someone fitter and richer would steal Oud away. Max intended to enjoy it while it lasted.

He reached to cup that sculpted ass in the palm of his hand when his mobile phone rang.

'Bugger.'

He glanced at the screen but didn't recognise the number. It could be a diplomatic emergency. Max couldn't afford not to answer it.

'Hello?'

'Max, it's Jayne.'

'Jayne? This isn't your number. Where are you calling from?' He must have sounded as annoyed as he felt.

'So, would you have answered if it was my number? Or I am interrupting something important?'

'Yes, no.' Max watched Oud roll out of bed and

disappear into the bathroom. 'Go ahead, Jayne,' he sighed. 'What is it?'

'I'm still in Pattaya working on the Maryanne Delbeck case. And I've stumbled across something that raises significant questions about the verdict of suicide.'

'Really?'

Max sat bolt upright, excitement and dread slugging it out in his head. While he took pleasure in his friend's investigative prowess, Maryanne Delbeck had died on his watch and re-opening the investigation would be a diplomatic nightmare.

'I'm still putting together the evidence but I need you to contact immigration at the US Embassy and ask them to put a hold on a visa for a recently adopted baby boy. Adoptive parents' first names are Leroy and Alicia.'

Was one diplomatic nightmare not enough for her?

'Jayne, I don't think you understand. I can't do something like that without just cause.'

'I have reason to believe the baby was stolen from his mother and his identity falsified.'

Max whistled.

'That would do.' He rubbed his temples. 'But where's your evidence? I can't recommend a NOID without something more concrete than your word.'

'A *noid*?'

'Notice of Intention to Deny. It's what the embassies issue when there's doubt raised about the legality of an adoption. It's a very big deal. Rarely happens in Thailand these days.'

'Well, does it have to be that formal? Couldn't you just have a quiet word with your counterpart in the US Embassy so they lose a form or something?'

Max sighed. 'I'm not promising anything, but I'll see what I can do.'

'You're a prince among men,' Jayne said.

Among men is where I'd much rather be, Max thought as he terminated the call.

He could hear the shower running—perhaps all was not lost. He slipped out of his boxer shorts and headed for the bathroom.

Jayne hung up the phone and sipped her plastic bag of iced coffee. It wasn't yet eight o'clock but she'd been busy. She left Rajiv sleeping, with a note promising to be back at six to take him out for dinner. On her way to Chai's office, she had dropped into an express photo lab and had Kob's photo duplicated, together with the shot showing Frank and Doctor Somsri with the adoptive parents. Next she found a street café serving rice noodle soup. While waiting for her breakfast, she consulted her English-Thai dictionary— she spoke Thai with greater fluency than she wrote it—and composed a short message that Mayuree would be sure to understand: 'I believe your son is alive. Please contact me as soon as possible.' She included her mobile phone number.

It was too early for the post office, but Wichit's nephew Chai was happy to add Jayne's letter, addressed to Kanchanaburi, to his office mail. It was his phone she'd used to call Max in Bangkok. He also proved to be a good source of information on restaurants in Pattaya.

She thanked Chai and set out for the centre, keen to make sure there wasn't any fallout from her confrontation with Chaowalit. She saw Frank on the way into the orphanage, but his brief greeting and leave-taking cry of 'God bless' gave her no reason to believe he suspected anything.

The day passed like any other. The Thai staff fed the babies, the volunteers played with the babies and Jayne cleaned up after the babies.

She parried another attempt by Dianne to invite her out and escaped at five on the dot. Back at Chai's office, she drafted a letter to Police Major General Wichit. She didn't plan to send anything until she had evidence, but it was an opportunity to collect her thoughts, get a handle on how the scam worked.

By his own admission, Frank knew which children in the nursery were sought after for overseas adoption—*look kreung* and Thai girls—and his first tactic was to pressure the mothers to give up their children. To Jayne's mind, this in itself pushed ethical, if not legal boundaries. When that didn't work, things got really interesting. The desirable babies were given a falsified identity and forged paperwork to make them eligible for adoption. Jayne recalled Frank saying they often held the children's official papers at the centre. This would come in handy when putting together the bogus identity: if the child was born in Krabi in Thailand's south, for example, the forged birth certificate would be sure to list place of birth as somewhere like Nakhon Phanom in the northeast, making it harder for the child's family of origin to be traced. Perhaps a counterfeit maternal death certificate was produced or a fake statement of relinquishment. Jayne assumed Frank and his associates would vary the details to avoid suspicion.

Perhaps the trickiest part of the operation was to account for the child's death when there was no way of producing a corpse. In the case of itinerant parents, excuses could be made about communication difficulties and time pressures. Where the mother was close at hand, as in Mayuree's case, exotic illnesses had to be invented and cremations expedited on public health grounds. Producing a fake death certificate was probably the easiest part of the operation.

Money would change hands. Jayne suspected the doctor and those behind him with access to official records took the biggest cut. Frank's reward would be more spiritual: the knowledge he'd saved innocent souls from their prostitute mothers and sent them to good Christian families in the West.

Frank would have to keep some sort of paperwork. But what use was falsified material to Jayne without proof it was falsified? She had no way of knowing under what name Kob was adopted out or what grounds had been fabricated to explain how he became an orphan.

What she could prove was that he wasn't dead. It followed that if she could get hold of Kob's death certificate, she could prove it was a fake. And that should be enough to keep Kob in Thailand, if not justify an investigation into adoption fraud at the New Life Children's Centre.

Frank Harding would have no reason to keep a copy of Kob's death certificate. However, Doctor Somsri who'd signed it would be obliged to keep a copy on file.

Jayne rummaged through her bag for the doctor's business card. She checked the address on her map: his consulting rooms were conveniently located within a few blocks of the orphanage.

'Death certificate for Kamolsert,' she typed. 'Check Dr Somsri's office.'

'Is it okay if I save a file on your computer?' she called over her shoulder to Chai.

'Sure,' he said. 'Save it to the desktop. I'll have a folder set up for you next time.'

'Thanks,' Jayne said on her way out. And because she knew it would reflect well on him added, 'I'll be sure to tell your uncle what a great help you've been.'

She called Rajiv to let him know she was running fifteen minutes late.

30

The *songthaew* took them along the winding clifftop road to a gateway dripping with fairy-lights. They continued on foot down a path lined with wax ginger flowers and lit with flaming torches, pausing to allow a peacock to cross in front of them. After a minute or two the tropical garden gave way to a neat lawn lined on three sides with thatched wooden huts, each one a private dining room.

Jayne and Rajiv left their shoes at the foot of a short set of steps and sat down on triangular floor cushions. Their low table was set with blue glazed plates and white linen serviettes folded into the shape of lotus buds, the bronze forks, spoons and chopsticks heavy enough to double as weapons. The air smelled of lemongrass and melancholic *look thoong* music hummed in the background. They could see white rabbits grazing on the lawn outside their hut.

'We've stumbled into Wonderland,' Jayne said.

'It certainly is wonderful,' Rajiv said. 'I am liking it very much.'

Jayne took his hand, held it for a moment.

'I'm glad,' she said, smiling.

Rajiv returned the smile. It had crossed his mind to

seduce her the second she returned from work to undo the night before. But he lacked the nerve. And the mood was wrong. A romantic meal, a few drinks, some conversation— this was better.

Jayne was wearing a black short-sleeved dress that made her skin glow. Rajiv wore a long cream-coloured *kurta* over white jeans, an ensemble Jayne joked made him look like a Bollywood star. At times they looked mismatched, him with not a hair out of place, clothes ironed and sandals polished, Jayne messy haired and rumpled with dirt under her nails. At other times, like tonight, they complemented each other. White on black and black on white, they'd be at home in the pantheon of Hindu gods with dualities like these.

As usual Rajiv let Jayne order the food—green papaya salad, steamed seafood curry and a chicken and bamboo shoot soup so spicy it silenced conversation for several minutes. Jayne didn't volunteer any more information about the case and Rajiv didn't ask in unspoken agreement to leave work aside for the night.

They talked about travel. Jayne had backpacked through India on holiday from university, seeing more of his country than Rajiv had.

'What was your overall impression?' he asked.

'Hardly a fair question,' she said. 'Every new place was different.'

'Did you enjoy yourself?'

'It got a bit overwhelming at times—' she paused to light a cigarette '—but I enjoyed myself. Enormously. I'd go again.'

'Would you ever live there?'

'Ah...' she wavered.

'You know,' he added quickly, 'if you were offered a good job.'

'I guess I've never thought about it before. I could live in India, though it would depend on where.' She paused to ash her cigarette. 'What about you? Would you want to live somewhere other than India?'

'Like where?'

'Well, Thailand for example.'

'Not sure.'

'What about Australia?'

'I don't—'

They were interrupted by Jayne's mobile phone. She looked at the number, a pained expression on her face.

'Sorry, Rajiv, I need to take this.'

She slid off her cushion, slipped on her shoes and wandered out on to the lawn, scattering rabbits in several directions. Rajiv followed her with his eyes, his stomach sinking.

He helped himself to one of her cigarettes and was halfway through it when she returned. She didn't remove her shoes. Rajiv knew what was coming.

'You need to be going, isn't it.'

'I'm so sorry about this—'

He held up one hand. 'Just one question.'

She raised her eyebrows.

'Do you want me to be staying or going, because if this will be your way of saying that you're too busy—'

She took his face in her hands. For a moment he thought she was going to kiss him, and wanted her to, despite his upbringing.

'I would much rather stay here with you,' she said. 'But I'm racing against the clock. That was my friend at the Australian Embassy. Mayuree's baby is headed for the United States the day after Chinese New Year unless I stop

225

it. Chinese New Year starts tomorrow. That gives me three days to find what I need, get back to Bangkok, brief the adoptive parents, and help Mayuree retrieve her son before they issue him with an immigration visa.'

'Please do not be worrying about me,' Rajiv said. 'It's okay.'

'Thank you.'

'Where is it you will be going?'

'I have to visit a doctor's surgery to pick up some paperwork.'

Rajiv glanced at his watch. 'After hours clinic, is it?'

'More along the lines of self-service.'

'Is breaking and entering normally something you are doing every day, Jayne?'

She shrugged.

'Are you needing me to come?'

'No offence, but it'll be quicker if I'm on my own.'

Rajiv exhaled. While he supposed there was a parallel between Jayne's cavalier attitude towards crimes against property and his own interest in hacking, Rajiv preferred to push legal boundaries from the safety of a computer.

'See you back at the hotel?'

'Within the hour,' she said.

31

A notice outside Doctor Somsri's consulting rooms announced business was closed for three days and wished customers 'Happy Chinese New Year' in Thai, English and Chinese. Alongside it a gold and red cardboard figure of a bull signified the Year of the Ox.

Jayne pressed her face against the window and could just make out the reception area. She crossed to the other side of the road to take in the whole, narrow two-storey building. She suspected the doctor's office was upstairs where the blinds were drawn.

The building was in a quiet *soi*, but a streetlight over the entrance ruled out picking the lock on the front door. It was tightly wedged between two neighbouring Chinese-style shop-houses: businesses on the ground floor, residences upstairs with small balconies overlooking the street. Jayne walked down a narrow laneway on the left to check out the back of the buildings and found them fused into a single concrete wall. No rear exits.

She returned to the street, convinced the surgery must have more than one entrance. She studied the three facades again. Apart from different paintwork and signage—one was a tailor, the other sold votive paper offerings for burning at funerals—the shop-houses were a matching pair, twins separated by the modern edifice of the doctor's rooms. All three buildings shared identical dimensions and most likely the clinic had once been a shop-house, too. Triplets.

Jayne knew from wandering the backstreets of Bangkok's Chinatown that while Chinese shop-houses look solid from the front, they were usually built around hidden courtyards to allow air and light to circulate. Multiple doorways led off the courtyard to rooms in the front and back sections, with upper storey rooms joined by a narrow bridge. In a row of shop-houses, adjoining courtyards created open space and enabled neighbours to mingle from one end of the block to the other.

She tried the laneway on the right and found an entrance to the courtyard behind the first shop-house. The ground floor windows were dark, upstairs the blue flickering light of a television. She sidled along the damp wall of the back half of the building. She froze at the brush of fur on her feet, glanced down to see a white cat with a small head and stub of a tail rubbing against her ankles. She slipped one foot under its belly, lifted it out of her way and continued inching towards the doctor's rooms. Her toe hit a wall where more courtyard should have been—it was the doctor's renovated building.

Jayne could see enough shadows to tell that the wall wasn't solid. She walked her hands along until they reached empty space. A swoop of her penlight revealed a narrow tunnel, no doubt grudgingly conceded to allow the neighbours to wheel their motorbikes through to the back of their houses.

The good news for Jayne was that on either side of the

tunnel were doors leading into the front and back sections of Doctor Somsri's surgery. The door to the back section was padlocked. The one closest to reception was not. She chose the path of least resistance.

'Chinese New Year,' Frank read aloud with distaste. The desk calendar was a gift from his colleagues at the Pattaya International Church. Why they insisted on acknowledging these pagan festivals was beyond Frank.

It wouldn't be a holiday for him anyway—the festival provided the opportunity to expedite another adoption. Chinese New Year would see a renewed influx of tourists to Pattaya and the whores would be busier than usual. This gave Frank more time to get the baby away and Doctor Somsri more scope to account for the infant's hasty cremation—such as lack of space at the morgue due to a spike in accidents connected to Chinese New Year festivities. It helped avert suspicion to keep the stories fresh.

Frank pulled out the files on the newest arrivals. It was always difficult deciding how long a child should be at the New Life Children's Centre before they were adopted out. The advantage with the newer ones was that their demise could be blamed on a pre-existing health problem. The disadvantage was it could spook others into withdrawing their children from care. They could minimise this, Frank surmised, by offering another round of health checks to the remaining children so that they didn't suffer the same fate as little...

He shuffled through the files.

'Pornpan Sasomsab,' he read aloud, 'A.k.a. Num, nine months.'

Where did they get these dreadful names? God willing,

the little girl would soon be given a decent Christian name.

Frank began the preparations, determined to demonstrate to Somsri and his backers that they could rely on him.

Jayne wore a chain of skeleton keys around her neck, the ultimate accessory of choice for the fashion conscious cat burglar. They were a gift from her friend Simone, formerly a teacher at the British Council in Bangkok. The card that came with them read, 'I did a deal with some shady East End types to score these for you, the perfect gift for a private investigator.' She was right: they were the perfect gift.

The lock on the rear exit of the doctor's rooms surrendered without a struggle and Jayne stepped inside, closing the door behind her. A few steps forward brought her alongside the reception area. She noted some filing cabinets, but had her money on the important stuff being in Doctor Somsri's office. She skirted over to the staircase, level with the front entrance. There was little chance of being seen but she checked the street all the same before creeping up the stairs two at a time.

The upper storey smelled of bleach, most of the space was occupied by consulting rooms. Jayne walked into one, scanned the contents of the cupboards and helped herself to a pair of latex gloves. The door to Doctor Somsri's office was locked but coaxed open easily enough. Jayne closed the door, pulled the blind aside to check the street again, thought about turning on the desk lamp, decided against it.

She used her penlight to inspect the desk. She found a ring-binder diary in a drawer and leafed through it. Nothing other than a few notes and numbers. Obviously not the doctor's appointment diary. She was about to toss it back but paused to check Wednesday 5 February, the date Mayuree's son was taken. There was an entry on that day: a few Thai letters—some kind of shorthand—and alongside the 19.00 appointment time, *khing*, the Thai word for 'ginger'. Some kind of code? She tore out the page.

She returned to the consulting room and pilfered some zip-lock plastic bags. She placed the diary page inside one and shoved it down her bra.

Nothing else of importance in the desk, she turned her attention to the filing cabinets. They were locked, pointlessly, as the key was blue-tacked to the back. Doctor Somsri didn't take the same precautions as Frank. Perhaps he had nothing to hide. Or nothing to fear.

His files were arranged in Thai alphabetical order, which took Jayne some time to decipher. The air-conditioning was off and she soon worked up a sweat. Most of the files were medical records. Jayne assumed the doctor would want the adoption-related paperwork to look routine and therefore would keep it among his general files rather than in a special location. Sure enough, there was no master file for adoptions. While he probably wouldn't file under the child's real name for adoption paperwork, she figured he'd have to for the death certificate.

There was no file for Kamolsert. Jayne wracked her brain to remember his surname, one of those long, elaborate Thai names that had grown over generations. She remembered it started with a vowel and one of the syllables was the Thai word for 'heavenly blessing', which had the unfortunate English transliteration *porn*. She scanned the labels, reading aloud as she went.

'*A-ss-a-wa-wat-ta-na-porn.*'

A mouthful, but that wasn't it.

'*At-ta-mang-porn.*'

Close.

'*A-porn-su-wan-na.*'

Apornsuwanna sounded right.

She pulled out the file and there at the top was what looked very much like Kob's bogus death certificate. The date checked out. Doctor Somsri's signature was in black ink beneath a red stamp in the lower right-hand corner. Jayne didn't stop to read the rest. She folded the certificate in half and sealed it in a second zip-lock bag.

Shots rang out. She ran to the window and peered around the blind. At the end of the street she saw sparks and smoke, heard more explosions, saw a crowd massing. Firecrackers. Chinese New Year festivities designed to scare away evil spirits so the good spirits can get to work bringing prosperity to the household or business.

Jayne let the blind fall and wiped her damp forehead. She glanced at her watch. It was taking longer than she'd thought. She returned the Apornsuwanna file to the cabinet drawer and was about to close it when she caught sight of the same Thai word that was in the diary. *Khing.* She pulled out the file. It contained adoption papers, in English and Thai, signed by Leroy King and Alicia King, co-signed by Doctor Somsri and witnessed by...

'Chao-wa-lit,' she read aloud.

'*Krup?*'

Jayne spun around. Standing in the doorway was Chaowalit and behind him Doctor Somsri. The fireworks had masked the sound of their approach. The King file fell from her hands, paper scattering at her feet.

'I can explain—' she began.

Chaowalit reached her in two strides, grabbed her and pinned her arms behind her.

'I knew you were a lying cunt,' he muttered in her ear, droplets of spit spraying on her face.

It was almost a relief when Doctor Somsri pressed a cloth against her face and she blacked out.

32

Jayne's head throbbed and her knees ached. Her eyes were closed but she was aware of an overhead light. She was in a lift. Its rattling motion increased the pain in her head and she groaned involuntarily.

'She's moving.'

A man's voice, in Thai, above her.

She went limp against the floor, willing her body not to shake.

'That's twitching, not moving,' said a second man's voice.

'I'm telling you, I saw her move.'

'And I'm telling you she's drugged. She's moving in her sleep, okay,' said the voice Jayne recognised as Chaowalit's.

'I could lose my job letting you use the service lift like this,' the first said, petulant.

'Shut up,' Chaowalit said. 'You're getting paid.'

The other man mumbled something as the elevator shuddered to a halt. A pair of hands grabbed Jayne under the armpits and dragged her out of the lift. She opened her eyes just enough to glimpse the elevator doors closing on a man in a chef's uniform.

It was humid: they were outside. Knowing Chaowalit was now alone and couldn't see her face, Jayne opened her eyes. The rooftop terrace looked familiar. Had he brought her back to the Bayview Hotel? Would he risk a second crime at the scene of Maryanne Delbeck's death?

A new surge of fear swept Jayne's body. A stabbing the previous year had convinced her to get fit, learn a few self-defence moves. But groggy and sore, she was in no state to put her training to use.

Chaowalit lowered her to the ground, then a swift, hard kick sent her tumbling into the swimming pool.

More pain ripped through her. She imagined the relief of drifting back into oblivion, but her body surged to the surface, gasping for air. Chaowalit was waiting, arm raised, a blunt object in his fist. Jayne kicked fiercely at the water, moving just out of reach, but his blow still struck her shoulder.

Adrenaline followed the pain turning her panic into fury. A few well-placed strokes took her to the middle of the pool and she turned, treading water, to glare at Chaowalit.

'What the fuck are you doing?' she yelled.

'Shut the fuck up!' the man shouted, running around the edge of the pool like a dog.

'I will not shut up, you murderous dog-fucker,' Jayne shrieked.

If he kept yelling at her, he'd do half the work of attracting attention.

'You little white bitch.' Chaowalit growled. 'Maybe this will shut you up.' He snapped opened a flick-knife, blade catching the light.

Jayne shivered, the scar on her arm tingled.

'Oh, come off it,' she said, trying to hide the waver in her voice. 'This is supposed to be a simple drowning accident, right? Your friend Somsri is probably preparing the autopsy report as we speak: dumb farang tourist drinks too much, falls into the pool and drowns. Maybe I knock my head on the side of the pool on the way in. No one will connect it with Maryanne Delbeck's death since I'm just another guest here, though at this rate the Bayview might think twice about letting female guests from Australia out on the roof after dark.'

Chaowalit sneered.

'Doesn't a stabbing spoil your plan?'

He looked from the knife in his hand to Jayne and back again.

'I'm good at improvising,' he said and flicked the blade back into the handle.

He reached down to pick up something from the ground. A Coke bottle. He held it by the neck and smashed the bottom on the side of the pool.

'There's more than one way to draw blood,' he said, jabbing the air. 'Here's an idea: dumb farang tourist hits her face on a broken bottle that was lying by the side of the pool as she fell in. Hideous injuries. Death by drowning will seem merciful.'

Jayne kept treading water, wondering how long she could keep it up, wondering if Chaowalit could swim.

'You're smart,' she said, a shameless attempt at flattery. 'Does Frank Harding know what you're up to?'

'None of Khun Frank's business,' Chaowalit said.

'So this is just between you and Somsri.'

Chaowalit said nothing.

'Do you do all of the Doctor's dirty work?' Jayne continued. 'Like, getting rid of Maryanne, for example?'

Chaowalit yelped with surprise. 'Is that what you think? Farang girl dies, son of a bitch like me must be behind it?'

'I meant it as a compliment,' Jayne said, inching her way towards the side of the pool. 'Her death has kept everyone guessing. Was it suicide? Was it murder? No one seems to know, but I think you do.'

'Why?'

'Because, as I said, you're smart. Smarter than people realise.'

Chaowalit considered this for a moment.

'I was there when Khun Maryanne died, but I didn't kill her.'

'Then who did?'

'You won't believe me if I told you.'

'Try me.'

'It was an accident.'

Jayne laboured to keep her head above water and her expression neutral.

'I believe you.'

Chaowalit shrugged. 'Doesn't matter if you believe me or not. You weren't there.'

'Was anyone else—apart from you and Maryanne, I mean?'

'Yes.'

'What happened?'

Chaowalit looked at the bottle in his hand and shrugged again. 'It was Sumet's idea.'

'Sumet?'

'Brother of that whore, Mayuree. He and Maryanne were, you know, *faen kan*.' He made a lewd gesture using the bottleneck and his fist.

'They were fucking,' Jayne said.

'Yes.' He raised his eyebrows in admiration of her command of the Thai vernacular. 'And planning to get married—or so he said. Problem is Sumet wanted Maryanne to take him back to Australia, but she wanted them to stay in Thailand. So Sumet hires me to proposition her.'

'What do you mean?'

'I had to make it seem like she'd been leading me on. It wasn't a stretch. I mean, she was always coming on to me, touching me, practising her Thai on me, you know. My job was to make her feel bad for being a little cock-teaser.'

'He paid you to do this?'

'Of course,' Chaowalit shrugged. 'I had to make Maryanne feel bad so he could come along and make her feel better. Only it didn't work out that way.'

'What went wrong?'

'Depends on how you look at it.'

Jayne touched the bottom of the pool with the tips of her toes.

'Tell me how *you* look at it, younger brother.'

'Okay,' he nodded. 'I look at it this way. Nice school teacher Sumet asks Chaowalit the thug to proposition *his* girlfriend. Does that sound like an act of true love to you?'

'No, not at all,' Jayne said.

She moved closer to the side of the pool, her weight resting on her feet.

'*Chai laew,*' he agreed. 'Chaowalit has met some bad types in his time. He knows a bastard when he sees one. Sumet didn't deserve Maryanne. She was too good for him. I set her straight.'

'Here? On the roof?'

Chaowalit nodded. 'Sumet phoned her and said to meet here for a romantic date in the moonlight. Plan was for

Chaowalit to choose that same evening to proposition her. I followed the first part of the plan: I was waiting in the lobby and followed her up here. Then I explained how Sumet only wanted to marry her to get to Australia. I said I wouldn't make her go back to Australia if she didn't want to.'

'So you did proposition her,' Jayne said, thinking aloud.

'I just told her the truth.'

'How'd she take it?'

'She didn't believe me. Then I showed her the money Sumet paid me to make her change her mind. She just kept shaking her head saying *no, no, no*. Then Sumet showed up and she fell to pieces. Accused him of all kinds of things I can only guess at—she was crying and talking fast at him in English.'

'How come the noise didn't bring other people to the roof?'

'She wasn't shouting,' Chaowalit said. 'She was quiet, sobbing.'

'More powerful than shouting,' Jayne said.

'*Jing jing*,' Chaowalit nodded, grateful to get it off his chest. 'Then she climbed over the railing. Things were getting way too heavy. I wanted to get the fuck out of there. But I was fixed to the spot. Maryanne is crying *do you love me or not* and Sumet is saying *I love you, I love you* and running towards her. I think she only meant to scare him 'cause she didn't seem like the type to...'

'What?'

'She didn't seem like the type to jump.' Chaowalit shook his head. 'She was too sweet, too *happy*.'

Jayne registered a change of tone, edged further away.

'That's what everyone says about her.'

'She was young, you know, and young girls make such

a fucking drama of everything,' Chaowalit said. 'If a boy wants a night out with his friends, the girl weeps and pouts until he changes his mind. If he forgets her birthday, she goes into depression because it means he doesn't love her. And if he gets sick of all the dramas and tries to break it off, she threatens to kill herself. It's all an act, you know, just a way of getting what they want.'

Jayne thought back over all the things she'd heard about Maryanne in the course of her investigation: that she was cheerful, upbeat, trusting, 'too confident'. She was also young, inexperienced and used to getting her own way. Sumet's betrayal, Chaowalit's clumsy offer to replace him— Maryanne would have felt as if the rug had been pulled out from under her. It wasn't a stretch to imagine her threatening to throw herself off the top of a building in order to punish both men. But did she mean to kill herself?

'Are you sure it was an accident? You don't think Sumet pushed her?'

'Nah,' Chaowalit shook his head. 'He didn't have the balls.'

'Not like you?' Jayne said.

'Not like me.'

Holding the bottle by the neck, he stepped into the shallow end of the pool.

'You don't need to do this,' Jayne said, backing away. 'I'm only interested in what happened to Maryanne.'

'That so?' Chaowalit tossed the broken bottle from one hand to the other. 'You should've just asked in the first place.'

'Can't we make a deal?'

'Bit late for that now.'

He started wading towards her.

'There's something you should know,' Jayne said, her

back pressed against the tiled wall of the pool. 'I've already sent my findings to the police.'

Chaowalit laughed. 'You think the cops are a problem? Somsri has half the Pattaya Police Department on the payroll.'

'I'm not talking about Pattaya,' Jayne said, groping for a ladder or foothold. 'I'm talking Bangkok. To my friend, a Police Major General.'

Chaowalit's expression darkened. 'You're a lying bitch.'

She caught sight of the ladder in the far corner. No use. She reached around, placing her hands on the edge of the pool, eyes on Chaowalit.

'This time tomorrow, Pattaya will be swarming with cops looking for you and Doctor Somsri. They'll want to talk with Frank, too. And let's see, who will be the fall guy for the operation? Can you see Doctor Somsri or Frank Harding defending a son of a bitch like you?'

Jayne hoped Chaowalit didn't see through the lie. She hadn't actually sent anything to Wichit and even if she had, it had taken tonight to confirm Chaowalit's involvement in the adoption racket. He was the link between the centre and the doctor's rooms. The courier.

'Enough fucking talk.' He threw the bottle. The glass smashed on the edge of the pool where her hands had been only seconds before.

Chaowalit took the knife from his waistband, flicked it open.

'Back to Plan A?' Jayne muttered in English.

She groped the side of the pool, pretending to hoist herself out. At the last moment, she plunged under the water, hit the bottom with her feet and pivoted towards the ladder in the corner. She heard the clatter of the knife hitting the tiles but couldn't see where it fell.

She surfaced without looking behind her, grabbed the parallel bars of the ladder and swung herself out of the pool in a move powered entirely by adrenaline. Her left shoulder screamed in protest. So did the ankle on which she landed. Badly. She stumbled, whimpering, across the terrace towards the elevators and pounded her fist on the button.

She could hear Chaowalit in the pool and glanced back. He'd ducked beneath the surface—he could swim after all—and was fishing for his knife.

She heard him come up, curse and duck under again. She watched the lights showing the elevator's slow ascent from the first, second, third, fourth floors.

The number nine was illuminated when Chaowalit yelled 'Gotcha!'

She looked back as he hauled himself out of the pool, weighed down by wet jeans. He'd cut his hands on the broken glass and came storming towards her with blood dripping from his fingers along the edge of the blade.

Her eyes darted from the lights passing the tenth, eleventh, twelfth floors, to the flashes of steel and blood.

A few seconds more, she might've made it. But he was too close and there were still two floors to go.

No. Only one. Thai hotels didn't have thirteenth floors because Westerners considered thirteen unlucky. A few seconds' grace. The elevator door opened and she dived in, expecting empty space, ready to spin around and claw at the buttons to close it. Instead, she crashed head first into someone.

She collapsed without knowing if she'd hit friend or foe.

33

She had to get the baby to sleep. She tried lying alongside him, but he was so small and slippery, he kept falling between the wall and the bed. She put him in a matchbox where he lay on his back, waving his arms and legs in the air like an overturned beetle. But she still couldn't get him to sleep because of the bright light shining in his eyes.

Jayne came around to find a torch in her face. She squeezed her eyes shut, blinked until the phosphenes subsided, opened her eyes.

The torch belonged to a woman in a white coat. Could she be back in Doctor's Somsri's rooms? She tried to push herself up but her arms were tied down. She wanted to scream but her voice caught in her throat.

The woman in the white coat held something to the side of Jayne's face and pushed a tube between her lips. 'Water,' she said. 'Drink.'

As Jayne drank she noticed the woman's name-tag. A good sign.

'Your arms are strapped down to stop you knocking out your saline drip. You've been thrashing around so much. It might have been the pain—you have a badly dislocated shoulder and a sprained ankle. We gave you some pain relief. We can probably untie you now.'

The straw still in her mouth, Jayne nodded, sending a spasm through her left shoulder blade.

'Do you need any more pain relief?'

She spat out the straw. 'Yes, please, that feels like a good idea.'

Her voice sounded as if she'd smoked a whole packet of cigarettes in one sitting and washed them down with a bottle of whisky. The local brand.

'Your Thai is good,' the doctor said, unruffled. 'The Police Major General told me it was.'

'Major General *Wichit*?' Jayne said. 'What's he doing in Pattaya?'

Doctor Penchan raised her eyebrows. 'You're not in Pattaya, Khun Jayne. You're in Bangkok. At the Christian Hospital.'

Jayne scanned the room, took in the crucifix on the wall. 'How—'

'The Police Major General will explain, once I'm confident you're well enough to see him.'

'I feel fine,' Jayne lied.

Her shoulder throbbed. Her ankle ached. It hurt to open and close her eyes.

The doctor put a velcro bandage around Jayne's upper arm, adjusted her stethoscope and pumped in air to check her blood pressure. The tightening of the armband made Jayne feel faint.

'I think we'll wait until your blood pressure goes up a little.'

Jayne had a thought that sent her blood pressure skyrocketing. 'Rajiv!'

'Would that be the Indian gentleman who brought these flowers?'

Doctor Penchan gestured at a bouquet on the shelf, a wonderful clash of red roses, yellow marigolds and purple orchids.

'I still don't understand—'

'You were unconscious for twelve hours. You came to briefly then fell asleep. It's no wonder you're disoriented.'

'What day is it?'

'It's Sunday February nine, but only just.' She glanced at her watch. 'It's three o'clock in the morning. Try to get some more sleep. Then I'll let your friend Major General Wichit speak with you. And the Indian man, too.'

Her voice was soothing, maternal. Jayne took the painkillers.

Police Major General Wichit removed his hat and took a seat. They'd elevated Jayne's bed and the drip was gone from her right hand, leaving behind a mushroom-coloured bruise. Her left shoulder was still strapped, but the colour had returned to her cheeks. She looked less deathly today.

'Let's talk in English,' he said, placing his hat on his lap. 'Where shall I begin?'

He meant it as a rhetorical question but Jayne dived in.

'Was it you in the lift?'

'Actually, it was my subordinate, Sergeant Thawon, whom you nearly bowled over, but I was in the lift, yes.'

'But how—?'

'My nephew, Chai. You left a file on the desktop of his computer, addressed to me. He thought it was important and sent it through by email.'

'The Thai police have email now?'

'Of course.'

'The letter wasn't finished,' Jayne said. 'They were just notes. I knew I didn't have a case until I had hard evidence.'

'Yes, but I ran a check on Frank Harding and there were irregularities. *Persona non grata* in Laos, charges of adoption fraud in the Philippines dropped for lack of evidence. It was enough to sound alarm bells. I could tell you were getting close and I worried you might be in danger.'

'But how did you find me?'

'Your, umm...'

'Assistant,' Rajiv chimed in, putting his head in the door. 'Good morning, Major General. Hello Jayne.'

Jayne's face lit up. 'Rajiv!'

'Good to see you looking better,' he said. 'Boss.'

Jayne smiled in spite of the pain.

'I'm sorry. Am I interrupting?' Rajiv added. 'Should I come back later?'

'Actually, I was just about to explain to Khun Jayne how I managed to find her at the Bayview Hotel. Would you like to take over?'

'Certainly.' Rajiv installed himself on the end of Jayne's bed in a manner not at all befitting an employee.

'Forgive me, Jayne, but it's only natural that when you were gone for so long, I should start to worry. I tried phoning you and someone answered but switched off the phone. I am thinking maybe I caught you in a tight spot where a ringing phone might be blowing your cover. In such a case, you'd be getting back to me, isn't it? I waited ten more minutes and when I still hadn't heard from you, I decided it was time to take action.

'So I go through your notes and find the number for the Children's Centre. Next I am asking our hotel receptionist,

Miss Yui, to please be phoning the centre pretending to be the mother of a sick child and asking for the name of the consulting doctor. Miss Yui is then obtaining his address from directory assistance.

'I impose on Miss Yui to assist me again by calling the Pattaya police on my behalf and report you as a missing person, last seen in the vicinity of the doctor's rooms. When I am leafing through your notes, I also find a mobile phone number for Police Major General Wichit. I recall you mentioned you had a friend who was a Police Major General and I am thinking this must be the one. Yet again Miss Yui is coming to my aid, calling Major General Wichit from my phone. We learn he can speak English and Miss Yui puts him on to me.

'I am surprised to learn that he is actually nearing Pattaya as we speak, coming to find you, Jayne. So I am giving him the address of the doctor's rooms. Finally, after all this excitement, I thank Miss Yui and step outside to smoke a cigarette. That is when I see you.'

'*What?*'

'I am about to light my cigarette when I see a car pull up behind the hotel. To my surprise, it is that guard from the centre who is getting out. I see him open the back door of the car and drag something out. It's *you*, Jayne. I am horrified. I am thinking they have killed you.

'Next thing a man dressed like a cook is appearing and the two men are carrying you towards the service lift.'

Rajiv paused, stared at the floor as he told the next part of the story.

'Perhaps you are thinking I should have run after them. But it is two against one and I know very well that I am no match for that guard. So I am doing the best I can. I am hitting redial on my phone, telling the Major General to get to the hotel. I am rushing back inside to raise the alarm, and together Miss Yui and I are trying to find a hotel guard to go up to the rooftop. But the guards are all convinced it is haunted by the ghost of the dead Australian girl. Before we can talk the guards into it, the police are arriving.'

'Your assistant is a very smart man,' Wichit chimed in. 'He saved your life. Thai people would say this now makes him responsible for you.'

Jayne stared past him, looking at Rajiv as she spoke. 'Where I come from, it's me who should feel grateful to him.'

Wichit looked from Jayne to Rajiv and back again. She seemed dazed, though whether due to the trauma of the assault or to Rajiv's story, Wichit couldn't tell. He hoped she understood that Rajiv had done the right thing—that she wasn't a hopeless romantic like his wife Sangravee, who equated heroism with the kind of egotistical acts of stupidity that in Wichit's experience usually endangered lives.

'We arrested Chaowalit on the spot,' he continued. 'At this stage, we're charging him with assault and intention to cause grievous bodily harm. This could be upgraded to attempted murder.'

Jayne closed her eyes. A subject for another time.

'The Pattaya police went to Doctor Somsri's rooms after they received Rajiv's call and found the building ablaze. They think the fire may have been caused by an explosion of chemicals stored on the premises.'

'Let me guess, all files were destroyed.'

'Yes.'

'Deliberately lit?'

'No way of knowing yet. The doctor admits he was there earlier in the evening and caught you snooping through confidential medical files. Says he asked his bodyguard to remove you from the premises as an intruder but when you fainted, he took pity on you and suggested Chaowalit return you to your hotel instead.'

'Un-fucking-believable.' Jayne shook her head. 'What about Frank Harding?'

'Disappeared,' Wichit said. 'We've got an alert out at every immigration checkpoint in the country but nothing yet.'

Jayne closed her eyes. No one said anything for a moment.

'The plastic bags,' she said suddenly, eyes wide open. 'In my clothes. Kob's death certificate. Did anyone find it and—'

'We have it,' Wichit said, 'but it doesn't prove much.'

'It proves Kob's death was faked.'

'Not necessarily. The only evidence you had of the baby being alive is a photograph, which could have been taken *before* he died.'

'But it wasn't!' Jayne shook her head, causing her to wince in pain. 'Kob is alive. He was handed over to an American couple named King—Leroy and Alicia—to be adopted. Surely the US Embassy can confirm seeing him since the photo was taken, after he's supposed to have died?'

'The embassy's closed until Wednesday for Chinese New Year,' Wichit said. 'We haven't talked with them yet. We can't, until we have incontrovertible evidence.'

Jayne sighed. 'I don't believe this.'

'They won't agree to an investigation without proof of significant irregularities. And we don't have that. At least not yet.'

Jayne closed her eyes. No one spoke.

'I'll get the evidence,' she said. She opened her eyes and

eased herself up. 'How soon can I get out of here?'

'That will be a matter for the doctors—' Rajiv began.

She held up her hand. 'I feel fine. Rajiv, can you figure out how I can get to Kanchanaburi and back by Wednesday?'

'Jayne, I don't think you should—'

'You're still my assistant, aren't you?'

Wichit could see it was time for him to leave. 'The doctor tells me you can go home within a couple of days,' he said, rising to his feet. 'I'll keep in touch.'

He patted Jayne carefully on the arm to avoid her bruises and shook hands with Rajiv.

'Take care of yourself, young man.'

'Thank you, Major General.'

And good luck, he added under his breath. I'm guessing you'll need it.

Both of them spoke at once.

'I've got to get out—'

'You've got to take care—'

They stopped, paused for breath, tried again.

'I'm so grateful—'

'I'm so relieved—'

They smiled.

Rajiv shuffled along the bed to get closer to her. He picked up her hand and traced around the purple bruise with his fingertips.

'When I saw Chaowalit drag you out of that car, I thought you were dead. You weren't moving...'

He looked away. 'I did not know what to do.'

'You did well.' Jayne patted his arm. 'Like Wichit said, you saved my life.'

She reached up to stroke his face. Rajiv kissed her gently

like she might break. She pulled him to her and kissed him so hard it hurt. She didn't care. She wanted to feel something, anything.

'Whoa.'

He pulled away, gave her a worried look. 'Jayne, what's gotten into you?'

'I'm just glad to be alive,' she said.

It sounded hollow but Rajiv smiled.

'So, *boss*,' he said, 'are you serious about going to Kanchanaburi?'

'I have to find Mayuree, bring her to Bangkok to explain to the Americans that she didn't relinquish her son. It's the best evidence I can think of. I just wish I knew how to get to the Kings as well.'

'Leave it to me,' Rajiv said.

'I was only joking about being my assistant.'

Rajiv held up one hand. 'Leave it to me,' he said again.

Jayne watched him go, jealous of his energy and enthusiasm, neither of which she had. She lay still for a long time, forgoing more painkillers, trying to sort through her emotions.

She knew Rajiv was right not to have jumped in and tried to save her from Chaowalit. That was the sort of foolhardy thing Jayne would have done and lived to regret.

Or not.

He was right when he said he was no match for the Thai guard. Jayne thought the same herself. That Rajiv was smarter, wittier, more handsome didn't matter. Chaowalit would have punched that mouth, smashed that beautiful face, beaten that fine mind to a pulp.

Rajiv was considered where Jayne would have been rash, methodical where she was impulsive, cautious where she was...what? What *was* the opposite of cautious? Brave? Or reckless?

Rajiv was right about everything.

So why didn't she feel anything for him any more?

34

Jayne was released from hospital the following afternoon. Her doctor, in collusion with Major General Wichit, insisted she attend a counselling session before they'd let her go. The counsellor was a buxom Englishwoman with hair too big, clothes too small and a voice too cheerful. She introduced herself as Candy, and Jayne wondered if she'd handpicked the name to go with her saccharine manner.

'So, how are you, Jayne?'

'Much better, thank you. Shoulder hardly hurts at all.'

'No, I mean, how *are* you, emotionally speaking?'

'Fine.'

'*Really?*'

'Does that disappoint you?'

'Of course not. It's just that you've recently survived a *life-threatening incident*,' she said, an implicit 'bravo' in her voice, 'and it's normal for people in your situation to experience a range of symptoms we psychologists refer to as *post traumatic stress disorder*. These include depression, mood swings, listlessness, inability to concentrate, insomnia, paranoia...'

Candy prattled on and Jayne tuned out, the whole

exercise beneath her. Private detectives didn't have counselling. Philip Marlowe would never have put up with this shit.

'...and sexual promiscuity,' Candy continued.

This caught Jayne's attention.

'Survivors may indulge in risky behaviours such as unprotected sex with strangers as a life-affirming act.'

Sounds good to me, Jayne thought.

'Some feel superhuman, as if nothing can touch them. At the other extreme, you may feel suicidal.'

In her mind, Jayne chastised the counsellor for her clumsiness: using the third person to describe activities at the fun end of the spectrum and the second person to describe suicide was hardly playing fair.

'Are you saying I should give in to all of these impulses or none of them?'

'Ah, Jayne, you still have your sense of humour. That's a good sign. I'm saying that these impulses and symptoms are *normal* for survivors of trauma. People experience one of three responses in the face of a traumatic incident: flight, fight or freeze. You fought back—that bodes well for your recovery. In the meantime, if you do experience any symptoms, please don't hesitate to contact me.'

She handed over her business card. Jayne glanced at it to be polite and suppressed a guffaw. Candy's surname was Sweet.

'I appreciate your time,' she said, rising to her feet.

'No, I appreciate *yours*,' Candy gushed.

They shook hands.

'Didn't have a choice,' Jayne said.

To her satisfaction, Candy looked wounded by this parting shot.

Jayne expected to find her apartment hot and musty after more than a week away. But the place was clean and cool, and there were fresh orchids patterned like leopard-skin in a vase on the dining table that doubled as her desk.

Rajiv.

The same impulse that took pleasure from slighting Candy wanted to toss the orchids in the bin—sending flowers could not make up for failing to step in to save her life—and this struck Jayne as a good thing. Instead of feeling nothing for Rajiv, she hated him. She was making progress.

Her mobile phone rang. Caller ID identified the man himself. Jayne let it ring five times, toying with the idea of telling him she never wanted to see him again.

'I found the Americans,' Rajiv said.

She made a snap decision for a stay of execution.

'*What*? How?'

'If I'm telling you, then you will not be needing me as your assistant any more and I will be doing myself out of a job.'

She wasn't in the mood.

'Just tell me.'

Rajiv cleared his throat. 'I checked the registrations of all the three, four and five star hotels within a short commute of the US Embassy. I am guessing a couple with a new baby are going to want to stay nearby, what with all the tearing down of the flyovers to make way for the new Skytrain, which will be making the traffic in Bangkok worse than ever.'

'Yes, yes. And?'

'Suriya Hotel,' Rajiv said. 'Soi Ruam Rudee, almost directly behind the US Embassy.'

'Great job. Thanks.'

'So does this mean you will be keeping me on as your assistant?'

His tone was playful, almost cocky. He was oblivious to the fraying of the thread from which he hung.

'That depends,' she said curtly. 'Have you organised the tickets to Kanchanaburi?'

'I've booked the train at seven forty-five tomorrow morning.'

'*Tomorrow morning*? You idiot! I told you I need to leave today.'

The vehemence of her outburst shocked them both into silence.

'I assumed you would be wanting to interview the Americans as soon as possible and kept this afternoon free for that,' Rajiv said after a moment, his voice calm and measured. 'I am thinking five o'clock is a good time to catch them at their hotel, given they have a small child. The last bus leaves for Kanchanaburi at seven o'clock, but from the Southern Bus Terminal across the river. You would be needing at least an hour, maybe two to get there on time, which you cannot do if you are meeting the Americans, isn't it?

'Correct me if I'm wrong, but I guessed sharing a minibus full of backpackers was not an option, which rules out a late departure tonight. And seeing as you would have to wait until tomorrow to leave anyway, I booked the train because it is one of the most scenic rail journeys in Thailand and I thought it would do you good.'

She could find fault with neither his logic nor judgment, which only made her hate him more.

'The buses leave earlier, starting from four in the morning, and it's a shorter journey than the train.' His voice remained infuriatingly calm. 'There's still time to change our itinerary if you want.'

'What do you mean *our* itinerary?' At last, a chance to punish him. 'Who said anything about you coming to Kanchanaburi?'

Rajiv sighed. 'My mistake.'

'If you want to make yourself useful, get me on a fast bus around six tomorrow morning,' she said. 'Make it a return ticket, same day. I don't have time for scenic fucking rail journeys.'

She heard the click of a cigarette lighter, a sharp inhalation, followed by another sigh.

'I will be dropping off your ticket later, Jayne. I'll slip it under the door. Call if you need to, but only when you are no longer angry with me.'

He hung up before he could hear her burst into tears.

Rajiv waited until four o'clock before setting out. He estimated Jayne would be heading across town by then to find the Kings and he wouldn't be tempted to check in on her.

The ferry from Banglampu carved a scalloped path along the Chao Phraya, cruising along the west bank before returning to the east bank at Tha Maharat, the jumping off point for the herbal medicine stalls and amulet market where his aunties shopped for potions and charms to heal their ailments, physical and spiritual. He wondered if the shamans' skills extended to mending wounded pride.

He was hurt but not surprised by Jayne's behaviour. She'd become distant and withdrawn since that night. It was almost a relief to feel her anger over the phone.

The trauma counsellor had warned him about this. She buttonholed Rajiv on his way out one evening to ask how he was doing. Rajiv said he was fine. She regaled him with statistics on the risk of marital breakdown amongst couples where one has survived trauma. Rajiv thanked her, explained that he wasn't married and tried to excuse himself.

'She'll probably hate you for a while,' Candy said. 'Don't take it personally.'

He stopped and looked at her.

'It's not rational. Grief and trauma never are. Hang in there. She'll get over it.'

Along the riverbank, houses were squashed together, overhanging the water as if pushed to the edge by buildings bigger and stronger than they were.

So far Candy had been right: Jayne hated him. Rajiv hope she would be right about Jayne getting over it, too. He would *hang in there* a little longer.

He alighted from the ferry and hailed a motorcycle taxi to take him to Jayne's apartment. Being her whipping boy was not a role that Rajiv relished, any more than being her assistant. But he was prepared to tolerate it if it got him what he wanted: to be Jayne's partner.

35

Jayne found the Kings in the hotel's rooftop café. They were sitting side by side, Alicia holding Kob in her lap. Jayne took a seat at a table close enough to watch them and hear their conversation without attracting attention.

The couple was older than she expected, Leroy's cropped hair speckled with grey. They looked exhausted and elated in equal measure, just like any new parents she supposed. There was a half-empty bottle of Budweiser on the table in front of Leroy, and an untouched glass of orange juice in front of Alicia. Strewn in between were a set of multicoloured stacking cups, a dummy, clumps of tissue and a teddy bear. Kob was playing with a string of beads around Alicia's neck.

'I think he likes us,' she said, planting a kiss on his forehead. 'I think he's decided his Momma and Daddy are okay.'

'Praise Jesus,' Leroy said. 'I don't know if I could've handled another day like yesterday. I'm not sure how much more singin' I had left in me, know what I'm sayin'?'

Alicia laughed and patted her husband on the knee. 'I just knew all that choir practice would come in handy some day.'

'It sure helps that he's a Bob Marley fan.' Leroy leaned towards Kob and sang the chorus of 'Three little birds'. Kob beamed, reached out to stroke the man's face.

Jayne was shocked. She assumed Kob would be fretting for his mother. He was happy. This would be harder than she thought.

'The counsellor was right,' Alicia said. 'She said the first couple of days would be tough. We were total strangers to him. Jesse needed time to get to know us.'

'And we're still getting to know him,' Leroy said. 'Like, how come he slept like a log that first night an' ain't never done that again?'

'He's just keeping his Momma and Daddy on their toes,' Alicia said, touching her forehead to Kob's. 'Right honey?'

Kob smiled when she pulled back and tilted his head forward to do it again.

'His appetite's improving,' Leroy said, watching them play.

He glanced at his watch. 'Actually honey, he's about due for a feed. You wanna take him downstairs or should I bring the bottle up?'

'Bring it up,' Alicia said. 'I don't want to spend a moment more than we have to cooped up inside that room. I can't believe no one told us about the national holiday. We could've come a week later and got outta here so much faster. But that would've meant one less week with our beautiful boy—' she kissed Kob's cheeks '—so it's worth it, isn't it my darling?'

Leroy took a swig of beer and rose to his feet. He and Cousin Tommy shared a similar build. If anything, Leroy was even broader across the shoulders. Not a man to mess with.

'Back in a minute.'

He bent down and kissed the boy on the top of his head, a gesture that seemed all the more tender coming from such a big man.

As Alicia watched him leave, Jayne caught her eye and smiled.

'He's a lovely baby,' she said, nodding at Kob.

'Thank you,' Alicia smiled.

'Mind if I sit with you for a moment?'

Alicia gestured at the chair Leroy had vacated.

'I'm Jayne Keeney.'

'Where you from?'

'Australia.'

'I'm Alicia,' she smiled, 'and this beautiful boy is my son Jesse.'

Jayne offered the boy a finger and he toyed with her silver ring.

'Actually, that's why I wanted to talk to you. It's about the boy.'

Alicia felt a sinking feeling in the pit of her stomach.

'What do you mean?'

'I'm a private investigator,' Jayne said. 'As painful as it must be for you to hear this, that little boy should never have been adopted. His name is Kamolsert, or Kob, and he was stolen from his Thai mother.'

'How dare you.'

She snatched Jesse away from Jayne's grasp. He startled and began to cry.

'See what you've done,' she hissed. 'Shh, there, there, my darling.'

Alicia held Kob over her shoulder and patted his back. Her mind raced with possibilities. Could there really be a problem with Jesse's adoption? They were led to believe the system was beyond reproach—another reason they'd chosen to adopt from Thailand and not Africa or South America where baby trafficking was rife.

No, nothing could go wrong. Not now. Not after all they'd been through. God wouldn't do that to them. God wanted them to have Jesse.

It had to be a shakedown. The Thais, infamous for their scams, were getting more sophisticated, even involving Australians.

Alicia faced the woman squarely and narrowed her eyes.

'I don't know who you think you are or what you think you're doing, but you should know my husband is an ex-Marine and he don't take kindly to blackmail.'

'Blackmail?' Jayne sat back in her seat. 'No, it's nothing like that—'

'We got papers,' Alicia cut her off. 'We got papers to show Jesse's mom is dead. We got proof he's ours.'

Jesse continued to cry. Alicia scooped up the pacifier from the table and put it in his mouth.

'Shh, it's okay my boy.'

'The mother's death certificate is a fake,' Jayne said, speaking quickly and quietly. 'The people at the New Life Children's Centre, Frank Harding and the Thai doctor, have got a racket going. They take babies placed in the centre's temporary care and turn them into orphans. They told Kob's mother he was dead. Faked his death certificate, too.'

'How come nobody at the US Embassy said anything?'

'They haven't been briefed yet. I'm helping the police put together the evidence to take to the embassy and—'

'No, no,' Alicia shook her head. 'This is all part of a trick. You can't fool me. I've been in Thailand before. Let me guess, the momma wants money and then she'll call off the cops, right?'

'The mother just wants her son back.'

Alicia sprang to her feet, drew herself up to her full height of five feet eleven inches and thrust out her chest.

'He's *my* son now,' she said. 'A good mother would never allow anyone to take her baby. I'm not about to lose mine.'

Jayne looked up at her.

'Look I know this must be hard for you. But, please, meet with the mother. Hear her side of the story. She'll be in Bangkok in the next day or two.' Jayne reached into her bag and placed her business card on the table. 'Here are my contact details. Call me anytime.'

Alicia watched her leave, picked up the card and shoved it in her back pocket as Leroy reappeared. He handed her a bottle of infant formula and clapped his hands to take hold of Jesse.

'He been cryin'?'

'He's just hungry,' she said, handing him over.

'Good thing Daddy's brought a bottle for his baby boy,' Leroy chirped.

Alicia realised her knees were shaking and sank back down on the couch, fighting panic. Leroy, focused on Jesse, was oblivious to her distress. She made a spur of the moment decision not to tell her husband what had happened.

She shook the bottle, removed the cap and handed it back to Leroy. Jesse reached for the milk and settled into his father's arms to drink.

Alicia gazed at her husband and son, forced herself to breathe, willed her heartbeat to slow down. Jesse sucked away at the milk, one hand on his bottle, the other reaching for the silvery hair poking out from the top of Leroy's shirt.

Alicia felt a wave of love and, hot on its heels, a surge of anger.

How dare anyone seek to discredit their family. It was disgraceful. Alicia would not stand for it.

'Honey, I know you said we need to watch what we spend,' she said, placing her arm around Leroy's shoulders. 'But do you think we could move to the Hilton for the last couple of nights as a treat? I mean, nothin's too good for our beautiful boy, right?'

She would stay one step ahead of the extortionists and by the time they cottoned on, she'd have her son far away, safe and sound.

36

Jayne slept fitfully, woke before her alarm, made her way in the dark to the Southern Bus Terminal. She arrived with twenty minutes to spare, the bus already idling in the departure dock. Despite the chill of the air-conditioning and the rousing smell of diesel, she fell asleep on the bus before it pulled out and didn't wake until they arrived in Kanchanaburi.

As she descended, she was swamped by a horde of dark, scrawny men offering tours to the Bridge on the River Kwai. She waved them aside and found a place that made fresh coffee, rural style, filtered through a calico bag and brewed in a stainless steel jug until it was thick and strong, served in a glass over two fingers of sweetened condensed milk. She chased it down with a bowl of rice noodle soup, as salty as the coffee was sweet.

Over her second coffee and first cigarette, Jayne reflected on her encounter with Alicia King. While the first to admit she knew nothing about being a parent, let alone an adoptive one, Jayne was surprised by Alicia's proprietary air, given Kob had been in her custody less than a week. Jayne had expected shock, denial, defensiveness in reaction to the revelations of fraud. She hadn't expected Alicia to accuse her of extortion. Did the American woman even care whether the adoption was legitimate?

Alicia was preparing to fight; Jayne could only hope that Mayuree was up to it.

She left the café and hailed a *samlor*—literally 'three wheels'—a kind of bicycle-rickshaw obsolete in Bangkok. Jayne directed the driver to Mayuree's address and climbed behind him. The bench seat was upholstered in blue and yellow vinyl with a cover that looked like the hood of a pram.

The gentle pace of the *samlor* gave her a feel for Kanchanaburi town, which after Bangkok and Pattaya belonged to another era. Gigantic trees dominated the skyline, the street signs were in the shape of fish, and no building in the town appeared taller than three storeys.

Rajiv had included information on the area with her bus ticket. She found a map and figured they were headed northwest, tracing the path of the Kwae Yai—the River Kwai. Mayuree's family home was located close to the town's most famous tourist attraction. The *samlor* driver pulled over in front of a freestanding shop-house on the main road. Mayuree must have been waiting for her. By the time Jayne paid the fare, the Thai woman was at her elbow, ushering her down the side of the house to a shaded garden at the back.

'The cleaner comes today,' she said by way of explanation. 'It's easier if we stay out of her way.'

Jayne nodded, though she neither saw nor heard any movement inside the house.

'My parents are not home,' Mayuree added. 'My mother thinks my father is visiting relatives, but he is really attending cockfights at a Mon village near the Burma border.' She allowed a tiny smile. 'My mother has gone to the temple. She's been going twice every day since Kob...since he was taken from me. I think she's trying to build up merit to pacify the *phi am* of the grandson she rejected.'

'*Phi am?*'

'She's been having trouble breathing. She thinks Kob's ghost is haunting her, sitting on her chest as she sleeps.'

'So you haven't told her he's alive?'

'Sister, to be honest, I'm not sure I dare believe it.'

'Oh, he's alive all right,' Jayne said.

She put a photo of Kob on the table between them, the same one she'd already mailed to Mayuree.

'This is not all we have,' she said. 'I've been investigating an adoption scam connected to the New Life Children's Centre.'

Mayuree nodded. They'd gone over this on the phone.

'I had reason to believe Kob was handed over to an American couple. Last night I traced them to a hotel in Bangkok near the US Embassy. And Kob was with them. I saw him with my own eyes.'

'And he was okay?'

'He was fine.'

'That's wonderful—' Mayuree began. 'But why are you telling me this? Why haven't you brought my son back to me? Where's my baby now?'

'Still with the Americans.'

'Didn't you explain to them—'

'Of course I did.'

'And?'

'They didn't believe me. They thought I was trying to blackmail them.'

Mayuree buried her face in her hands and shook her head.

'They've applied for a visa to take him to America,' Jayne said. 'The embassy is closed for Chinese New Year until tomorrow. We still have time to get to them. But you have to confront them, Mayuree. You're the only one who can get Kob back.'

Mayuree thought about her little son in the arms of strangers and felt *sia jai*. 'Sorry' in English, but much stronger in Thai. Not merely sorry. The heart was altogether lost.

'We'll take the bus to Bangkok today,' Jayne was saying. 'You need to bring as much evidence as you can—things that belonged to Kob, photos of the two of you together, messages addressed to both of you—anything that helps prove you're his mother.'

Mayuree thought of her bag tumbling from the motorbike as she left Pattaya, splitting open as it hit the ground. Her heart sank further.

She took her hands away from her face and looked at Jayne. 'I'm not sure I have anything left.'

'It doesn't matter. Your family and friends can swear that you're Kob's mother and didn't consent to his adoption. I know a lawyer who can help with that stuff free-of-charge. The most important thing is for you and Kob to be reunited. No one will be able to refute your claims once they see the two of you together.'

They sat in the dappled sunlight of the garden for a moment without speaking.

'How can you be so sure?' Mayuree said, staring at the ground.

'What do you mean?'

'I mean maybe Kob's already forgotten me. I wasn't a good mother to him. I left him with strangers. I didn't protect him. I *lost* him.'

'That's not true—'

Mayuree cut her off. 'You don't understand, Khun Jayne. You don't know me. Kob is better off where he is now. He's destined for a rich country with two parents to care for him. *Laew teh duang.* Thai people believe it always comes down to fate.'

Mayuree didn't look up but she heard her farang companion groan and mutter something in English.

'Do you mind if I smoke?' Jayne asked.

'Please.'

Jayne lit a cigarette, drew back and exhaled in a long, smoky sigh.

'Look, maybe I'm just a farang who doesn't understand Thai culture. But with all due respect, I think what you just said is *bullshit.*'

The English expletive gave Mayuree a jolt. She raised her head. Jayne was seated in profile to her, colour in her cheeks.

'You love your son, sister, and he loves you. I know you tried to spend time with him, resisted the pressure to give him up. I saw your apartment in Pattaya and the effort you made to keep it clean and welcoming for him. I know the long hours you worked in order to build a future for him.'

She turned to face Mayuree.

'I don't know you well but I know enough. You're a good mother, Mayuree, and Kob's rightful place is with you. And if you're going to call it fate, make sure you've read it correctly that it's your fate to let someone steal Kob away rather than stand up and fight for him.'

She butted out her unfinished cigarette.

Mayuree struggled to contain her emotions. No one had ever told her she was a good mother. She felt the strong beat of a heart she thought was lost.

'This lawyer who will help me free-of-charge. Is that because she's no good?'

For the first time since she arrived, Jayne smiled.

'On the contrary, people like you and me could never afford her fees. She owes me a favour. So you'll come to Bangkok with me?'

'Can you give me a few hours?'

Jayne glanced at her watch. 'Think you can make the three o'clock bus?'

Mayuree nodded.

Jayne took out her phone, hesitated.

'There's one other thing I need to know, sister,' she said. 'Where's Sumet?'

37

Sumet paused by the pond at the base of the Little Hill Cave Temple to watch a father and his infant daughter try to coax fat, indolent carp to eat the pellets they proffered. It was an exercise in merit-making to feed the fish, but the carp were not obliging. An old woman was faring better at a nearby shrine, where an ancient monk muttered blessings over her bowed head. On the ground between them was a cloth laid out with offerings of incense, candles and flowers. Sumet recalled how it grated on Maryanne that women and monks were forbidden to touch.

Not even to be allowed to pass something directly to a monk without making him unclean, he could hear her say. *How's that supposed to make me feel?*

It's because women are so much more powerful than men, he told her ghost. *Surely you can see that now.*

But in death as in life, she wouldn't see reason. She was too strong-willed—part of what Sumet found attractive about her. Had his sister Mayuree been more like Maryanne, she would never have allowed herself to get into the trouble she did. The problem for Sumet was never Maryanne's character. The problem was one of fit.

Phit fah, phit tua, as the saying goes. 'Wrong lid, wrong box.'

Maryanne's behaviour was at odds with what was expected of women in Thailand. She was neither patient nor accommodating. She was passionate, laughed out loud and treated everyone as an intimate friend. While Sumet might be able to tolerate this, others would not. She didn't belong in Thailand and never would.

Maybe Sumet didn't belong in Australia either, but he could adapt. Sumet was used to farangs whereas Maryanne, by her own admission, had grown up in a part of Australia where there were no Asians. For these reasons, he should've been able to convince her that the best option for them once they married was to live in Australia, not Thailand. But she wouldn't listen.

During one of their more heated exchanges, he bit back the urge to ask what good there was in marrying a farang if it meant having to stay in Thailand.

Sumet had lived with his parents in a Kanchanaburi shop-house with ceiling fans, cold running water and a kitchen on the back veranda. He'd supplemented his paltry teacher's wage with work as a tour guide and translator. His family had no political connections, nothing to get him ahead in life. But he was good looking and spoke English well, which made him a good catch. At least, that's what the older Australian woman who took him to bed after one memorable tour told him. So when his sister called to ask for help with the new baby, Sumet followed her to Pattaya, where he could meet a nice, wealthy farang girl.

Mayuree told him about the orphanage where farang girls volunteered, and he advertised his services there as a Thai language teacher, sure that only very wealthy people could afford to work for nothing. When Maryanne answered his ad, he thought his prayers had been heard. She was sexy and fun and her family was rich. Sumet figured once they moved to Australia, with her contacts and his language skills, it wouldn't take long to get him a job in the family business. He would be able to buy everything they wanted, even a car. After a while he would send for Mayuree and Kob. He had it all planned.

But Maryanne refused to live in Australia. *We've got love*, she'd say. *That's all we need.*

Sumet knew for a fact it never was, but he was in too deep to walk away. He grew desperate as he glimpsed a future in which his responsibilities increased but not his income.

Since Maryanne wouldn't listen to reason, he had to play on her fears. He didn't want to, but he was starting to panic. He came up with an idea to undermine her confidence, leave her off-balance enough to lean on him for support. In her vulnerable state he'd convince her they were better off in Australia. No one was supposed to get hurt.

But Sumet's plan went horribly wrong, leaving him with a *phi tai hong tong klom*—most fearsome of ghosts—at his back, and a karmic debt it would take the rest of this lifetime as a monk to atone for.

He turned his back on the pilgrims and made his way past the gold Chinese lions that guarded the entrance—the male on the left playing with a ball, the female on the right with a paw on her cub—and headed up the hill to his place of meditation.

The name Tiger Cave Temple suggested a secret refuge concealed by dense jungle where a man on the run might hide out undiscovered for years. So when, after a twenty-minute ride from Kanchanaburi town, her motorcycle taxi driver pulled over at the foot of a hill behind several tour buses on a stretch lined with crowded restaurants, Jayne thought she was in the wrong place. The driver assured her that this was Wat Tham Seua.

A steep green and gold *naga* staircase leading to the summit was swarming with Chinese New Year holidaymakers posing for photos with the temple's great terracotta tiled *chedi* tower in the background. A meandering path off to the right offered a less crowded climb. Jayne passed half-constructed shrines, picnic platforms, a peacock aviary, and a nondescript gash in the hillside sign-posted as the entrance to the Tiger Cave. She emerged near the summit opposite a snack stand. Grateful to live in a country where no site was too sacred to serve refreshments, she purchased a plastic bag of iced tea and sipped it through a straw as she sauntered up a short flight of stairs to the main terrace.

The vision that greeted her was a lustrous gold Buddha large enough to cradle a ten-year-old child in the palm of his outstretched hand. His crossed legs rested on a platform of concrete lotus petals, and at his feet was a giant alms bowl fed either side by a conveyor belt.

A row of vendors opposite the Buddha sold flowers, incense, candles and coins. Jayne watched as a Thai woman and her child fed a stack of baht coins into the little metal dishes attached at regular intervals to the conveyor belt, which transported and deposited these offerings into the oversized alms bowl. Low-tech, high-kitsch, gloriously Thai.

To the left of the Buddha was a gaudily painted concrete tiger with a big head. To the right was a Bodhi tree hung with brass bells and coloured sashes. Beyond the tree a terrace opened on to a breathtaking vista of the Mae Klong

River valley and Kanchanaburi town in the distance.

Jayne could have lingered, but the monks in yellow, orange and ochre robes arranged like a string of marigolds on a nearby bench reminded her of her purpose. She approached a young man at one end of the row.

'*Phra ka*,' she said, using the honorific reserved for monks, nobility and Buddha images. 'Can you help me? I've come to see *Phra* Sumet. His sister Mayuree sent me.'

'You'll find him at Wat Tham Khao Noi,' the young monk said. 'He goes there to meditate.'

He gestured into the distance, and Jayne realised he was referring to a pagoda on top of another hill.

She nudged her way through the crowds on the *naga* staircase and descended to find her *motercy* driver. He ferried her as far as the base of Wat Tham Khao Noi, which although its name translated as Little Hill Cave Temple, was another steep climb. She followed a path that passed through buildings guarded by fierce stone warriors and connected with a staircase that zigzagged towards the summit, its balustrades formed by sculpted dragons spewing water.

As she neared the top, she paused on a small sheltered balcony to wipe the sweat from her face. The view looked away from the river over ripening rice paddies dotted with white herons to limestone cliffs beyond. Branches of frangipani trees stretched towards her like hands. There was hardly a sound, just birds and the breeze. This was more like the quiet retreat she'd imagined for Sumet.

Reluctantly she turned from the view to ascend the last steps to the pagoda and found herself face-to-face with a young monk whose resemblance to Mayuree was unmistakable. He had the same heart-shaped face and almond eyes but he was prettier than his sister. His smile turned his eyes into little half-moons and revealed straight white teeth. There was far more stubble on his head than on his chin. He looked so innocent, Jayne almost felt guilty for what she was about to do.

'*Phra* Sumet?' she said.

The man's smiled wavered but he nodded. He sat down on one of the bench seats lining the balcony and gestured for her to take the seat opposite.

'*Phra*, my name is Jayne Keeney,' she began. 'I'm a private detective. I'm trying to help your sister to get her son back.'

Sumet nodded.

'I was actually hired by the father of Maryanne Delbeck to look into her death.'

He blanched, nodded again.

'You don't seem surprised to see me?'

'I've been expecting you.'

He had a sweet, almost childish voice.

'Did Mayuree warn you I was coming?'

'No,' he said. 'I should say I wasn't exactly expecting *you*, Khun Jayne. But I knew it could only be a matter of time before someone came.'

'Why are you hiding, *Phra* Sumet?'

'Because people will think I killed Maryanne.'

'Why would people think that?'

'I cannot talk about it,' he said, smoothing his robes.

Jayne knew there were dos and don'ts required of monks.

'Is it about sex?' she whispered.

He coloured and shook his head.

'Money?'

He nodded.

'Maryanne's money—did she give it to you?'

276

He nodded again.

'She gave it to me for safe keeping,' he whispered. 'She worried her father would take it back once she told him about us.'

'Told him what about you?'

'That we were going to get married.'

'And were you really going to marry Maryanne, *Phra* Sumet?'

'I wanted to with all my heart.' He stared out over the rice paddies. 'But then she died and I was left with…'

'Her money.'

He nodded. 'People will think I killed her for it. So I ran away.'

'Where's the money now?'

'I cannot talk about it.'

Jayne felt her cultural sensitivity radar short-circuiting.

'Surely you don't want the police to come and arrest you, disrobe you in front of all the *Sangha* and take you into custody, just so you can talk about Maryanne's money?'

Sumet rubbed the patches of stubble where his eyebrows had been.

'Most went to the police in Pattaya to keep my name out of the report. I gave the rest to the temple.'

'Minus what you paid Chaowalit to scare Maryanne, you mean.'

Sumet swallowed hard, his Adam's apple pressing the closely shaved skin of his throat.

'That was a mistake.'

'I won't argue with you there,' Jayne said. 'You know none of this looks good.'

Sumet bowed his head, contemplating his situation.

'Where's Maryanne's diary?' she said.

He tightened his grip on the shoulder strap of his *yahm*, a square bag cut from the same cloth as his monk's robes.

'*Mai khao jai*,' he whimpered.

'I think you understand exactly what I'm talking about,' Jayne said. 'The diary, *Phra* Sumet.'

She held out her hand.

He opened his mouth to protest, closed it, and angled his body away from her. In keeping with rules prohibiting monks and women from touching, he took a small package wrapped in a white *pha biang* from his bag, turned back to Jayne and placed it on the bench between them.

Jayne loosened the scarf to reveal a blue notebook. Maryanne had listed her contact details, passport number and email address on the front page. There was also a note in English and Thai offering a reward for the diary's safe return.

'You've read it.'

It wasn't a question. Sumet pressed his chin to his chest.

'Did you kill her?'

He shook his head and laughed the way Thai people did to mask their distress. 'I don't know.'

'What do you mean?'

'I don't know. I feel responsible for what happened. Does this mean I killed her?'

'Did you push her off the hotel roof?'

'No,' he said, his voice steady.

'Then what happened?'

'She lost her balance. She was getting headaches, feeling dizzy, especially at night. She should never have climbed up there and I...I couldn't reach her in time.' He looked up, tears welling in his eyes. 'The look on her face when she fell: she was so scared.'

Jayne looked away. She'd expected Sumet to be a young gold-digger with a swagger and a jaded take on how all farang women were crazy. She'd come to their meeting fully intending to see him charged with obstructing justice, if not manslaughter. Instead, she found herself pitying this haunted monk.

It crossed her mind that it could be an act, albeit a convincing one.

'Can anyone else verify the headaches and dizziness?' she said.

Sumet sniffed. 'It's in the diary. And she mentioned it to the doctor in Pattaya.'

'Doctor Somsri?'

'No, Maryanne avoided him. She didn't want anyone connected with the centre to know about the baby. She saw another doctor, a woman.'

'Baby?' Jayne said. 'What baby?'

The monk gave her a sad smile. 'Our baby.'

Sumet watched as Jayne headed uphill towards the pagoda. Having come this far, she told him, she might as well go all the way to the summit and the temple. Her determination and bravado reminded him of Maryanne, but Jayne was tougher, wouldn't scare as easily. After all, she was a seasoned private investigator: the only person to have connected him to Maryanne's death.

It surprised him that she wanted to keep his name out of a revised verdict, but Sumet had given up trying to understand farang women. He was simply grateful to spare his parents the scandal of being linked to a dead farang, and avoid the media scrutiny that would inevitably expose his sister and her bastard child. He told himself this was why he'd fled to the monastery in the first place: to protect his family. But he was flattering himself.

The temple was the only safe place for Sumet. Maryanne's ghost would not let him off as lightly as Jayne had done. A *phi tai hong tong klom* by its very nature could never do that. It was bad enough to be a *phi tai hong*, a spirit shocked into being through sudden, violent death, but to die young and pregnant as well—that doubled the ghost's power. Only by donning the robes of a monk and living in the sanctuary of a temple could Sumet stand any chance of surviving in the presence of a spirit that strong.

He gathered the hem of his robes and made his way back down the stairs, the ghosts of his former lover and unborn child riding on his shoulders.

38

Jayne gave up trying to read the diary on the motorbike ride back to Kanchanaburi. She asked the driver to take her to a nearby floating restaurant—an open-sided bamboo raft with a thatched roof—moored on the riverbank in view of the famous bridge. She ordered a soda with lemon, lit a cigarette, opened the notebook and began to read.

Maryanne's diary was a combination of travelogue and self-analysis, written in a style similar to her letters home: naïve, a little clumsy, at times conceited. But Jayne found qualities to admire.

She scanned the initial reflections on Pattaya—'sleazy', 'gross' and 'not what I expected'—paying more attention to the descriptions of her work at the New Life Children's Centre and the people she met. Frank was 'totally dedicated', Connie 'hard working and serious', the other volunteers 'nice people but mostly older than me and a bit stand-offish'. The children were 'adorable'. Her impression was that Maryanne might not have accepted the post if she'd known what Pattaya was like. But she enjoyed the nature of her work at the centre and tried hard to get along with everyone. Perhaps too hard.

Sumet first rated a mention on Monday 3 June 1996

when she answered his ad for Thai language lessons. He walked into their meeting carrying his nephew Kob, making a favourable impression. Within a week, they'd gone on a date. It was Sunday, and Maryanne mentioned that Mayuree usually spent Sundays with her son. Jane tore a strip of paper from her notebook and marked the page as evidence to build up Mayuree's case against the Kings.

A week later Maryanne and Sumet were dating again. Maryanne admired Sumet for standing by his sister and helping care for her baby. She was also attracted to him. *'I think Sumet likes me but it's hard to tell,'* she wrote on Sunday 23 June. *'Thai people are so polite. I think he wanted to kiss me yesterday. I know I wanted to kiss him.'*

A week later they did kiss, late at night on Jomtien beach. Reading between the lines, Jayne figured Mayuree must have spent the night with her son, leaving Sumet free to pursue the budding romance. The following day, Maryanne checked out of the serviced apartment the centre had chosen for her, and moved into the Bayview Hotel because she *'needed more privacy'*.

The following weekend, in her bed at the Bayview Hotel, she and Sumet had sex for the first time—ever, for Maryanne.

At last I feel normal. What a relief! I was so sick of saying no, and for what reason?—Because I might die and go to Hell for having sex outside of marriage? If my time in Thailand has taught me anything it's that God has more important things to worry about.

I wonder if Sumet knew it was my first time.

I feel amazing. I think I'm in love!

The journal entry was dated '*Sun 7/07/96 – 3 am.*' There was something endearing at the thought of Maryanne sneaking out of bed to record the event while Sumet slept. Jayne experienced her first genuine twinge of sorrow for the life that was lost in the fourteen-storey fall from the Bayview Hotel rooftop.

Maryanne appeared to settle into a routine. Monday to Friday she worked at the centre, first in the orphanage and later with the boarders. Sundays were spent with Sumet, mostly in bed. Jayne skimmed over the graphic details.

Maryanne and Sumet occasionally went out to dinner during the week, usually with Kob in tow, and sometimes saw each other at night when Mayuree wasn't working. Whatever the case, Maryanne's feelings for Sumet eclipsed everything else around her.

Sad news this morning. I arrived at work to learn that eight-month-old Koong, one of the boarders in the nursery, had died overnight, apparently from some kind of blood disorder (maybe AIDS-related?). It was sudden, though he'd always been a bit on the scrawny side.

I love working with the babies, but it's a good reminder not to get too involved. Like they taught us at uni, you have to maintain a professional distance or else you burn out too quickly and are no use to anyone.

Frank's said the centre will help pay for the funeral. Apparently cremation is the done thing in Thailand. I'll probably go along to pay my respects, unless they hold it on Sunday. Sumet and I don't get enough time alone together as it is.

Her mention of the death of another infant a month later was little more than a passing observation, wedged between a lexicon of words and phrases she was learning in Thai, and more lengthy descriptions of what she and Sumet got up to in bed.

Despite Jayne's initial suspicions, there appeared to be no connection between Maryanne's death and the adoption racket at the New Life Children's Centre. Maryanne took the explanation of the infant deaths on face value and didn't question them, preoccupied as she was with Sumet.

They were planning to get married, and hot on the heels of this decision came the suspicion she might be pregnant. In a diary entry dated Tues 27 August, Maryanne noted that her period was late *'and I'm NEVER late'*. She was concerned how Sumet might react, but hoped it wouldn't matter as they'd already decided to get married.

'Sumet told me women in Thai villages often get pregnant first just to prove they can, then marry in a hurry,' she wrote. *'Maybe this will happen to us.'*

Maryanne took a pregnancy test the following week with a positive result. She was thrilled and so was Sumet. After breaking the news to him, she wrote in her diary, *'This is the happiest day of my life.'*

The diary proved that Jim Delbeck's instincts were right about his daughter: Maryanne had never been suicidal. Her death was a regrettable accident. Jayne should have been able to hand over the diary and close the case. But it wasn't that simple.

Monday 16 September 1996

Sumet and I had our first argument last night. I want to live in Thailand after we get married. Turns out he assumed we'd be moving in with my parents in Australia. As if.

I'm in two minds about whether I want to see the look on Dad's face when he learns that his first grandchild is going to be half-Asian. The shock would serve him right for being such a racist.

On the other hand, why would I want to put myself or Sumet through that? I'm not sure I ever want to take my Thai husband and our baby anywhere near my family home. They live in Ipswich, for God's sake, the heartland of Pauline Hanson, the woman who stood up in Parliament last week and said she believed Australia was "in danger of being swamped by Asians". It's all over the papers here.

I tried explaining this to Sumet but I'm not sure he understands. I mean, he understands what I'm saying—his English is excellent—but I'm not sure he believes me. It's hard to talk about what's going on in Australia. It makes me feel ashamed.

In Thailand mixed race children are considered beautiful and lucky. They call them look kreung *or 'half-and-half kids'. All the top Thai models and actors are* look kreung. *As I said to Sumet, I want our baby to grow up in a country where his or her ethnic mix is celebrated, not condemned.*

If he met my father he'd understand. No doubt Dad would use the occasion to crack a few racist jokes about 'gooks' and 'slopes', egged on by Ian in his usual role as Dad's arse-licker. And Mum would do her usual thing of keeping her mouth shut for the sake of a quiet life.

I can't trust them to see Sumet for the beautiful, gentle, caring man he is. They'd see him as one of those Asians they risk getting 'swamped by'.

Sumet worries too much about money. He thinks that

he won't be able to provide for me. It's a big part of his motivation for moving to Australia. I don't care about that stuff and I don't expect him to provide for me. I can find work here in Thailand teaching English. In fact, it's a lot easier for me to find work here than it would be for Sumet to find work in Australia.

Maybe I'll get to prove myself once we visit his family in Kanchanaburi. It sounds like such a nice place and I really like the idea of living there.

I wonder if Dad will disown me.

Sunday 22 September 1996

Sumet and I had another argument about Australia last night. I thought given his parents' attitude to poor Mayuree and her baby, he'd have a bit more empathy. But he doesn't seem to believe it's that bad. Perhaps I should take him home to meet the family. Then he'd see for himself. But I really don't want to and anyway we can't afford the airfares.

I could ask Dad for the money I suppose, though I wouldn't put it past him to refuse to pay for Sumet's ticket, even if we married. And I wouldn't go without Sumet— no way!

Maybe I should blackmail Dad, offer to spare him the humiliation of having to introduce his 'slope' son-in-law and 'half-caste' grandchild to all his One Nation voting mates in exchange for paying us to stay in Thailand.

I'm tempted to cut all ties with my family, make a fresh start. It would upset Mum, but it might also give her an incentive to crawl out from under her rock. I reckon she'd visit us once the baby is born, even if meant lying to Dad about where she was going.

On the other hand, maybe it would force Dad to

confront his prejudices to see his darling daughter happily married to a Thai man.

I wish I could trust him more.

And I wish Sumet would just accept that I'm happy to live in Thailand. I'm tired of arguing. We go round and round in circles about the same things, over and over again.

Speaking of circles, I've been getting a lot of headaches over the last week. Dizzy spells, too. Once or twice I stood up too quickly and almost passed out. Dr Apiradee says these are normal symptoms for the first trimester of pregnancy, and I should consider myself lucky I don't have morning sickness. But I feel so tired.

I wish I could tell someone else about the baby, but if word got out—and it would, the Thais are terrible gossips— I'd lose my job at the centre, and I need to keep working there for as long as possible. It's awful, but I make more from my volunteer allowance than Sumet used to earn as a teacher.

We need all the money we can get, especially if we're going to rent our own place. I mean, I'm keen to visit Sumet's family but I don't want to live with them.

Thurs 26 September 1996

After what seems like weeks of fighting, Sumet and I had a lovely time last night. Romantic dinner followed by a moonlight walk along Jomtien Beach, where we first kissed, first told each other 'I love you'. I can't believe it was only three months ago!

If someone told me when I left Australia that within a few months I would fall in love with a beautiful Thai man and be having his baby, I wouldn't have believed it. But here I am, and I couldn't be happier.

287

Within five days of writing this, Maryanne was dead.

Jayne closed the diary and let it fall on to the table, imagining the ripples it sent through the floor of the floating restaurant.

She phoned Police Major General Wichit and briefed him on her find.

'I can't fathom how something as significant as Maryanne's pregnancy could have been left out of the autopsy reports,' she said.

'It wasn't. I have the Thai report here—' she heard the shuffling of papers '—and it's on page two: deceased was approximately eight weeks pregnant at the time of death, foetus normal.'

'Well, it didn't rate a mention in the English version. A significant detail to get lost in translation, don't you think?'

Police Major General Wichit cleared his throat. 'Perhaps my colleagues in Pattaya didn't deem it relevant to the autopsy findings in light of Doctor Somsri's testimony regarding Maryanne's mental health.'

'Which we now know to be false. I'm guessing Somsri fabricated the depression to account for Maryanne's death— to keep Chaowalit out of it and protect his standover man.'

'Highly likely,' Wichit said. 'But at the time my colleagues had no reason to doubt the word of a doctor.'

'Surely Maryanne's pregnancy had a bearing on their findings?'

'Not so much as to change the verdict. The police had the corpse of a young girl, unmarried, pregnant and reportedly suffering from mental instability. In other words, a classic suicide.'

'Then surely they would have mentioned the pregnancy to corroborate their case.'

'Perhaps whoever finalised the translation dismissed that as a minor detail in order to spare the girl's family.'

'Minor detail?' Jayne spluttered. 'How could someone make that sort of judgment call? If I were Maryanne's parents I'd be outraged.'

'But you're not a parent, Jayne, and it might interest you to know that in similar circumstances the authorities in your country issue two death certificates: one does not specify cause of death so can be used for administrative purposes without causing families distress.'

Wichit was pulling rank on her in more ways than one.

'I believe my colleagues acted with the best of intentions based on the available evidence.' he added. 'Of course, if Maryanne's parents wish to lodge a formal complaint—'

'They don't know about it yet. I haven't had time to tell them. And...'

'And?'

'I haven't figured out what to say.'

'Hmm.'

She could picture him nodding.

'I'm worried what Maryanne's father might do to Sumet. I want to keep him out of it.'

'So perhaps you can empathise with whoever edited the English version of the autopsy report after all?'

That it was a question not a statement gave him away. She knew it was Wichit himself who'd made that judgment call, and that he was thinking of his own daughter when he did it.

'My client has a right to know his daughter didn't commit suicide.'

'Of course.'

There was another moment's silence.

'If Chaowalit makes a sworn statement that he witnessed Maryanne fall, we can get a revised verdict of accidental death without the diary and without bringing Sumet into it,' Wichit said. 'We can let sleeping dogs lie, yes?'

This idiom translated into Thai sounded stranger than most because Thais only ever associated dogs with people as an insult. Jayne smiled in spite of herself.

'I need to think about it,' she said.

39

With more than an hour before she was due to meet Mayuree at the bus depot, Jayne summoned a waiter and asked for a beer, a packet of cigarettes and a plate of *pad thai*, in that order.

She sipped the beer, smoked a cigarette and leafed through the diary. The simplest course of action was to hand it to Maryanne's father. He'd employed Jayne to prove his daughter hadn't committed suicide, and the diary would make him feel vindicated.

But that's not all it would do to him: the truths it contained might do serious damage. Then again, if Jim Delbeck were the racist prick the diary suggested, why should Jayne care? On one level, it would be satisfying to drop those bombshells on Maryanne's behalf.

The arrival of the fried noodles provided a distraction, but she only managed to pick at the food. She pushed aside the plate and lit another cigarette. A motorised long-tail boat raced along the river, ferrying a group of tourists towards the bridge. Water lapped at the raft in its wake and the restaurant rocked.

Jayne remembered Rajiv's notes and fished them out

of her bag. He had customised a guide to Kanchanaburi for her, photocopying items of interest from travel guides, history books, newspapers and magazines. Jayne failed to understand why he kept trying to please her when she treated him so badly. At the same time, she felt guilty he wasn't there with her. Kanchanaburi was his kind of place.

To punish herself, she read every page of his notes. She learned that Kanchanaburi province, known as Thailand's Wild West, boasted some of the country's highest waterfalls and largest sanctuaries, where elephants and even tigers roamed in the wild. Signs of human habitation dated back ten thousand years, and in the thirteenth century Kanchanaburi had been an outpost of the mighty Angkor empire. While the Thais visited for the spectacular scenery and floating discos, the major attraction for Western tourists was the province's World War II history. Under the command of the Japanese Imperial Army, some 16,000 Australian, British, Dutch and American prisoners of war had died building the Death Railway from Thailand to Burma. Their stories were commemorated with museums and monuments from Kanchanaburi Town to as far away as Hellfire Pass in the province's northwest, their remains interred at two Allied War Cemeteries.

More than 70,000 Asian labourers also died building the Death Railway, press-ganged from colonial Malaya, Burma, Thailand and what is now Indonesia. There were no monuments to them, only a mass grave allegedly covered by an orchard of limes and banana trees.

Jayne put down the notes. Did she have the right to punish Jim Delbeck for being racist when even here Asians were treated as second-class citizens? And what about Maryanne? Though she lamented her father's racism, she wasn't above prejudice herself. No one ever was. And it was inconclusive from her journal entries whether she intended her relationship with Sumet to drive a wedge between her and her father, or to test his love.

Jayne checked her watch and signalled for the bill. A light breeze sent her notes drifting to the floor. She gathered them up, put them into her bag and reached for the diary. The front cover had blown open, revealing Maryanne's name and contact details. Jayne stared at it for a moment, picked up her phone and called Rajiv.

From the moment Uncle returned to the bookshop, he'd been on a mission to subvert Rajiv's carefully computerised system and restore his own eclectic regime. It started with small acts of resistance—moving the keyboard aside to make room for his receipt pad, pens and carbon paper, 'forgetting' to return books to the shelves so they amassed in piles on the front desk—and soon developed into a full-scale rebellion. Rajiv arrived one morning to find towering stacks of books where a shelving unit had been and the computer disconnected at the wall. He turned the computer back on but his efforts to enter data were frustrated by tacky keys. Something had been spilled on the keyboard. Sabotage.

After an hour spent trying to consolidate records without use of the letter 's', Rajiv was ready to tear his hair out when Jayne called. Mumbling something about a new keyboard to his uncle, he excused himself for the rest of the afternoon. Uncle smiled and squeezed his shoulder as if he couldn't be happier.

Jayne gave Rajiv a précis of the contents of Maryanne's diary, including Maryanne's email address. She asked him to access it, gave him a list of possible passwords and said she would call again once she got back to Bangkok. There was no small talk, no reference to their previous conversation. She told him nothing about Kanchanaburi and he knew better than to ask.

He took it as a good sign that she called; he was useful to her, maybe indispensable. It brought him closer to realising his ambition of becoming her partner in the detective business—a partnership he needed to secure sooner rather than later, given the return of Uncle.

He had to tread lightly. Jayne was fiercely independent and the notion that his skills were important to the business had to come from her. He needed to earn her respect without making her resent him.

At the same time, Rajiv needed to stand up for himself. He'd put up with being treated badly in light of the traumatic events in Pattaya. But he couldn't let her walk all over him.

Trouble was, Rajiv felt himself falling in love with Jayne. The full force of his feelings struck him when he saw her unconscious in the hospital. He wanted to win her over, but as his actions on that fateful night in Pattaya had shown, Rajiv wasn't romantic hero material. Not for him the lead role in *The Ramayana*, the Thai version of which, *The Ramakien*, he was currently reading to see how it differed from the Indian epic poem. He was no warrior-hero like Rama or his brother Lakshman. What Rajiv had to offer was brains not brawn. He was more like the monkey king Hanuman, whose cunning and resourcefulness were central to the heroes' success. He took heart from Hanuman's prominent role in *The Ramakien*, and hoped Jayne, like the Thais, appreciated the merits of cleverness and trickery.

He could have gone to an internet café nearby on Khao San Road, but the one on Silom was cleaner and faster. That it was close to Jayne's apartment was an added advantage in case he found anything of significance that needed to be printed out and taken to her later that evening.

It was still early enough to get a seat on the ferry. He handed ten baht to the conductor as she shuffled along the aisle, rattling the coins in her metal cylinder. Rajiv scanned the books in his bag: a history of the Death Railway, an Australian crime novel called *Kickback* that he'd picked up for Jayne, a bootlegged copy of a hacker's manual, and an English translation of *The Ramakien* that he fished out and resumed reading.

40

It took them two hours to get from Kanchanaburi to
Bangkok's Southern Bus Terminal, and another hour
in cross-town traffic to reach the hotel where the Kings
were staying. Jayne would have deferred the confrontation
until the following morning, but Mayuree couldn't wait
to be reunited with her son. The closer they got, the more
agitated the Thai woman became, compulsively checking
her reflection, sniffing a menthol inhaler and dabbing at her
eyes with tissues. Jayne worried that Mayuree would lose all
self-control once she saw Kob, but decided that might not
be a bad thing. An emotional outburst might be just what it
took to move Alicia King.

Still, she wanted to spare Leroy and Alicia—not to
mention Kob—the trauma of a surprise attack and asked
Mayuree to wait in the lobby while she paged them.

'They checked out already,' the receptionist said.

'When?'

'Early this morning.'

'Shit,' Jayne muttered under her breath. 'I don't suppose
they left a forwarding address?'

An embarrassed laugh told her no.

Jayne glanced at Mayuree perched on the edge of a chair, shredding a wad of tissue in her hand. She punched Rajiv's number into her phone.

'Jayne, I have been waiting on your call. I managed to hack into Maryanne's account and—'

She cut him off. 'Rajiv, I'm in trouble. I'm at the Suriya Hotel with Mayuree, but the Kings checked out this morning. Alicia must've been spooked.'

'Do you want me to start checking for them at other hotels in the vicinity? They still have to take the child to the US Embassy tomorrow, isn't it?'

'Would you?' She made no attempt to hide the gratitude in her voice. 'I'm not sure how much more Mayuree can take.'

'And you, Jayne. Are you okay?'

'I'm okay,' she said. 'Thanks for this. And Rajiv, I'm sorry about—'

'We do not have time for that,' he said. 'I must be hanging up so I can make the inquiries.'

She turned to find Mayuree hovering behind her.

'Where's Kob?' she hissed. 'Where's my son?'

'He's not here,' Jayne said. 'The Americans have changed hotels. They won't be far away. That was my assistant on the phone. He's going to call back in a few minutes with their new location.'

Mayuree shook her head. *'Dichan pai mai dai.'*

'I'm not going,' Mayuree said. 'And I don't want you to go after them either.'

'What do you mean?' Jayne said. 'Without you, we have no case.'

'You don't understand, Khun Jayne. I tried explaining

when we were in Kanchanaburi. *Laew teh duang.* It is my boy's fate to go and live in America. He is lucky. It's his karma. It's my fate to have lost him.'

Jayne put a hand on Mayuree's arm.

'Look, it's been a long day. Let's go back to my place, get some sleep, come back early tomorrow and—'

Mayuree shrugged off the hand. 'You're not listening to me. I'm telling you, my son is better off without me.'

'*Mai khao jai.*' Jayne shook her head.

'I don't expect you to understand.'

'But you're his mother.'

Mayuree stared into the distance. There was a bronze Buddha on a shelf behind Jayne, pointing the fingers of his right hand to summon the earth goddess to wring a flood of water from her hair and engulf the demons sent to tempt him. Mayuree looked into the face of the Buddha and knew she'd been a mother only in name. She'd placed her son in an institution when he was six months old and had barely seen him since. She was too proud to send him to her family in Kanchanaburi where he'd have had a better life, even under her mother's disapproving glare. She even let herself be duped into believing he was dead. A good mother would have stood up to the doctors, nurses and farangs and refused to believe it without proof. But not Mayuree.

'How can you say that, Khun Jayne, when you know nothing about me?'

There was venom in her tone. It wasn't just about Jayne. It was about all the times she'd failed to stand up to farangs who'd pushed her around. John who made her turn tricks to get him out of debt. Curtis who deserted her when she was pregnant. Frank who pressured her to relinquish her son then lied to her about him being dead. And Maryanne, who brought such promise into their lives, only to ruin it all with her foolishness.

If it wasn't for Maryanne, she and Sumet could have kept Kob out of institutional care. They'd managed all right before Maryanne came along. Mayuree should have known that once she lost Sumet it was only a matter of time before she'd lose Kob, too. Maryanne's ghost would never let Mayuree keep her baby when she'd been robbed of her own.

'Go to hell,' she told them all.

Jayne's cheeks flushed red. 'I'm sorry you feel that way, sister.'

'Not half as sorry as I am for letting you talk me into this. I should've known better than to trust a farang.'

'But—'

'I've wasted enough time. Don't follow me.'

Ignoring the hurt on Jayne's face, Mayuree straightened the bag over her shoulder, turned and strode out the door of the hotel. Her heart ached for the loss of her son, but she could not fight fate. He'd been given a chance at a better life, far from the reach of vengeful ghosts. And this time Mayuree would do the right thing by him.

She'd become a good enough mother to let him go.

41

Jayne's face burned, she could hardly breathe. Like the time decades earlier when instead of swinging out on a rope into a river, she'd lost her grip and landed flat on her back in the dirt. *You've had the wind knocked out of your sails, sweetheart,* her Dad had said, rubbing her back. *You think it's your body hurting, but it's mainly your pride.*

She had no idea how long she stood in Mayuree's wake. The next thing she knew Rajiv was at her side.

'I found them,' he said. 'I found where the King family is staying and—'

She stopped him with a raised hand and shook her head.

'Mayuree?' he said.

She nodded. 'Let's get out of here.'

They found a coffee shop nearby. She let Rajiv order while she lit a cigarette. She smoked half of it trying to figure out what she said to trigger Mayuree's change of heart. She dialled the woman's number. No answer.

The coffee arrived and she looked up to see Rajiv watching her across the table. He raised his eyebrows and tilted his head, a delicately posed question.

'Mayuree doesn't want us to get her son back,' Jayne

said, tipping the ash from her cigarette.

'I am guessing that much,' Rajiv said. 'But why?'

Jayne sighed. 'She thinks it's Kob's destiny to live in America, that he'll be better off. She doesn't think she's fit to be his mother.'

She drew back hard on her cigarette, her words spilling out with the smoke. 'I guess Alicia and Leroy King feel the same way. Doesn't matter that the kid was stolen. He's better off with them. And behind the scenes is that arsehole Frank Harding and his lackeys at the centre in Pattaya, preying on women like Mayuree, telling them how much better off their children would be without them. It's no bloody wonder she feels unworthy. Mayuree would have no reason to believe people like her ever get justice. We've got to prove her wrong.'

She butted out her cigarette and started gathering up her things. 'I need to call my friend Max at the Australian Embassy. Maybe he can come with us to confront the Kings to prove it's official.'

Rajiv cleared his throat. 'You just said Mayuree doesn't want us to pursue the matter.'

'Yes, but I can't believe she meant it. It's just symptomatic of how little control she's had over her life.'

'And you think it would be helping matters to take control from her in this instance, too?'

'What do you mean?'

'By suggesting we ignore Mayuree's decision, we are giving ourselves the right to take the control away from her again.'

Jayne frowned. 'Maybe we know better in this case.'

Rajiv leaned over and took her hand. 'Jayne, have you considered that Mayuree might be right—that the baby *is* better off?'

She recoiled from his touch. 'Are you serious?'

Rajiv held up his hand. 'Please do not be jumping down my throat. As your assistant, I'd do everything in my power to assist you in pursuing this case if that is what the client wanted. But I come from a different world than you. And in my experience—' he paused to find the right words '—as someone raised in a country even poorer than Thailand, I humbly suggest the child may have a better life with people who have the means to shelter him from the sort of...strife that is beyond his mother's control. And I think Mayuree knows this, even if you don't.'

Jayne slumped in her chair. She had expected Rajiv to support her. As an Indian national, surely he'd take umbrage at the assumption a child was better off growing up in the West? Instead he was using his Third World credentials to suggest she was in the wrong—the exploiter, the one who failed to understand. That made it twice in an hour she'd had such an accusation levelled against her.

She'd longed for Rajiv to stand up to her. But not like this. Not to make her doubt her own judgment. She needed confidence to survive in a place where her values were at odds with the majority, and resist the pressure to assimilate or leave. She needed confidence to succeed in her work, too, to trust her instincts. Jayne hated Rajiv for undermining her.

More than that, she hated him for being right.

Jayne straightened her shoulders and signalled for the bill. Rajiv knew he had to act quickly.

'I am sharing your frustration,' he said. 'But we can still build the case against those people at the centre in Pattaya to prevent them from continuing to prey on women like Mayuree.'

'We don't have much of a case without Kob,' she shrugged, taking out her wallet.

She was angry, readying herself to walk out on him again. Rajiv's experiment in standing his ground was falling well short of winning her over. He needed to change tack.

'I do have something for you—'

He was cut off by the ringing of her mobile phone. She glanced at the screen.

'Hello Police Major General.'

She turned her profile to Rajiv but stayed at the table.

'The mother has decided not to pursue the case,' she said flatly.

'No need to try and sound surprised, Police Major General,' she added after a beat. 'You warned me it was a long shot. I guess all that leaves us with is the search for Frank Harding and—'

Something Wichit said stopped her mid-sentence.

'You've found Khun Frank?'

She spun around to face Rajiv again.

'Floating face down in Pattaya Bay,' she repeated.

'*What*?' Rajiv gasped.

She held up her hand, frowned into the phone. 'What do you mean *no leads*? What about Frank's involvement in the adoption scam?'

Rajiv strained to hear what the Police Major General was saying.

'So they all get away with it except Chaowalit?'

'...'

'You're not thinking of dropping the charges against him?'

Rajiv's eyes widened.

'...'

'I'll get back to you.'

303

'What was all that about?' Rajiv asked.

'Frank Harding's dead and so is the case against the New Life Children's Centre.'

'At least that means the adoption fraud stops, isn't it?' Rajiv said.

Jayne shook her head. 'I doubt it. Frank might have been the front man, but I strongly suspect Doctor Somsri and whoever's behind him were the ones pulling the strings. Chances are they'll live to defraud another day.

'Meanwhile, I'm trying to get a revised verdict into Maryanne Delbeck's death, but the only way I can do that without exposing Sumet is to allow the police to cut a deal with Chaowalit, which means he'll probably walk on the assault charges.'

'Why not expose Sumet?' Rajiv asked.

'I can't see anything would be gained by it,' Jayne said. 'He knows he made a terrible mistake and he's trying to make amends. I honestly believe he'll do more good in the monastery than he would in prison. But then again, what do I know? I'm just an insensitive farang.'

Rajiv ignored the dig.

'Besides,' she added, 'bringing Sumet into it means going public on his relationship with Maryanne. And you can imagine what the press here and in Australia would do with that. This probably sounds stupid, but I feel like Maryanne was let down by everyone she loved, and I just want to do the right thing by her. I'm not protecting Sumet. I'm protecting Maryanne.' She sighed. 'I wish I knew what she'd have wanted.'

'I may be able to help.'

Rajiv reached into his bag and handed her a sheaf of print-outs.

'From Maryanne's email account, the contents of the inbox and sent items folder. Unfortunately, I could not retrieve deleted items as they had already been removed from the server. It's a common default setting and—'

'Too much information,' she said, shuffling through the paper. 'Did you find anything interesting?'

'In the drafts folder.' He indicated the page at the bottom of the pile. 'A message saved but not sent.'

She read through the text and smiled.

'You're a genius.'

Rajiv nodded his head. 'So you're no longer angry with me?'

'I didn't say that.'

He shrugged and lit a cigarette, an emotional smoke-screen.

'Jayne, I need to—'

'Look, Rajiv—'

They both spoke at once. He nodded for her to continue.

'I'm feeling crappy about the way I've treated you. To be honest this document—' she waved Maryanne's email in the air '—makes my life a hell of a lot easier. And I'd like to do something for you in return. Can you meet me tomorrow morning at seven-thirty at Bangkok Noi station?'

'Bangkok Noi station? What will I be doing?'

'Tell your uncle you've had a tip-off about a cache of war histories from a book dealer in Kanchanaburi.'

'Kanchanaburi?'

'Yes,' she said, smiling again. 'Shouting you a trip there is the least I can do.'

'Shouting?'

'It means the trip is on me—I'm paying. Think of it as a bonus.'

Rajiv walked home through Pahurat's laneways with a spring in his step. He might not be hero material but he was smart and resourceful, just like Hanuman the Monkey King in *The Ramakien*, which he had finished reading that afternoon.

As in *The Ramayana*, with Hanuman's help, Rama rescues his beloved wife Sita from the demon king Ravana. But in the Indian version, Rama is so tortured by doubts about Sita's fidelity, she allows herself to be swallowed up by the earth to prove her love to him. In the Thai account, Rama and Sita get to live happily ever after.

Rajiv took it as a good omen.

42

Dear Sarah,

It's been so long since I last wrote, you must have given up on me. Sorry. When I explain what's been going on, I think you'll understand.

Remember a couple of months ago I told you about Sumet, the guy I was seeing? Well, things have become pretty serious. Actually, that's the understatement of the year. Truth is, we're planning to get married and we're having a baby.

Don't freak out! I know it seems sudden, but it feels totally right. From the moment I met Sumet, I felt like we were destined to be together.

I know we're young and have only known each other a short time (blah, blah, blah), but Thailand has taught me that life is too short to hesitate when you find what you really want. In the time I've been here, two babies have died at the centre where I work. Makes you realise how important it is to seize the day.

We're planning to live in Thailand. Sumet says we can get a relative of his to come and live with us to help cook and clean after the baby is born, which sounds good to me!

Obviously I'll want to bring the baby to Australia at some point to meet you and the rest of the family, which is where you come in.

Sarah, I need to ask you a BIG favour. You know you're my favourite aunt (grovel, grovel), and we've always had a lot more in common than either of us have with Dad. Could you please help me tell Mum and Dad about Sumet and the baby? I know Dad will go ballistic and I just don't want to have to deal with it. I figure if you break it to him, give him the chance to vent his spleen, I can talk with him after he's calmed down. Would you do this for me?

In case you're wondering, I feel fine. I'm 12 weeks' pregnant, which the doctor says is out of the danger zone. You're the first person to know after me, Sumet and Doctor Apiradee.

My darling auntie, I promise I'll name the baby after you if it's a girl, though we don't know what we're having. I honestly don't mind, though Sumet wants a girl. I think you'd really like him, Sarah. And I'm sure if you could see how happy I am, you'd be happy for me.

Always your loving niece,
Maryanne

43

Kanchanaburi's infamous floating karaoke bars were moored indecently close to the JEATH War Museum, named for the key players involved in the construction of the Death Railway: Japan, England, Australia, America, Thailand and Holland. Jayne couldn't help wondering how the ghosts of the Allied POWs, Asian labourers and their Japanese captors felt about the flashing lights and reverberating din. Did the ascendancy of karaoke—literally 'empty orchestra'—make the Japanese ghosts feel superior? Did the others sit on the riverbank and shake their heads to think they fought and died for this?

'Let's go there for dinner,' Rajiv said.

'Are you serious?'

He wiggled his head. 'The one called Mae Klong is supposed to have the best food.'

As part of atoning for her recent behaviour, Jayne had left the itinerary to Rajiv. He'd booked separate floating huts for their accommodation and barely allowed Jayne time to put down her bag before whisking her off to spend the afternoon exploring the town's attractions. Not exactly romantic, but as angry as she'd been with Rajiv, as confused as he sometimes made her feel, Jayne was attracted to him. More than ever. She proposed the trip to Kanchanaburi with the idea it would either make or break them. So far the signs were not great. She hoped her luck would improve over dinner, but a karaoke restaurant didn't bode well.

She picked out the Thai script for 'Mae Klong' from one of several floating huts lining the docks. The main room had two walls, one flanked by a large wooden bar and lined to the ceiling with bottles of alcohol on shelves backlit with pink neon. The other wall at right angles to the bar contained a small, darkened stage with a television to one side and a cordless microphone resting in a stand. The restaurant was otherwise open-sided, with clusters of tables and chairs between the bar and stage and the kitchen on the upper deck.

Over a meal of jungle curry spiked with whole red chillies and sprigs of green peppercorns, they de-briefed on the Maryanne Delbeck case.

'You know, Maryanne wrote in her email that she was twelve weeks' pregnant, but she was only eight weeks at the time she died. She drafted that letter four weeks before she intended to send it. She must have felt so lonely.'

'Hmm,' Rajiv murmured. 'And it was written the day before she died, isn't it?'

Jayne raised her eyebrows. 'You've been paying attention.'

Rajiv smiled and helped himself to one of her cigarettes.

'So what have you decided to tell the family?'

'My report to Jim Delbeck will attribute Maryanne's tragic death to a case of high jinks gone wrong, and explain that Maryanne's friends were too scared to go to the police. I'm counting on him to understand, given his prejudices about Thai cops. At least I'll be able to reassure him Maryanne was never suicidal. And I'll send the official paperwork showing the revised verdict of accidental death.'

'And if he wants to take it further?'

'I've thought about that. If Jim Delbeck wants someone to blame, I reckon the best bet is to dangle Doctor Somsri before him. After all, the doctor defrauded everyone by fabricating Maryanne's mental illness.'

Rajiv whistled through an exhalation of smoke. 'Nice touch.'

'Yeah, we might yet put him out of business—at least temporarily.'

Jayne pushed aside her plate and reached for a cigarette.

'I also want to send Maryanne's email to her aunt. I'll leave it to her to decide how much more Maryanne's parents need to know. And I'll ask for her postal address so I can mail her the diary. Is it possible to add a note to the email?'

Rajiv wiggled his head. 'Of course. I am thinking it's about time you obtained an email account.'

'You're determined to get me using it, aren't you?'

'Up to you,' Rajiv said, 'How long do letters from Australia normally take?'

'Between one and two weeks.'

Rajiv wiggled his head again, a gesture Jayne had come to realise could mean as many different things as a Thai smile.

'I guess if the Thai police are using email, it can't be that hard, right?'

Rajiv smiled and held a lighter to Jayne's cigarette.

'At this rate, I really will have to put you on the payroll as my assistant.'

His smile faded.

'I am not wanting to be your assistant,' he said. 'I am wanting to be your partner.'

Jayne opened her mouth to protest but Rajiv held up his hand.

'Please, let me be putting forward my case. You are a very clever detective, Jayne. You are bold and intuitive and this, combined with your ability to speak Thai, makes you very successful. But you are disorganised—'

'Hang on a minute—'

He held up his hand again. 'I cleaned up your apartment when you were in hospital, and if you don't mind me saying, your files were a mess.'

Rajiv was right. Paperwork had never been her strong suit.

'I can help with that and more. I have excellent research skills, I am good at problem solving, and I can teach you to use modern technology to improve your business.'

'Like how?'

'Like using the internet—you can do background checks, look up addresses, make travel bookings. The possibilities are endless.'

Jayne toyed with her cigarette. Rajiv had a point. As more private detective services opened in Bangkok, she was at risk of becoming outmoded.

But did she want a partner? She'd never given it serious consideration. Yet looking across the table, it struck her that if she *did* want a partner, Rajiv would be perfect.

'What about the bookstore?' she said.

'Uncle is already coming back and taking over.'

'Meaning a return to the old regime?'

Rajiv raised his eyebrows.

'What about visas, work permits, that sort of thing?'

'My responsibility,' Rajiv said. 'I share the work and the risk.'

This explained his recent behaviour, both his eagerness to please and his choice of separate rooms at the guesthouse. He wanted to be her business partner, nothing more. Maybe it was for the best. Why then did she feel disappointed?

A waitress appeared to clear their table. Jayne glanced around the room and realised that while they were talking, the restaurant had not only filled up, it had started floating.

'I guess that's one way to guarantee we stay on for after dinner drinks,' she said as a second waitress appeared pushing a small trolley loaded with ice buckets and a selection of mixers.

'Shall we get a bottle?'

'Why not.'

She ordered Sang Som, the more drinkable of the local whiskies. The waitress returned with the bottle, measured out two capfuls into each tall glass, topped them up with ice and soda and added a slice of lime.

'What shall we drink to?' Rajiv said.

Jayne thought for a moment.

'To partnership,' she said, raising her glass.

'Partnership,' he agreed.

'On a trial basis,' she added. 'I'm not sure it'll work.'

'I am willing to give it a try if you are,' Rajiv said.

Jayne drank deep from her glass, wishing it were more than a business partnership they were toasting and reflecting on the irony of having missed the boat on romance yet again whilst literally drifting out into the middle of a river.

Rajiv picked up a plastic folder that had materialised on the drinks trolley.

'The song menu,' he said. 'Perhaps we should start with a duet in honour of the occasion.'

Jayne looked up at the stage, now bathed in light. The

television was playing a karaoke DVD without sound, images of a Chinese couple frolicking beside a waterfall.

'My problem with karaoke in Thailand,' she said, 'is the lack of Oz rock options.'

'Meaning?'

'No Cold Chisel. No Angels. No Hunters and Collectors.'

'I'm not familiar with those artists,' Rajiv said, scanning the song lists. 'I am usually finding something I like. My problem is I'm terrified of microphones.'

It was on the tip of Jayne's tongue to ask if that were the case why he'd insisted on dining at a karaoke bar when the music intervened.

An enthusiast from Japan took to the stage to sing 'Careless whispers'.

'Not an easy song,' Jayne said, leaning close to speak into Rajiv's ear. 'I was forced to sing it once when I was tailing a Singaporean man.'

'What happened?'

'The audience sighed with relief when I finished.'

'No, what happened to the Singaporean man?'

'His Thai wife was suspicious about the amount of time he spent away from home. Turns out there was no other woman, only a passion for karaoke. I encouraged my client to take singing lessons.'

Rajiv laughed loudly enough to be heard over the music.

Next a member of the same party performed 'I'll be there', a ballad made famous by the Jackson 5.

Rajiv studied the song menu in earnest while Jayne topped up their drinks.

'A bit of Dutch courage,' she said, raising her glass.

Rajiv matched her toast. 'Do you know why it's called Dutch courage?'

She shook her head.

'It is in honour of the seventeenth century traders from the Netherlands who fortified themselves with alcohol before sailing up the Thames River to leave food for Londoners besieged by bubonic plague.'

'Now you're just showing off.'

Two girls took to the stage to sing a Thai pop song about loneliness and heartache. They were followed by four Thai men, who crowded around the microphone for a passable cover of 'I swear' by All 4 One.

This started something of a boy band trend. A second group chimed in with 'Back for good' by Take That, followed by a threesome singing 'How deep is your love?' by the Bee Gees.

Rajiv excused himself to use the bathroom. Jayne eyed a nearby table where a group of farangs—Australians, British and Irish judging by the accents—were egging each other on but hadn't quite reached the requisite level of drunkenness to perform.

Centre stage was seized by a Filipino man who sang 'I will always love you', sounding so much like Whitney Houston, Jayne could have sworn he was lip-synching.

At this point the Australian-British-Irish contingent took their turn. First a threesome, arms draped around each other's necks, stumbled through a rendition of 'Love me tender' that would have Elvis turning in his grave, assuming he was in fact dead and not hiding out in Thonburi as the Bangkok rumour-mill would have it. Next two of them sang a cringe-worthy version of Tom Jones's 'Delilah', flat notes reverberating through microphones held too close.

At this point it occurred to Jayne that if Dante were writing his *Inferno* in the twentieth century, surely one of the Circles of Hell would involve being trapped in a karaoke bar in the middle of a river with a group of drunken, tone-deaf men. She vowed to have a word with Rajiv about his choice of venue when she realised how long he'd been gone. Surely he hadn't jumped ship?

She lit a cigarette and tried to look nonchalant as she scanned the room. More music started up, a piano riff with the hint of electric guitar in the background.

'I can't fight this feeling any longer/ And yet I'm still afraid to let it flow.'

She recognised the song, an eighties classic.

'What started out as friendship has grown stronger/ I only wish I had the strength to let it show...'

Jayne looked up at the stage where Rajiv, his collar turned up, was holding the microphone with two hands and singing like a rock star. To her surprise, he had a wonderful voice.

She liked his choice of song, too, a romantic ballad about a man falling in love with a woman he'd been friends with for some time. She wondered how much, if anything, she should read into the lyrics. Perhaps he was just a big REO Speedwagon fan. Perhaps this was nothing more than his signature karaoke song.

'And even as I wander/ I'm keeping you in sight.'

But the thought that he might mean anything by it sent her heart racing.

'And I'm getting closer than I ever thought I might.'

As the electric guitar ramped up for the chorus, Rajiv stepped down from the stage.

'And I can't fight this feeling anymore/ I've forgotten what I started fighting for.'

A spotlight followed him as he walked among the tables.

'It's time to bring this ship into the shore,/ And throw away the oars, forever.'

People laughed and clapped as he serenaded them. A group of Thai girls giggled and shrieked as if Rajiv were the real deal. He reciprocated by touching their outstretched hands as he passed, like a rock star acknowledging the fans in the front row. Jayne almost expected one to leap from her seat and throw herself at him.

He filled a musical interlude with more pop star moves, pounding his heart, pulling at the air with his fist, and spinning on one leg. It was a side of his personality that Jayne had never seen. Her cigarette burned out in the ashtray in front of her. Jayne was captivated.

The electric guitar subsided, and Rajiv came to a standstill on the floor amidst the tables. He closed his eyes.

'My life has been such a whirlwind since I saw you./ I've been running round in circles in my mind.'

He opened his eyes and looked directly at Jayne.

'And it always seems that I'm following you, girl./ Cause you take me to the places/ That alone I'd never find.'

There could be no mistaking the significance of the lyrics now.

'And even as I wander,/ I'm keeping you in sight.'

He gestured towards her.

'You're a candle in the window/ on a cold, dark winter's night.'

Heads turned to see who he was singing to. Jayne felt the rare sensation of a blush as Rajiv moved closer.

'And I can't fight this feeling anymore...'

Several groups of patrons waved lit cigarette lighters in time to the music. Jayne felt overwhelmed, but by what emotions she couldn't tell. Part of her felt mortified. Another flattered. Did she dare believe that Rajiv felt the same way about her as she did about him?

'*And if I have to crawl upon the floor/ Come crashing through your door—*'

The notion of him crashing through anyone's door made her laugh out loud.

'*Baby, I can't fight this feeling anymore.*'

She laughed so hard, she cried. But that didn't seem to faze Rajiv.

He stopped in front of her, crouched down on one knee so their faces were level and pulled a white handkerchief from his pocket. He wiped her tears, all the while singing a final '*Woo-oo*.'

As the music faded, he kissed the damp handkerchief and held it to his heart, a gesture that was pure Bollywood. The entire room burst into applause.

Jayne's head was spinning. It was the most ridiculous, romantic gesture anyone had ever made for her.

Rajiv stood up and handed the microphone to the nearest waitress. He flashed a grin to acknowledge the crowd and resumed his seat. He was covered in sweat and when he reached for a cigarette his hands were shaking.

In that moment, Jayne understood that bravery came in many forms, and that courage such as Rajiv's was rare.

Their eyes met. She raised her glass to him and smiled.

She smiled at him again when, several hours later, they slid out of their clothes and stood, skin to skin, in her floating hotel room. Moonlight filtered in through an open window facing the river, enough to illuminate the sweat on Rajiv's brow. When he touched her, his hands were still shaking.

'First times are over-rated in my experience,' she

whispered. 'Let's just get it over with so we can relax and enjoy what happens next.'

'I think I love you,' he said.

He took her face in his hands and kissed her.

All ghosts fell silent.

Acknowledgments

My thanks to Andrew Nette, with whom I share life, a child and at one stage even shared a desk during the writing of this book. Beloved partner, valued reader and talented writer.

Thanks to Christos Tsiolkas who makes my life and my books better.

I'm grateful for the research assistance provided by Randall Arnst in Bangkok, which enriched this book, despite some outlandish requests on my part.

Kathryn Sweet did a great job again of checking and correcting my Thai transliterations; any remaining inaccuracies are my responsibility alone.

Alison Arnold and Caro Cooper at Text Publishing responded with enthusiasm to the manuscript and provided spot-on editorial advice to improve it. My thanks to Michael Heyward and all at Text for welcoming me back.

I am grateful for the love and generosity of my friends Angela Whitbread, who helped bankroll my fieldwork in Thailand in 2008, and Mary Latham, who opened her house as a writer's retreat when I needed it.

I'd also like to acknowledge those in Phnom Penh

(where this book was written) who shared their experiences of overseas adoption and in their determination to ensure their adoptions were legal and ethical, helped me to imagine what might be involved in illegal, unethical adoptions.

I drew on two excellent sources of information on Thai life and culture: Richard Barrow's blog Paknam Web—Richard Barrow's Life in Thailand (www.thai-blogs.com) and *Very Thai: Everyday Popular Culture* by Philip Cornwell-Smith and John Goss (River Books, Bangkok, 2005).

Thanks also to: Atchariya (Fon) and Pratyaporn (Pern) Thongklieng for their list of Thai names and meanings; Ying for allowing me to use the story of her name change; Sarah Rey and Sonja Horbelt for German translations; Harriet McCallum for advice on post traumatic stress; Haydn Savage for the Buddha of Wednesday afternoon; Palani Narayanan for the perfect song for the karaoke scene; and Richard Fleming for excellent legal advice.

And for inspiration I thank Dinesh Wadiwel, who should have won the karaoke prize at the Alice Springs Memorial Club that night in October 2004.

Finally, thanks to my beautiful daughter Natasha for tolerating all the time I spend writing stories when I might be reading to you instead.